In Your Dreams

Gary,

Hope you enjoy the read.
It might be fiction, but
my friends say it could
happen.

Make sure Leo gets a chance
to browse this as well.

R. Penny

Ghostdance

To order additional copies, please contact us.
BookSurge, LLC
www.booksurge.com
1-866-308-6235
orders@booksurge.com

RON
TERBORG

IN YOUR DREAMS

A NOVEL

2004

In Your Dreams

"Okay, it's just a dream. And dreams don't bite, do they?"

This Work Is Dedicated To All Budding Writers, Good Or Aspiring To Be Good. Remember, The Spoken Word Fades As The Sound Wave Fades, But The Written Word Is Forever. Carpe Diem, Baby.

Lest I Forget, A Special Thanks To My Lovely And Understanding Wife, Jude, For Letting Me See This Thing Through.

CHAPTER 1

Rolly Timmons knew he was asleep. Deep down, way deep down, he knew the thing creeping toward him was the beginning of his Dream. Opening credits, so to speak, for the latest figment of an overactive imagination. All he had to do was wake up, and the thing would go away ... again. Another nightmare chucked into the dream dumpster. Yet, here it was, basically the same theme as last night, and the night before, and the night before. And, each night, the dream-thing moved in a little closer before Rolly could force himself awake.

The episodes had started a little over a week ago. Last Friday, he had experienced a mild nightmare, something to do with being chased by a faceless man/person/thing. On Saturday, the same phantasm visited, only stayed longer—and showed more of itself. Sunday night, Rolly voluntarily woke himself for the first time because the being got too close. That was a turning point of sorts. On subsequent nights, he had snapped out of the nightmare, always in time. But, tonight was just a little different. Tonight his curiosity overrode his will to wake. And the presence crept closer and closer until it was god awful way too close.

Okay. Wake up

Nothing. No response. Until now, his subliminal command had always worked. Rolly would dream whisper the magic words, then wake drenched in sweat, more recently in urine. Last night he woke just as his bladder finished baptizing a three-foot radius of his king-size bed. But, at least he woke up. Tonight, the command wasn't working. Tonight, as he sank deeper into sleep, the dream was winning.

REM-sleep enveloped Timmons, dragging him to the stage of rapid-eye-movement slumber that introduced his nightmare full-fledged and in living color. Close, closer. Now, the thing lightly caressed his face for the first time. Icy tinsel draped his body. Tiny strips of silver cold slid against his bare arms and down his exposed back.

A rotting face leered at Rolly from deep within a death-black cowl. Breath flavored with the musty aroma of something long dead cascaded over Rolly's head, forced its scent into his nostrils. Skeletal fingers reached out across the dirty-hued background, clicking as they grabbed at the dreaming man.

Wake up now! Wake up, wake up, wake up!

Locked in the horrid, fascinating dream, Rolly struggled to escape. He pivoted helplessly, his right foot caught in some kind of painless dream bear trap. Subconscious thoughts of flight vanished, replaced by an immediate, very real need for survival. As he watched, the phantasm approached, slowly, stealthily, its fingers now curled like bony eagle talons.

Rolly spun again, unable to flee with one foot glued to the fantasy earth. Now, razored claws grasped at his throat. He was caught! Brittle hands of dull white bone encircled his neck, sharing their touch of cold death and sepulcher smell.

Wake up, goddammit! Oh, wake up, please! Breath scraped through his constricting throat. Dream world images dimmed as the spectral fingers began squeezing life from Rolly.

Wake up, wake ... Abruptly, the dead fingers loosened, skittering away from the floundering man's throat. Rolly dream-watched in horrid fascination as the phantasm

2

struggled backward, its jerky arm motions flailing against an unseen assailant. Bony fingers slashed helplessly at its own neck, ripping away stringy, gouged strands of desiccated flesh. The dingy cowl slithered from its corrupted head, revealing torn lips parted in an enraged silent scream.

Only then, directly behind the thrashing specter, did Rolly glimpse his savior.

CHAPTER 2

Daniel Gray Wolf woke abruptly, as was usual after a tough battle within the dream world. Rubbing his pounding temples, the Dream Catcher glanced at the bed next to his.

Rolly Timmons slept peacefully, no longer the slave of bad dreams.

Knowing his own nurturing sleep and dreams wouldn't come for hours, Gray Wolf eased off the cot, careful to avoid the built-in squeaks that accompanied the rickety bed. Timmons was at ease and did not need to be disturbed by Daniel's restlessness. The battle with Rolly's nightmare had exhausted him, sapped the strength he normally reserved for such encounters. *Are these things getting harder, or am I just getting older?*

Daniel shuffled into the bathroom, quietly closing the door behind him. Rummaging through the medicine cabinet, he located the near-empty bottle of aspirin. Popping the safety lid into the sink, Gray Wolf expertly tapped a small pile of pain relief into his hand then lifted them to his mouth. He didn't notice the bitter chalky taste as he dry-chewed the tablets, a habit developed twenty years ago when he got into this business full time. Swallowing the grainy residue, Gray Wolf turned from the sink and bumped into Rolly Timmons.

"Whoa, shit! You gave me a start, boy. I was trying not to wake you up."

"It's gone," Timmons replied. "The nightmare's gone and I don't think it's coming back."

"Hey, that's good, Rolly. I'm glad for you."

"You don't understand, Mr. Gray Wolf," Timmons explained, grasping the older man's arms. "I mean the dream is really gone. I can feel it!"

"I do understand, son," Gray Wolf said, gently loosening the clutching fingers from his sleeve. "I was there, remember? And call me Daniel, after what we've been through, okay?"

"Daniel, I don't know how to thank you. I mean, how do I pay you for something like this? Anything—anything you want!"

"Well, Rolly, I've kinda had my eye on a new Ford pickup. You think you could see your way clear to thanking me with one of those?"

Timmons swallowed rather abruptly, a stammered response forming on his dry lips, when the Dream Catcher interrupted him.

"Just kidding, son. It's kind of a custom that I don't accept pay for what I've done. Maybe you can buy me a cup of coffee next time we meet."

"Jeez! You had me going there for a minute," Timmons sighed. "Yeah, coffee. I can handle that."

"Okay, Rolly," Daniel said as he sidled past the younger man. "Next time we meet, it will be under happier circumstances, I guarantee."

"I sure hope so, Mr. Gray ... Daniel. You know, I said the dream was gone. I just have this feeling. But what if it should come back?"

"Rolly, trust me," Gray Wolf admonished softly. "I do a good job. Old Mister Drybones won't be back anymore. Now get outta here and take care of that young family of yours."

Timmons picked up his stylish sports jacket, dusted imaginary specks from the lapels, then strolled to the exit as Gray Wolf watched. Opening the door, Rolly Timmons looked back a final time. "Thanks again, Daniel. This takes a big load off my mind."

Gray Wolf dismissed the man with a friendly wave of his arm, turning back toward the bathroom even before the outside door clicked shut. Grabbing the aspirin bottle, he poured three more tablets into his shaking palm.

"Twenty-six year old stockbroker—hundred thousand a year. Man, I'm in the wrong business," Daniel mumbled as he crunched the pills between even, white teeth.

Gray Wolf busied himself with cleaning the sparsely furnished bedroom, hoping a more natural activity would dislodge the lances piercing his head. It was always like this after a dream episode. Sometimes the pain would be minimal, easily fixed with a couple of Bayer's. With other episodes, like tonight, a handful of Darvon couldn't cut through the discomfort. Instead, he would unnecessarily straighten up the already fastidious room, willing his mind to blot out what he'd just been through.

Daniel Gray Wolf, despite the rigors of his calling, didn't look thirty-eight years old. Raven black hair bore no sprinklings of silver, his one hundred and seventy-three pounds fit in all the right places on a six-foot frame. One distinguishing feature, a small hereditary birthmark in the shape of a spider, adorned his otherwise unremarkable face. The purple-brown blemish was barely noticeable. Only upon closer examination could viewers distinguish the Dream Catcher mark situated in the hollow of his right temple. It was a badge Daniel wore with reluctance and, after sessions like this evening, some fear.

Gray Wolf was *Yuwipi*, the Lakota word for shaman, or

keeper of dreams. In the last ten years, his people had come to call him *Ihanbla Gmunka*, Dream Catcher, because the literal definition was more accurate. Possessor of a paranormal ability, yet the ability was his purely by heredity. He had not studied for it, had not earned it or won it. He could trace his lineage back twenty generations and each first-born son had the endowment.

A gift of pain and anguish for the bearer. Daniel sourly mulled his heritage as he finished the needless household chores.

Dreams were integral to a Sioux culture filled with spiritual awareness and mysticism. Great significance was placed on a warrior's dreams. Children were named because of what the father or mother visioned. Sometimes the dreams proved frightening in their prophecy, leading more than one Sioux brave to a premature death because he blindly followed a vision foretelling his demise. But, a warrior willing to share his nightmares found obvious relief in *Ihanbla Gmunka's* intervention.

The birth of the Spider Dream Society, or Iyuptala Iktomi, was a natural advent. Although all creatures were revered as gifts from *Wakan Tanka,* the Great Spirit, spiders bore an especially honored place in Sioux culture. Dream catchers were initially silken spider webs gingerly cultivated, then re-attached with equal care to hoops of red willow. An intact, finished piece held powerful medicine. The belief was this webbed hoop filtered all dreams entering a warrior's lodge. Good dreams passed freely through the lacy openings, while bad dreams were captured on the sticky strands and held until daylight could dissipate them. Yet, these webbed hoops were fragile, easily broken. Cultural progression demanded a more resilient dream catcher, a man capable of capturing bad dreams.

8

History does not tell how the first *Ihanbla Gmunka*, or Dream Catcher, was chosen. Evidence points to an even more ancient line of shaman, noted for their mystical and spiritual powers. Always the firstborn son, a Dream Catcher performed normal tribal functions. Sometimes he was a warrior, sometimes a hunter. Daily activities and responsibilities took priority. Yet, the gift was to be shared willingly when a member of the tribe experienced recurring nightmares. Tradition, and typical Sioux modesty, did not allow the bearer of this ability to be overly compensated for his act. A choice piece of dog meat or a finer cut from the buffalo was the accepted payment.

Each of the Haken-Siouan stock, the tribes comprising the Seven Tribal Council Fires, had a Dream Catcher. Because of the short life expectancy of a Sioux warrior, these gifted men typically married early in an effort to produce an heir. If a tribal Dream Catcher was killed in battle, or died prior to his son being capable of assuming the role, other stocks within the Council shared their granted one, as long as his absence didn't interfere with tribal affairs. Language was not a great barrier even though three distinct tongues were spoken: Dakota in the south and east; Nakota in the north; and, Lakota in the west. The tribes had been conversing for centuries and the language distinctions were no greater than a New Yorker talking to a Texan. The lineage, and legend, progressed for nearly four hundred years but gradually diminished as red and white nations grudgingly commingled. White science and white beliefs had all but driven the Dream Catcher to extinction. Except Gray Wolf. And he was teetering.

By choice, Gray Wolf had never married. He wanted a wife, a family, but did not want to pass the *Ihanbla Gmunka* stigma on to a son. *Don't want to do for my kid what you did*

9

for yours, Papa. Daniel reminisced what the 'gift' had done to Raymond Gray Wolf, his father.

The elder Gray Wolf had perished inside long before his actual death, a withered husk eaten up by other people's problems. Born in the late 1920's, Raymond Gray Wolf valiantly adhered to traditional Lakota values and lifestyle, miring himself in nineteenth century culture. He married young to produce an heir, though was not successful until the ripe old age of twenty-seven. The world progressed around him. Technology enhanced the media. Television became popular and broadened peoples' imaginations. Along with the modern outlook came new catalysts for dreams and nightmares. Yet Raymond persisted with his bow-and-arrow mentality. The combination proved lethal. Raymond was ill equipped to fight modern nightmares from a war pony. Hobbled by his less than stellar successes, the mystique of the Dream Catcher ebbed from the Oglala Sioux society. Nightmares did not decrease, but calls for help dwindled until Daniel came of age in 1971. Raymond Gray Wolf gratefully died two years later.

Now, twenty years into his calling, Daniel wanted no part in continuing the legacy. He carried on his obligations because ties with his fellow Native Americans were strong. Thanks to modern times, the blend of red and white cultures mandated he make himself available to those outside the Siouan stock. At first, he only helped those recommended by a tribal elder. But, as his underground reputation grew, so did his clientele. He was now dream catching, on average, twice a week. The toll was beginning to show.

CHAPTER 3

Daniel woke at six thirty, just as he did every Saturday. Climbing out of bed, he stretched, luxuriating in the absence of the pounding headache that had stalked him all the way to his own dreams. Quickly showering, he dressed in his weekend garb; clean blue jeans, short-sleeved sports shirt and tennis shoes. Slipping a bolo tie over his head, he adjusted the beaded emblem until it hung loosely below the open shirt collar.

"Breakfast," he mumbled, opening the refrigerator door. Bleak contents peered out at Gray Wolf as he searched the chilled interior for anything resembling morning fare.

Daniel inventoried the possibilities. "No eggs, no bacon, no potatoes. Is that meat loaf and gravy or lasagna? Hell, looks like you get to treat yourself to breakfast at the club, Gray Wolf."

Decision made, Daniel grabbed his wallet and keys, then exited the house. He paused long enough to inhale the late-August smells of rural Rapid Valley. Scents of fresh-mowed grass mingled with the tang of nearby cattle. Gray Wolf appreciated the pungent mixture. "Beats the hell out of cement plant smoke and landfill," he offered in backhanded compliment as he slid into his four-year old truck. Gray Wolf's one concession to luxury was his Elks Club membership. Though he infrequently used the grounds privileges, he was recognized as a regular mealtime customer. The clubhouse was only two miles from his home, a four-minute trip even under bad conditions. As he drove, brief thoughts of last night's encounter seeped into his mind, bringing with them the light twinge of a headache. Gray Wolf shook his head clear of the image.

"Ham and eggs'll take care of me this morning," he murmured, gently rubbing the birthmark on his temple.

"And hash browns," he added as a medicinal afterthought.

Gray Wolf wheeled into the sparsely filled parking lot. At seven o'clock in the morning, the normal crowd wouldn't be showing up for at least another hour. He would have the dining room almost to himself. Daniel parked next to a silver Cadillac, taking extra care not to bump the glossy exterior as he opened his door. Whistling a nameless tune, he sauntered into the club foyer, appreciating the ever-present air conditioning. He peered into the dining area, looking for the hostess.

"Good morning, Mr. Gray Wolf," a voice boomed from behind.

Daniel turned to see a bald-headed man stroll out of the bathroom and toward the dining area. The gentleman was obviously set for a round of golf, red short-sleeved polo shirt offset by a pair of loudly resplendent black, green and red plaid trousers.

"Well, good morning, Dr. Nagel. Early tee time this morning?"

"Have to get in a full eighteen before eleven. I'm lecturing at the Sheraton this afternoon."

"One of these days I'll unlimber the ol' sticks and bring this course to its knees," Daniel responded.

Edwin Nagel studied the man in front of him, a habit picked up from years of directing psychoanalysis. "Are you meeting someone for breakfast, or would you care to join me?"

"Thanks, but I've got to eat and run. I'm going to the reservation later this morning."

"I see," murmured Nagel, further studying Gray Wolf's face. "I suppose you'll be conducting a little of your *craft* while you're down there."

"Just going to visit some old friends." It wasn't actually a lie. Then again, it was just not the whole truth. He made himself available to his reservation friends if the need was there.

"I thought you'd given up your dream watching career."

"No, sir, I still help where I'm needed as a *Dream Catcher*."

"I see," Nagel said again, moving conspiratorially close to Gray Wolf. "It seems as though you haven't heeded my warning about this unsafe custom. Unlicensed and untrained practice of therapy is against the law, need I remind you."

"I can appreciate that, Dr. Nagel. Need I remind you, I don't practice anything? I've got this baby down pat. I don't counsel, I don't charge, and I don't have repeat customers. Seems to me you're the one who's 'practicing' around here, what with your multi-sessioned bullshit because you can't get it right the first time!"

Nagel's face abruptly matched his shirt color as he hissed, "Gray Wolf, I am a licensed psychiatrist in the state of South Dakota, well-respected among my peers, and have authored several papers on dream therapy. I have eight years of medical school and another twenty-some years of ongoing training behind me to back my decisions."

"Well, Doc, I only got four hundred years of dream catching history behind me. Sorry if that isn't enough for you … and don't say 'I see' to me again, because you don't."

"We'll meet again on this subject, Mr. Gray Wolf. Now, if you'll excuse me, my table is ready." Furiously, Edwin Nagel trounced into the dining room.

"Have a nice breakfast, Doctor," Daniel offered after the departing man. "And listen, if you need any tips about this dream stuff, just give me a buzz.

"Fuck it," Gray Wolf growled, no longer hungry.

Outside, the early morning breeze soothed the Dream Catcher's angry spirit. Muted sounds of lawn tractors working the golf course buzzed a calming melody. Breathing deeply, he inhaled the smells of tranquility before hopping into his pickup. Leaving the parking lot, Gray Wolf decided today might still be a good day after all.

Five minutes later, he was heading southeast on Highway 44 toward the reservation. The planned weekend visits with his brethren always brought pleasure, particularly his ritual meeting with Leo Red Hawk, a tribal elder. Red Hawk was ninety-eight years old and still in control of his mental faculties - very much in control, Gray Wolf thought.

Driving through the rolling countryside, Daniel thought about the old man. Red Hawk had been his friend, a father figure and confessor, for most of his thirty-eight years. When Gray Wolf lived on the reservation with his family, old Leo had been the source of much knowledge and wisdom.

Daniel had been close to his father, but Raymond Gray Wolf's view of things had soured as the dream catching onus weighed heavier on his mind. Red Hawk offered what Daniel's father could not; an uncluttered outlook.

Leo Red Hawk was a traditionalist—up to a point. He valued the old ways, yet was wise enough to enjoy creature comforts provided by the white man's technology. Leo didn't live in a tipi, didn't dress in buckskins, and he didn't shun the electricity that powered his portable television. His philosophy was, "I can think better in a warm house, with warm clothes on."

Gray Wolf found himself grinning as he thought of the old man. "Yeah, Leo, you're a trip."

An hour and a half later, Daniel cruised into the township of Badger, although the word township was a bit strong for the scope of this community. Two stores graced the main street. A combination liquor and grocery outlet, and a hardware-millinery shop provided the major manmade bumps on an otherwise unremarkable rolling landscape. Surrounding the one-story buildings was a handful of randomly scattered houses and trailers. Poverty was evident. The most recent coat of paint on any structure was at least twenty years old. But, Gray Wolf didn't notice the deterioration. Instead, the beauty of the country and the free-living style adopted by the twenty plus residents caught him. He pulled in front of the liquor store and set the parking brake.

Ten percent of the township's population sat on two rockers in front of Badger Liquor and Grocery Emporium. A pair of middle-aged gents rocked and enjoyed the shaded porch and soft wind.

"Mornin', Daniel," greeted the older of the two, holding out his weathered hand.

Gray Wolf grasped the leathery fingers. "Mornin' yourself, Mr. War Pony.

"Mr. Yellow Feather," he further acknowledged, shaking hands with the other rocker resident.

"Must be Saturday already, huh?" offered William Yellow Feather.

Gray Wolf chuckled. "Yeah, sure must be. You know Dakota Steel wouldn't let me off on a weekday just to visit you old coots."

"You here to see Leo?" asked Gilbert War Pony unnecessarily. "Probably down at his house, you know."

"Gilbert, you old fart," Yellow Feather cackled. "Leo's always down at his house. Hell, the man don't come out no more 'cept to see young Gray Wolf here back to his truck."

Ignoring his friend, War Pony asked, "So, what's the word in the big city, Daniel?"

"Aw, you know, the usual stuff. Ain't enough tourists to support all the businesses. Mayor wants to pump another couple of pennies into the coffer with a city sales tax raise. I come down here to get back to reality."

War Pony and Yellow Feather chortled. Gray Wolf rarely missed a weekend in Badger, yet the conversation was basically the same each visit. The porch dwellers had come to expect Daniel's dry repartee. It was summertime, and the talk was of tourists and taxes. Come winter, they would expect Gray Wolf to bemoan Rapid City's snow removal program. Each knew it was a game; public relations at work with the small-town boy lamenting his adopted big town.

"Well, gents, I gotta step inside and boost your economy a bit," Daniel said, pulling open the screen door and leaving the old roosters to their clucking.

Inside the emporium, the mid-morning heat dropped all of three degrees, aided by a lethargic overhead fan. Daniel sauntered over to the counter.

"Mornin', Mr. Trudeau."

The storeowner turned around from where he had been busily dusting shelves. "Hey, Daniel. Must be Saturday, huh?"

"Must be," Gray Wolf started out of habit. "You know Dakota Steel wouldn't ..."

Trudeau interrupted with a wave of his feather duster, "I know, I know. I heard you say that to those two monuments on my front stoop. Just wanted to yank your chain a little. So, what can I get for you today, Daniel?"

Gray Wolf surveyed the cluttered shop, "Well, let's see. I'll take a carton of those Camel straights, a six-pack of Coors, couple cans of that Dinty Moore stew if you got it, a loaf of bread, and hey, you get any of those cans of smoked oysters in? Kinda thought I'd surprise Leo. He seems to like them."

Trudeau began gathering the requested articles, as much from memory as by Gray Wolf's direction. "Uh, Daniel? Leo said not to surprise him with any more of them oysters. Kinda give him the shits and he don't move as fast as he use to."

Gray Wolf laughed at the image of a ninety-eight year old man trying to make it to the outhouse in time. "Okay, did he say what I should surprise him with?"

Trudeau grinned, "'Course he did. Said you could maybe pick up some fig bars to bind him up a bit."

"Load 'er up then, Mr. Trudeau ... and a package of your finest Fig Newtons, please."

Gray Wolf watched the wiry storeowner amble toward the counter with his armload of supplies. A solid, honest man, Ralph Trudeau was three-quarter Oglala Sioux, despite the surname inherited from a French mining engineer grandfather.

Daniel paid for the groceries and, sack in hand, picked up the two extra cans of cold beer that had magically appeared on the counter. He pushed through the screen door and handed the frosty brews to the porch inhabitants.

"Well now, ain't this a pleasant surprise?" Gilbert War Pony asked, passing a pale yellow can of Coors to his rocker partner.

"Get off it, you old buck! Only time you'd be surprised is if I didn't bring you a beer. Hell, your wife would probably kiss me for not remembering a weekly peace offering."

Gilbert took a long pull from his beer before answering, "Kiss her, take her home with you. Yer welcome to her, Daniel. Why the hell do you think me and William spend so much time here?"

Grinning, Daniel opened the pickup door and shoved his groceries in. "Take it easy, gentlemen."

"You too, *kola*," the men chorused before returning to their own conversation.

Pulling out of the parking lot, Gray Wolf thought back to the conversation. In the whole interchange, only one Lakota word was used. *Kola* ... friend. He knew War Pony and Yellow Feather were now conversing in their native tongue. Their use of English was in deference to his non-resident status. True, Daniel was raised in these parts, but had moved on to better himself. He would always be welcome, but was no longer a reservation citizen.

Thirty seconds later, he wheeled into Leo Red Hawk's dusty driveway. Letting the truck engine idle, Gray Wolf looked over the ramshackle affair Leo called home. Several different colors of tar shingle decorated the exterior walls while patched tin served as a roof. Yet, proudly perched atop the shanty, an antenna reached toward the sun. Daniel couldn't feel sorry for the occupant. Leo had been happy in this house for eighty years.

Shutting off the ignition, Gray Wolf pulled the groceries out after him. Still twenty feet from the house, he could hear the television blaring inside. Yes, Leo was obviously home. Daniel ignored the rusted doorbell. Even if it worked, the buzzing would never have been heard above the racket pouring out of the old Sears portable television. Knocking on the dirty glass window, Gray Wolf peeked into the murky interior.

Leo Red Hawk, eyes glued to his favorite Saturday

morning show, sat passively in a ruptured lounge chair. Only a periodic smile indicated he was awake, or alive. Movement at the door caught his attention more than the knocking. Raising a gnarled, brown hand, Leo beckoned Gray Wolf in before resuming his steadfast watch.

Daniel set the bag on the kitchen counter before sidling over to where Red Hawk sat. "What are you watching, *Tunkasila?*"

"Lone Ranger. Did you bring beer?"

Gray Wolf pulled a can of Coors from behind his back and popped the top. Handing it to the old man, he said, "So, how have you been this week, Grandfather?"

Eyes never leaving the television, Red Hawk answered, "I am old, your oysters make me shit when I am not ready, but life is good."

"Have you been eating properly?"

"I must be—my toilet is always full. Goddamned oysters. You didn't bring me more, did you?'

"No," Gray Wolf laughed. "Mr. Trudeau told me about the problem. I did bring you a little surprise, though."

"Fig bars, I hope," the old man countered, snatching a quick glance at Daniel before resuming his television sentry duty. "Watch with me now. We will talk more when Lone Ranger is over."

Daniel sat down beside his ancient friend and studied the timeworn noble profile. Leo Red Hawk was a relic, a true remnant of the nineteenth century. Thick, gray hair fell to the old man's shoulders; always the same length for as long as Gray Wolf could remember. Winter or summer, the old Sioux wore a long-sleeved flannel shirt, buttoned tightly to the neck. Suspenders and belt held the faded blue jeans in place midway between belly button and crotch. *You'll never make the cover of Gentlemen's Quarterly, Grandfather.*

The old man stirred in his chair as the closing credits rolled across the screen. "Perhaps you would get me another beer, Daniel."

Gray Wolf retrieved two cans, opening them and handing one to the old man. Lifting the other can to his lips, he swallowed the icy liquid until it stung his throat. Setting his half-empty can on the table, he glanced at the credits scrolling across the dusty television screen.

"How can you still get the Lone Ranger when it's been off the air for years?"

The ancient one chuckled a rheumy reply. "The television spirits know what I like. At four o'clock, I will watch Rin Tin Tin. But, you did not come to talk of an old man's entertainment."

"We will talk of what you want, *Tunkasila*.

"Tonto."

"Tonto, *kola*?" Gray Wolf asked, caught off guard.

"Yes, we must speak of Tonto, the Lone Ranger's faithful Indian companion. He is bad for the red man's image, Daniel. Did you know Tonto means 'stupid' in Spanish?"

Gray Wolf could only answer with a chuckle. There was no telling where the old man was headed with this philosophical discussion.

"It is good to hear you still speak the language, *kola washta*," Red Hawk continued. "I feared you would lose your red heart when you moved to the white city. I should know better. Your heart is still here; always will be here. You are not a Tonto, and that is good."

"This is my home, Grandfather," Gray Wolf said simply.

"Are you married yet, Daniel?" the old man asked rhetorically. "Have you given us another *Ihanbla Gmunka*, a Dream Catcher?"

"*Tunkasila,* I was just here last week, and the week before, and the week before that. Why is it you ask me the same question when you already know the answer?"

Red Hawk sipped from his can before speaking. "I have hopes that one week you will surprise this old man. I will not be around for another ninety or one hundred years and I grow impatient."

"Grandfather, you know my feelings on this. I don't want my son to go through what I saw happen to my father; what will probably happen to me."

"Now you are being selfish. You are also being a little Tonto, if you get my meaning. I believe I will start calling you that ... Tonto."

"Listen, Grandfather, I ... "

"No," the old man interrupted. "It is you who needs to listen. Listen to your remaining true brothers and sisters. Many of our ways are gone. Our men become more interested in casinos and bingo halls than tribal affairs. You have a gift, Daniel, as did your father and his father. But your talk makes me afraid."

"What is it you fear, *Tunkasila?*"

"I fear death, but not in the way you think. When I die, I fear the Lakota will die. And that will be the end of things. I'm a tired old man whose only enjoyment is television and visits by his good friend, Daniel. The Other Plain will be a welcome sight for these eyes. I will be among my old friends, among the Lakota I remember as a child. But, I fear you will be left with only a piece of your heritage. We are quickly running out of flag bearers, my friend."

CHAPTER 4

Daniel's visit with Leo Red Hawk lasted until four o'clock when, true to his word, the old man rustled out of his lounger long enough to turn on the television set. Thirty-five year old images of Rusty, Sergeant Biff O'Hara, and Lieutenant Rip Masters leaped to the screen in vivid black and white. Rin Tin Tin, the Wonder Dog, appeared on cue, nuzzling young Rusty's smiling face.

Red Hawk resumed his comatose state, fixedly staring at the figures of a bygone era.

Gray Wolf excused himself with a brief farewell, quietly closing the door behind him. The weekly ritual had varied little, except for the meat of the conversation. Red Hawk's statement weighed heavily on Daniel. *We are quickly running out of flag bearers.* Shoulders slumped, he trudged the short distance to his truck.

There was much truth in the old man's words, Gray Wolf surmised as he drove toward Rapid City. He had an obligation to his tribe, to anyone who sought his help. Daniel would never shirk that responsibility; he just didn't want to prolong it. Thankfully, this visit had been free of outside conflict. An understanding existed. If Daniel's ability were needed, he would be contacted at Leo's home. Part of him was relieved that no knock had come to Red Hawk's door while they conversed. But, the old man's continued plea left him with ambivalent feelings about his decision to end the Dream Catcher legacy. *Damn you, you old coot! Why do you have to play on my guilt?*

Daniel's sense of heritage was strong but his need for self-preservation remained equally solid. His floundering decision to terminate the *Ihanbla Gmunka* was not based on selfishness, but to protect any male offspring should he ever get married. Fragments of his conversation with Red Hawk sifted into his thoughts.

"*Tunkasila*, Grandfather, please listen to me. The world has changed. There are men out there who can fight nightmares without experiencing the pain; without their sons having to feel the pain."

"What do you know of pain, my son? I am ninety-eight years old, yet I remember *Chankpe Opi Wakpala*, Wounded Knee, as I remember your last visit. I was five years old, a boy of only twenty seasons, when the blue coats killed my family and much of your family. They put me in a boarding school, made me learn the white man culture and language, even cut my hair so I would look like the white man. I was never treated as an equal because I was a red man, a savage. But, they could not change my heart, Daniel. I am Lakota, Oglala Sioux, and I am proud. Now, are you as proud?"

It's always so simple for the old timers. I've been there, Daniel; I've done this, Daniel. Can you say the same, Daniel? Damn you, Red Hawk. You're beginning to make sense.

Gray Wolf slipped out of his funk as he neared the outskirts of Rapid Valley. Tonight was relaxation night. He longed for a restful evening at home without care, worry, or mission. Pulling into the driveway, Daniel had already mentally pulled the tab on a cold can of beer and propped his feet up. *Tomorrow, I'll mow the yard and trim the hedges just like a normal guy,* he thought.

Opening the door to his compact bungalow, Daniel whistled a stanza from his favorite nameless tune. Things were going to be all right. Tonight was his—then he heard the unmistakable beeping of the answering machine.

"Shit, piss, crotch! You better be one of the guys from the bowling league wanting me to sub," he warned the offending machine.

Daniel re-wound the tape, willing the voice to be Bob Hackett's. Punching the play button, he waited tensely for the message to start. "Hello? Mr. Gray Wolf, my name is Myra Ohlsen. You were referred -"

"Shit!"

"—by my neighbor, Mrs. Long Bear ... "

"Double shit!"

"You see, my daughter, Trina, has been having bad dreams for some time now and I don't know where else to turn. Please call me at -"

Gray Wolf hastily wrote the Ohlsen number down. He poised his finger above the erase button, thinking how easy it would be to make Myra and Trina disappear.

Are you proud of your heritage, kola?

"Don't start with me now, Red Hawk!" Daniel fumed at the imaginary voice as he dialed the Ohlsen number. "C'mon, don't answer. Don't be home. Please don't."

"Hello?" a dusky, feminine voice inquired.

"Mrs. Ohlsen ... Myra Ohlsen?"

"Yes, speaking. Who's calling, please?

"Daniel Gray Wolf, ma'am. I'm returning your call."

"Oh, Mr. Gray Wolf, thank you for calling so quickly. I was talking with my neighbor, Thelma Long Bear. We've been friends for such a long time. Anyhow, I was telling her about my daughter, Trina's nightmares. Poor girl really can't seem to shake them. Thelma mentioned your name and said you had experience in such things."

Gray Wolf waited a few moments until he realized the woman was done speaking. "Yes, Mrs. Ohlsen, I've had experience in dealing with bad dreams. How long has Trina been having her nightmares?"

"Well, off and on, for about three weeks. More recently though, she's been having them every night for the past few days. Maybe three or four?"

"Are they bad enough to wake her, Mrs. Ohlsen?"

"Oh, my goodness, yes! She wakes up crying because they're so vivid."

Daniel pondered whether to delay meeting with the Ohlsens. One more night wouldn't hurt the young girl and he could certainly use the rest.

"Can you bring her out this evening?" he surprised himself by saying.

"Ummmm, Mr. Gray Wolf," Myra Ohlsen said hesitantly. "Trina's confined to a wheelchair and has a special orthopedic bed. If it's not too much trouble -"

"That won't pose a problem, Mrs. Ohlsen. What is Trina's normal bedtime?"

"Well, she usually goes to sleep about ten-thirty."

"Fine. How about if I stop out at ten this evening? That will give me a few minutes to get to know Trina. Just idle chatter, you know? Could you give me your address in Canyon Lake Heights, please?"

"Sure, it's—wait! How did you know where I live?"

"You said you were a neighbor of Thelma Long Bear. I know where Thelma lives."

Writing down the address, Daniel pictured the upper class neighborhood, immediately scribbling '4 MPA' beside the directions. A little game he played in solitary, MPA stood for Mercedes Per Acre, and was Gray Wolf's personal census observation. A silly game used as a stress reliever, but never shown to the customers. The Ohlsen's 4 MPA rating put them in the one hundredth percentile, the elite, of his census.

"OK, I've got it, Mrs. Ohlsen. I'll be the Native American guy in a red 1989 Ford Pickup at your doorstep tonight at ten. You see any other description, and I'd ask for identification if I were you. Oh, by the way, if there isn't a second bed in Trina's room, I'd appreciate a cot or rollaway. If nothing's available, I have my bedroll I can bring."

A relieved Myra Ohlsen gushed, "Thank you, Mr. Gray Wolf. Trina and I really appreciate this. Of course, I'll take care of the extra bed."

"Until tonight," Daniel concluded, hanging up the phone while punching his leg with the other hand.

"Gray Wolf, you horse's ass. Why can't you take some time off?" *Wait, you don't want to answer that, kola. Leo's probably tuned into this frequency.*

Daniel checked his watch, noting it was five-fifty. His immediate need was to fix something bland for supper. Eating food too spicy and the after effects could interfere with this evening's work. He rarely had nightmares of his own, but would not tempt the fates by loading up on fried pork rinds, tacos, or similar fare.

"Coupla soft boiled eggs and wheat toast ought to take the edge off." Gray Wolf set about his supper preparations, humming to himself.

***

At nine-thirty, a freshly showered Daniel Gray Wolf left his home. The trip to Myra Ohlsen's residence wasn't far, maybe twelve miles, but there were only two major east-west roads traversing Rapid City. Both routes required driving through the city's business district. Due to the later hour, Daniel chose Omaha Street because it bypassed the heaviest downtown traffic. In a span of fifteen minutes, he had driven from his rural Rapid Valley home, through the minimal congestion of Rapid City's commercial area, and was now on Jackson Boulevard, a long residential span leading to the far west end of town. The Ohlsen's lived in Canyon Lake Heights, an elevated, exclusive area overlooking the lake and park bearing the same name.

"High rent district," he mumbled appreciatively, wheeling the pickup through narrow, winding turns as he rapidly gained elevation. Near the top of the hill, he spotted the Ohlsen mailbox. Slowing, Daniel carefully maneuvered onto the flagstone driveway, stopping directly in front of the sprawling ranch-style house. As he set the parking brake, he noticed the living room curtains part briefly. Somebody, probably Mrs. Ohlsen, was checking on his arrival.

The front door swung open as he stepped onto the porch. Myra Ohlsen looked every bit as good standing in the doorway as she sounded on the phone. Tall, tanned, and stylishly coifed, she held out her hand in a friendly greeting.

"Mr. Gray Wolf, a pleasure meeting you. Please, come in before the bugs eat you alive."

"Thank you, ma'am, and call me Daniel. I have to say, you must be mighty sure of your surroundings, opening the door to a stranger like you do."

Myra smiled, then in a stern voice, called, "Max!"

Immediately, a huge German shepherd appeared at her side, teeth bared, deep growl rumbling in its throat.

Daniel nearly fell off the porch in surprise.

"Friend, Max." The monster canine sat beside his master's feet, then wagged his tail for Daniel's benefit.

"I'm a trusting sort, Daniel, but not **that** trusting, okay? I hope Max didn't frighten you too badly."

"Whew! Nothing that a couple of stiff shots of bourbon wouldn't cure. Never mind, I'm just joking.

"So, can I come inside now?" Gray Wolf continued. "Or do I wait for Max' permission?"

"Of course, come on in. And call me Myra, okay? Just make yourself comfortable on the couch and I'll get Trina."

Daniel watched the attractive lady disappear through a hallway before turning his attention back to the waiting dog. Max had taken up sentry duty six feet from the couch.

"Let's make a truce, *kola sunka*. I stay a perfect gentleman and you don't bite my arm off. Shake on it?" Gray Wolf extended a tentative hand.

Max took two steps, sat down, and promptly placed his giant right paw in Daniel's hand.

Satisfied with the ritual, Daniel turned his attention to the expensively furnished interior. Mauve leather couches formed an L-shape against stuccoed walls adorned with a profusion of genuine oil paintings. Solid cherry book panels surrounded a massive marble fireplace at the far end of the room. Plush, spotless white carpet formed a woolen snowscape throughout the living area.

Gray Wolf sat back and admired the opulent surroundings. Despite the obvious wealth of the owner, he had to admit she was not the least pretentious. His study was interrupted by a soft whirring sound emanating from the hallway. He glanced up to see a motorized wheelchair rolling toward him.

Trina was a younger version of her mother. Delightful blue eyes peaked out from beneath a mop of carefully curled blonde hair. A warm, friendly smile graced the woman-child's freckled face. Despite the wheelchair, Trina looked in remarkably good shape, her legs showing no signs of atrophy. Daniel rose and walked to the girl, extending his hand.

"Trina," he said, noting her firm handshake. "I'm Daniel Gray Wolf and I'd like to visit with you a little. Your mother tells me you've been having some problems in an area I might be able to help with."

"Nice meeting you, Mr. Gray Wolf," Trina replied, a smile even in her voice.

"Let's go to the couches where we can all be comfortable," Myra suggested. "Daniel, please just sit wherever you like. Trina will be right behind you."

Gray Wolf sat down at the same station he had initially taken, watching as Trina skillfully maneuvered the mechanized chair into place in front of him. Daniel started the conversation.

"For openers, I'd like to tell you both a little about what I do. I'm not a psychic so I don't know what you're thinking, or what the future holds. I'm not a doctor, so I can't tell you what your dreams might mean either. What I do have is a hereditary ability to visit other people's dreams and work out their problems. I'm very good at what I do."

"Mr. Gray Wolf ... Daniel ... my Mom says that's what you prefer to be called. Will I know you're there, you know, in my dream?"

"Well, Trina, some people do and some don't. See, I don't come riding in on a great white stallion very often. From what I've been told by those who do see me, my presence only adds to their feeling of safety and comfort. The whole session is usually over quickly. What people have a tendency to remember most is not having a nightmare anymore."

"So, how do you get into my dream? I mean, how do you know when to come in and take care of the problem?"

"Good question, but I don't have an exact answer for you. From what I've read about dreams, you're most susceptible to nightmares during your deep sleep stage. It's sometimes called D-sleep, or REM-sleep. Both mean the same thing. REM stands for rapid eye movement. I guess that's the best way the doctors could describe the dreaming period. Anyhow, I fall asleep pretty easy and, by being near the person having bad dreams, I'm able to join them and take care of the situation."

"Should Trina tell you a little about what her nightmares are about, Daniel?"

"Only if she wants to. It's not really necessary. The real reason for this visit is to make sure my dream companion feels comfortable with me. I sure as heck don't want to scare a person I'm working with by popping in all of a sudden unannounced."

"I feel really comfortable with you already, Daniel. I mean, you're friendly and soothing and I like the way you talk about things. I just know you're going to be there to help me. I mean, all I want is for this stuff to go away, okay?"

"Okay," Gray Wolf responded with a smile. "Now, do either of you have any questions?"

"Yes, umm, what happens if I don't have my nightmare? I've read where people in dream therapy sometimes don't have bad dreams because they know someone is there; kind of a guard, you know?"

"That's why I don't usually come visit until we're sure the dream is a recurring one. You're going to go into your bedroom now, by yourself, and go to sleep. You've had this bad dream for several nights in a row. I think we'll lick the problem tonight without any problems. Just trust me, okay? I've done this many, many times."

Trina's face lit up with relief as she touched the wheelchair controls, swiveling the machine in a hundred and eighty degree turn before wheeling off down the hallway. "See you on the other side!" she called over her shoulder.

Hearing her daughter's bedroom door close, Myra Ohlsen's smile faded as she looked at Gray Wolf. "Do you really think you can help her? This is the perkiest she's been in several days. I'd hate to see her hopes dashed."

"Like I said, Myra, trust me. I'm batting a pretty good average. I've been a Dream Catcher for twenty years now and haven't had any repeat customers. We'll take care of Trina's problem."

"So, what do we do now?"

"We wait. The first hour or so is not critical. Her nightmares won't start until she's had a chance to enter deeper sleep."

"But, you know, Daniel, sometimes Trina cries out right after she's gone to sleep. Sometimes she wakes up moaning. Isn't this the nightmare acting on her?"

"No, I don't think so. Again, I've read a little about this subject. What you describe are symptoms of night terrors, a completely different animal. But, let me ask you, when she wakes up during these early episodes, does she remember what woke her up, or does she usually just fall back asleep?"

"No, she always goes right back to sleep. Doesn't seem to remember what the dream was about."

"Then, those are the night terrors I mentioned. Absolutely normal ... you have them, I have them ... we just don't recall waking up unless someone's there to tell us about it."

"Can I offer you something. Coffee—a drink, maybe?"

"No, thank you, Myra. It's best if I don't take on anything right now. After we're through, then maybe a cup of coffee, or something stronger, depending on how I'm feeling.

"Right now," Gray Wolf continued, "We just wait for

Trina to fall asleep. You can start checking on her periodically in about an hour or so. Look for signs of deep sleep, like Trina not being disturbed when you open her door; check her eyelids to see if there's movement. I won't be needed until then. In the mean time, you just do what you normally do … or we can visit. Whichever you prefer. I've brought a book, so I can definitely occupy my time."

"Oh, I have so many questions I'd like to ask you, but they're all just for my own satisfaction. It probably would be best if I finished up some work in the kitchen. We're having a bake sale after church tomorrow and, like a dummy, I promised to donate a couple dozen cookies."

"Go right ahead," Daniel said, pulling a paperback from his attaché. "I've got ol' Louie L'Amour to keep me company for awhile."

Engrossed in the book, Gray Wolf was surprised when Myra approached him, wringing her hands nervously.

"I think she's ready, Daniel. When I checked in just now, her eyelids were jumping all around. Poor baby, I hate to see her going through this."

Rising off the couch, Daniel lightly touched Myra Ohlsen's shoulder. "Easy now. I'm not going to take her appendix out. This will be finished before your next batch of cookies is done."

Gray Wolf followed Myra down the hallway to Trina's bedroom. Pausing at the door, he whispered, "Leave the door open if you like so you can peek in from time to time, but don't do anything to disturb the girl or me while we're asleep. Trina may move about some. I probably won't, but don't be alarmed by what you see, okay? She's just dreaming and is in no real physical danger."

Myra squeezed Daniel's hand, smiled briefly and walked back down the hallway toward the kitchen.

Guided by the dim nightlight next to dresser, Daniel made his way over to the sleeping girl's side. Checking her eyes, he nodded in satisfaction. Trina was in a deep slumber. Carefully, he sat down on the trundle beside the young girl's bed. Shucking his tennis shoes, Gray Wolf reclined on the cot and effortlessly fell asleep.

***

Daniel arrived in a park like setting. Lush trees tinged with autumn reds and oranges surrounded him. He peered out from the thick foliage and saw a narrow dirt path. At the far end, walking toward him, was Trina. *She can walk in her dreams*! Gray Wolf remained hidden in the brush, not wanting the girl to notice him. As he watched her approach, two young men came into view from the bushes opposite his vantage point. Daniel tensed, readying himself in case these boys were the cause of her nightmare. Yet, all he could sense was Trina's delight in the boys' company. They joined her on the path, one on each side, and began walking with her. The three teenagers were talking, enjoying each other's company, though no conversation was audible.

Stopping directly in front of Gray Wolf's hiding spot, the taller boy, good looking and blond, leaned over and kissed Trina lightly on the lips. Laughing, she tilted her head toward him and drew his face down against hers, kissing him with more ardor. On her right, the shorter black-haired teen put his arm around her waist, then placed his head against hers.

Still kissing Trina, the blond boy casually slipped his hand inside her blouse. The dark-haired lad reached down and touched her right knee, slowly sliding upward, bunching her skirt in a V-trail behind his ascending hand. Attaining the juncture of her thighs, his hand disappeared amongst the folds of clothing. Gently, almost synchronized, the boys lowered Trina to the ground, their hands never leaving the hidden spots of their ministrations.

Experiencing a minor voyeuristic discomfort, Daniel nearly withdrew from the sexual fantasy in front of him, yet felt compelled to stay. His attention turned back to the three, Gray Wolf watched Blond Hair unbutton the girl's blouse, stroking her exposed breasts. Trina reached for the boy's belt buckle, magically undoing his pants in the process. Dark Head unclasped his own jeans and lowered himself between her spread legs.

This isn't a nightmare. She's having fun. Gray Wolf's eyes continually drew back to Trina's legs; healthy legs now circling Dark Head's back. *Just a few more minutes, and if nothing bad happens ...*

Trina's shrill scream cut into Daniel's mind. It was not a sound of pleasure, instead full of fear and pain. He couldn't see what was causing her distress. Both boys had their backs to him. *Hold on, Danny-boy. She's been here before. Wait and see what the problem is.*

Trina struggled to free herself, kicking at the dark haired boy who still furiously pumped between her legs. Her hands beat at Blond Hair's stomach and chest as he forced his hips against her face. With a violent wrench, Trina dislodged her assailants. Scrambling to her feet, she began running down the path to Daniel's right. The boys turned to pursue her, startling the Dream Catcher with their changed appearance.

Arms stretched out in front of him, Blond Hair walked woodenly, stiff-legged after the frightened girl. Dulled eyes stared sightlessly. His slack-jawed mouth spread in a grin bordering on rictus. Beside him, Dark Head suddenly metamorphosed, face elongating into a feral snout as coarse black hair sprung from his body. Hunching over, the were-thing scrabbled after Trina's retreating form.

Trina fell. Not tripped. Just fell. She tried to rise as the monsters closed in, but couldn't. Her legs no longer supported her. Screaming again, she pushed herself backward, desperately trying to avoid the boy-creatures bearing down upon her. *Now!*

Gray Wolf leaped from the bushes, swinging a machete at the tall blond zombie. Blade connected with neck bone, severing the head with a satisfying sound of snapping vertebra and tearing flesh. Drunkenly, the headless torso wandered in circles, stiffened arms stabbing at nothing in particular. With a faltering footstep, the body slammed to earth, quivering as blackish-red blood splashed from the gaping hole where the head used to be.

Dark Head, the were-wolf creature, turned his attention to Daniel, snarling as he crouched into attack position. Springing, Dark Head slashed a razored claw toward Gray Wolf's head, narrowly missing as the Dream Catcher spun to one side. Enraged, the beast gathered itself for another assault, muscles bunching beneath the matted body fur. Inch-long fangs gleamed with saliva that dripped from the dream monster's gaping yaw. Daniel fortified himself against the attack, stooping until his eyes were level with the beast's.

Howling in triumphant hatred, the were-thing launched, spreading his powerful arms in anticipation of a death embrace. The attack met mid-air resistance as the creature skewered itself onto a silver-bladed lance. Momentum pushed the gravely wounded beast forward, his bristly body sliding down the length of the shaft and into Daniel's waiting arms. Weakened but still formidable, Dark Head scraped at Gray Wolf's arms and chest with its lethal claws. Fending off the snapping jaws with one hand, Daniel looped his other arm behind the beast's head, driving a silver dagger into the shaggy neck. Without a whimper, the brute collapsed at Gray Wolf's feet.

Exhausted, shaken from the attack, Daniel turned toward the fully clothed Trina. Still on the ground, unable to get up, she stared at the Dream Catcher with a growing wonder. *She's waking up!* Quickly, Gray Wolf ran into the orange-leafed forest.

***

Daniel woke, then stretched, wincing at the deep pain in his arms and chest. Souvenirs from the were-thing. He knew, from previous encounters, there would be no marks on his body. Dreams don't leave marks. But they could leave psychosomatic impressions.

Ignoring the bone-deep aches, he looked across the brief space between his trundle and Trina's bed. The girl snored gently, no more nightmares filtering into her sleep pattern.

With an effort, Gray Wolf sat upright, once again stretching against the very real twinges in his muscles. Slipping into his tennis shoes, he quietly exited the room, shutting the door behind him. His watch told him it was just after two in the morning, yet the living room lights burned brightly. He shuffled down the hallway into the welcoming light signifying another person was still awake. The tantalizing aroma of fresh-brewed coffee hung in the air. Daniel saw Myra Ohlsen, curled up on the couch, reading his Louis L'Amour novel.

Myra looked up with a start as he entered the living room.

"Goodness, you are quiet! Is everything all right?"

Gray Wolf nodded and said, "I'll take a cup of that great smelling coffee, if you don't mind."

Myra scurried into the kitchen as Daniel plopped onto the

sofa. Reaching down, he stiffly tied his tennis shoes, grunting with the effort. He straightened up and achieved a more natural pose as Trina's mother walked into the living room with two steaming mugs.

"Thanks," he murmured, accepting the proffered cup.

"Did everything go okay? You didn't have any problems. Trina's nightmares are all gone now?"

Daniel raised his hand against the onslaught of questions, gratefully sipping at the hot brew, before answering, "She's fine, Myra. Trina's a strong girl and we worked out her problems with very little effort." *You lying turd! You haven't felt aches like this in years.*

"Oh, Daniel, I don't know how we'll be able to thank you. Mrs. Long Bear said you don't take compensation for what you do. I think that's a shame, but she said it's some kind of tradition thing."

Gray Wolf nodded, sipping more of the delicious coffee. "The coffee's payment enough, thank you. I'm glad I could help."

"This lifestyle must be terribly hard on you; on your wife, Daniel."

"Naw, I haven't found anyone to put up with me yet." *Always modest, aren't you, kola? Why don't you tell Myra how you're really feeling?*

"I just find this all so fascinating, especially now that it's over and Trina's cured. I mean, it all seems so mystical, your powers and everything."

"I guess I don't think about it that much anymore. It's just an ability I've had since birth. It's meant to be shared. Nothing mystical about it from my standpoint."

Initial tendrils of the expected headache touched his forehead. Reaching into his jean pocket, Daniel removed a tiny cellophane containing three aspirin. Tearing the bag open, he popped the pain relievers into his mouth, crunching the tablets into a moist powder.

Myra Ohlsen noticed the ritual and asked, "Do you have a headache? Is that a normal thing after—after what you've just done?"

"Yeah, it's pretty normal. Tonight's not so bad. Like I said, Trina's strong and she gave me a lot of help."

"I suppose you really can't talk about what happened in there; sort of doctor-patient privilege."

"Well, not being a doctor, I can't lay claim to that privilege. But, I guess if Trina wants to talk about it, she would be the best source.

"Listen, Myra," Gray Wolf added, rising from the comfortable sofa, "I'd better be getting home, and you look like you could use some sleep as well."

Daniel had felt the slight uneasiness, that minute discomfort he was so familiar with. His job was done and people were relieved, but they now wanted to be just with their family.

Myra held the door open as he slung the attaché strap over his shoulder. "She's really okay now? Thelma Long Bear says you are really, really good. No repeat visits?"

"Would Thelma speak with forked tongue, Myra? Relax, and take care of Trina. She's a real sweet kid and her dreams will be good ones. This nightmare is gone for good." Gray Wolf left the house, offering a small wave in farewell.

"Thank you again," Myra called out as Daniel approached his truck.

Gray Wolf lumbered into his pickup and hit the ignition. As he sat in the idling truck, he watched to make sure Myra Ohlsen closed and hopefully secured her door. Only when he saw the front light blink off did he put the truck in gear, smoothly pulling out of the flagstone driveway.

The pain in his arms and chest had subsided, while the headache hung around near the back of his skull just enough to be remembered. At least Trina was free of her nightmare. The attackers wouldn't be coming back. Gray Wolf was positive the problem had been solved. Adolescents and children were the most susceptible to his ability, most likely due to their ingrained acknowledgment of adults being the authority figures. Adults, even in their dreams, sometimes questioned his ability to end their nightmares.

"Thank God she was just a kid," he murmured, wheeling onto the main thoroughfare after descending from Canyon Lake Heights.

CHAPTER 5

Thankfully, Sunday proved to be a no-brainer. Receiving no calls for help, Gray Wolf spent the day relaxing, shopping to stock up on sorely needed groceries, and then relaxing some more. Two straight nights of dream catching had definitely put a dent in his energy reserve.

By Sunday evening, Daniel felt basically human again. Unwinding in front of the television, he quickly went to sleep, not waking until the next morning.

"Shit, seven-thirty already!" Gray Wolf stretched once, popping his vertebra back into alignment before stiffly hobbling into the bedroom. Work started at eight o'clock, leaving no time for breakfast, let alone a shower. "Hope I don't offend too many folks." Changing quickly into Docker slacks, golf shirt, and deck shoes, Daniel exited the house five minutes later. His job was on the far northwest side of town; Dakota Steel and Supply, the region's largest producer of steel beams. Fourteen years with the company had netted him the manager's slot in the drafting department. His job, just like that of the seven draftsmen working for him, was to break down the intricate architectural blueprints presented the company. Beam by beam, his staff drew scale models for the steelworkers, carefully marking the location for bracket holes, weld plates, everything necessary to erect the architect's creation. Once drafted, the finished sheet was run through the blueprint machine, producing multi-copies for use in the fabrication plant.

Although the job was boring at times because of the repetitiveness, at least his take home check made up for the long hours pushing a mechanical pencil across a t-square. He secretly enjoyed the non-competitive atmosphere, the quiet time alone in his office. His crew was seasoned, making his supervisor's role all the easier.

Gray Wolf clocked in as the timer clicked to 7:54. *Hell, I had time for some toast.*

The workday went smoothly; no interruptions except the normal harried calls from fabrication requesting explanations on why a bracket was to be mounted as drawn. Surprised, Daniel heard the end-of-day rustlings outside his open door. Five o'clock sharp and these guys are outta here. *Me too!*

"Hey, Daniel, want to join us for a beer?" asked Jimbo Freeman as he passed by.

"Where you headed?"

"Me and a couple of the guys thought about going to the Casino Bar. Happy Hour starts about now, so it's two-fer time."

"Yeah, sounds good. Hey, I'll meet you guys down there, okay? Need to finish up this sheet first."

Gray Wolf leaned back on his stool, looking over the near-complete drawing. "Hell with it," he muttered. The drafting guys were three days ahead of production anyway.

Putting away his tools, Daniel punched out and headed across the parking lot to his sweltering pickup. As he opened the door, a faint wave of hot air fanned out, mingling with the slightly cooler exterior temperature. Gray Wolf hopped gingerly into the cab, careful not to touch the burning vinyl with his exposed arms. Cranking up the ignition, he flipped the air conditioner to maximum, holding his palms against the vents until cool air flowed.

"That's the trouble with this damn town," he muttered out of habit. "Can't leave the windows down because of the thunderstorms. Can't roll the windows up or you'll broil yourself.

"God, I love this place!" he yelled, slamming the door shut and rumbling out of the parking lot.

Gray Wolf arrived at the Casino Bar ten minutes later. The place was crowded, not unusual considering the sweltering outside temperature and the fact it was Monday. Or Tuesday. Or Wednesday. The day didn't really matter. Scattered calls for drinks, barely discernible over the country western music blaring from the jukebox, kept the two harried waitresses running from bar to tables.

Daniel nudged his way through the noisy crowd, searching for his friends. He found them at the far end of the bar, sipping their usual bottles of Budweiser. No stools were vacant, so Gray Wolf stood behind his three co-workers, raising his hand in an attempt to catch Dusty, the bartender, looking up from her drink ministrations.

Jimbo Freeman solved the problem. "Hey, Dusty, bring Daniel a Bud!"

Seconds later, an uncapped Budweiser slid down the counter. Daniel stuck his hand out, expertly stopping the frosty bottle in front of him.

"So," Gray Wolf yelled casually at Freeman. "Come here often, sailor?"

Jimbo responded with a raised middle finger before turning his gaze back to the impotent television set mounted overhead.

"How the hell can you pay attention to the TV with all this noise going on?" Gray Wolf shouted in his friend's ear.

"Soccer," Freeman responded with equal volume, pointing

at the flickering images. "Can't understand the fuckin' announcer anyway."

"Yeah, right. Thanks for the beer. I'll get the next round."

Daniel sauntered off, looking for a quieter place to nurse his beer. He spied a vacant spot in the far corner, away from the jukebox and blaring television. Shouldering through the bar crowd, he shuffled a roundabout path to the table and plopped down in one of the chairs. Chilled air flowed onto his head from the vent directly above. Gray Wolf leaned back, luxuriating in the cool.

"Excuse me, but this is my table."

Daniel looked at the speaker, a youngish man with thinning blond hair.

"Pardon?"

"This is my table. See, my beer's still sitting here. Had to go to the john."

"Okay, friend," Gray Wolf answered. "Sorry, but I didn't see anyone sitting here and it was out of all the noise, so I kind of moved in."

"Hey, I know what you mean," Thin Hair said." Listen, I don't mind sharing. You want to finish your drink here, go right ahead."

"Thanks, I think I will. Name's Daniel Gray Wolf."

"Steve Abrams," Thin Hair responded, shaking Daniel's extended hand.

"Hot one out there today, Steve. The beer sure goes down easy, doesn't it?"

Abrams nodded in agreement as he tipped the beer bottle to his lips.

Gray Wolf studied his table partner's profile while the man's attention was focused on the icy brew. Abrams looked to be about thirty, his thin hair and round tortoise shell glasses not quite able to cloak the boyish features. He was dressed in blue jeans, western shirt and cowboy boots, but it looked more like a uniform than his standard wear. *Stevie, you're not a for-real cowboy, are you? I'd say you're an accountant ... maybe a bookkeeper ... maybe a lawyer.*

"So, what do you do for a living, Steve?"

"Me? Nothin' much, you know? Just kinda hangin' right now."

Gray Wolf heard the nervousness. What was it, tension, fear, or embarrassment? Hell, some guys got defensive over not having a job. Maybe Steve was one of them. Daniel was about to change the subject, make small talk, when Abrams spoke.

"How about you?"

"Huh?"

"How about you—what do you do?"

"Oh, I run the drafting department at Dakota Steel," Gray Wolf answered, no false modesty in his voice.

"Dakota Steel ... that's here in town?"

So, you're an out of towner, Steve-O. "Yeah, on the northwest end. Big place, lots of steel. Can't miss it."

Abrams smiled at the subtle humor, the first time any look resembling relaxation had crossed his face.

"I gather by your question you're not from around here, Steve. Just passing through on vacation, or what?"

"No, I moved here a couple of weeks ago. Why?"

There's that nervous voice again. Pretty close to a defensive question.

"No reason. Just making small talk until the barmaid comes by with another tall one. Can I buy you a beer?"

"No. No, thanks. I probably should be going. Got to be somewhere by eight."

"Are you going to the dogs?"

"What the hell's this about dogs?" Abrams asked, almost belligerently.

"Whoa, pardner," Daniel soothed. "I meant are you going out to the dog track, you know, the Black Hills Greyhound Race Track. That's about the only thing happening on a Monday night in August unless you're a movie fan."

Abrams sighed as he rubbed both hands across his face. "Hey, I'm sorry. You just caught me by surprise with the dog thing. I've had trouble getting any sleep because I dream about dogs."

Oh, shit, kola! You sure know how to pick your drinking partners. Get your ass outta here, Gray Wolf.

"No problem, Steve. I'm sorry if I got you upset," Daniel said. "Well, looks like my buddies are waving for me. I owe them a round.

"Listen, thanks for sharing your table," Gray Wolf continued, easing off his chair. "Maybe I'll see you around."

Abrams grabbed Gray Wolf's arm, gently but insistently, "Hey, Daniel, I didn't mean to scare you off, okay? I'm just a little irritable from lack of sleep."

"Don't worry about it, pardner," Gray Wolf smiled, pulling his arm loose. "See you around, okay?"

Daniel felt Abrams' eyes on his back as he sidled toward his friends. He knew the eyes followed him up to Jimbo Freeman's side; watched him as he put his hand on Freeman's shoulder.

Jimbo snatched a glance at Gray Wolf, then quickly diverted his attention back to the tube. Pointing a finger at the screen, Freeman yelled, "Soccer ... never could understand the fucking announcers ... or the game."

"Yeah," Daniel yelled back. "You said that before!"

"What? Can't hear you with all the fucking noise."

"I said I'll see you tomorrow." Daniel called equally unintelligible good byes to his other two friends before heading toward the door.

Outside, the late summer heat assaulted him. Though nearly six-thirty, it was still hotter than hell, but at least it was quiet. Gray Wolf yawned at the sun hanging above the western hills. One beer had never made him tired before. Sluggishly, he walked to his broiling pickup. *Must be the heat getting to you, kola.*

Starting the reliable Ford, he cranked the air conditioner on high, placing his palms against the vents as he yawned again. *Hell, maybe it was your beer buddy.* Gray Wolf caught the tail end of Rapid City's infamous rush hour traffic as he headed east toward home. Nine cars at a stoplight, at the same time, constituted gridlock in the spacious community of fifty thousand souls. Ten minutes out of the Casino Bar, Daniel pulled into his driveway. Ten minutes later, he was asleep, and not in front of the television this time.

CHAPTER 6

One of two things woke Daniel Gray Wolf. Either it was the alarm clock or the telephone. Punching at the clock didn't silence the ringing, so Daniel groggily answered the phone. "Hullo?"

"Is this Daniel Gray Wolf?"

The voice was familiar, though Daniel couldn't yet put a face with it. "Yeah, speaking. Who's this?"

"Uh ... Steve Abrams. Remember, we met at the bar earlier this evening?

"Yeah, sure I remember. Seems like only hours ago. What can I do for you at eleven forty-three in the evening?"

"Well, Daniel, after you left the Casino, I got to feeling kind of bad for the way I acted. You know, jumping down your throat and everything. Anyhow, I went up and talked with your friend, Jumbo, the guy who points at the TV and swears a lot?

"Jumbo, sure ... and?"

"I wanted him to apologize for me, you know, when you got to work or something. Anyhow, Jumbo said –"

"That's Jimbo! Jimbo Freeman ... not Jumbo, for chrissakes. But please, go on now that you've got me awake."

The sarcasm apparently went over Abrams' head because he continued, "As I was saying, **Jimbo** said something to the effect, 'Aw, don't worry about it. If the Dream Catcher took offense, you would have known.'"

Oh Lord, here it comes. Thanks, 'Jumbo'. "He's right, Steve. I took no offense, so no need to apologize, okay? It's late now, I was asleep, and I have to go to work early in the morning. Good night, Steve -"

"Wait! Daniel, I need your help. Freeman told me about what this dream catching thing means. Said you take care of people's nightmares. I told you about the dogs tonight? Gray Wolf, I need help with the dogs!"

There it was ... the request. *You can't turn the guy down, kola. You don't know him, but you can't turn him down because now he's asked.* Gray Wolf was stuck.

"All right, Steve, but not tonight."

"Hey, that's fine! I mean, I won't be able to go to sleep tonight anyway. How about tomorrow night; can we meet tomorrow night? I'd prefer your place. I've just got a little Eighth Street efficiency with a bedroom big enough to fall into and hit the bed."

"Yeah, my place is fine," Daniel said, then gave directions to the grateful man.

Hanging up, Gray Wolf had an uncomfortable feeling about the pending session. He'd definitely talk to Freeman tomorrow about referring strangers. Jimbo knew the rules, probably even remembered them when he was sober. But, that wasn't the major problem. Steve Abrams was.

"Who are you, Abrams?" Gray Wolf said aloud. "There's something strange about you I can't put my finger on."

Lying back down, Daniel stared into the darkness as he tried to sort the mixed feelings.

No sense worrying about it tonight. Tomorrow will come soon enough and it will just be another session. One more headache, one more cure. You've done this hundreds of times, kola. This one's no different.

Even as he fell asleep, Gray Wolf knew the mental pep talk was bullshit. There **was** something different about this one.

Daniel didn't wake again until six-thirty, having passed the remainder of the night in a dreamless, restful sleep. Usually optimistic upon waking to a day of sunshine, his outlook was somewhat dampened as he remembered last night's sleep-interrupting conversation.

"Aw, man," he groaned into his hands as he sat on the edge of the bed. "Is this how it's going to be from now on? Hell, I might as well set up a tent and a couple of cots at the fairgrounds; post a big-ass sign that says 'I Kill Bad Dreams For Free'."

Mood set, Gray Wolf trundled off to the bathroom. Fifteen minutes later, wet hair clinging to his head, Daniel was driving toward downtown Rapid City. Having only himself to take care of, he found it convenient to eat breakfast out several mornings a week.

Daniel entered Tally's Restaurant shortly before seven. The little cafe on the corner of Sixth and St. Joe had been a landmark for as many years as he could remember. Situated in the heart of the business district, Tally's was blessed with a brisk trade because of its fast, tasty meals and plenteous coffee. Sliding into a booth, Gray Wolf's spirits picked up considerably as the prospect of eggs, bacon, and hash browns produced an anticipatory growl in his stomach.

Daniel sipped his coffee and stared out the window as early day Rapid City came to life. At seven in the morning, most of the traffic could be attributed to non-retailers; lawyers, doctors, business men, making their way to offices that wouldn't open for another two hours. Retailers typically didn't pull in until just before their nine o'clock opening hour.

A movement to his right brought Gray Wolf's attention back into the restaurant. He looked up at the figure standing beside his booth.

"Good morning, Doctor Nagel. Up with the birds, I see." The 'I see' added in deference to Nagel's constant use of the term.

"Good morning, Mr. Gray Wolf. Would you care for some company?"

Daniel looked around the half-empty diner, noting the availability of several booths and counter seats. Had the restaurant been full, he would have been compelled to allow Nagel to join him. The obvious vacancies made his decision much simpler.

"Sure, pull up a napkin." *Gray Wolf, you wuss! Why don't you just tell him to screw off?* "Always room for one more."

Daniel watched the fastidious psychiatrist produce a handkerchief and dust imaginary crumbs from the vinyl seat before sliding his eight hundred dollar suit pants across the surface. *Now he's gonna purse his fingers and stare at me with those shark eyes.*

Edwin Nagel steepled his fingers, resting his chin on the fleshy spire, as he looked unflinchingly into Daniel's eyes.

"I just thought I'd let you know," Nagel offered, "I sent a letter to the AMA about your unauthorized activities."

"Aw, and you didn't let me check the spelling first?"

"I see. Humor ... yes, that's good. Enjoy it while you can. I don't think you'll feel quite so jovial after the American Medical Association issues a friendly cease and desist order."

"Well, let's see, Dr. Nagel, this is late August, right?. If they respond to you as quickly as they have to me in the past, I should be hearing from them in early September. Next year, that is."

"Your tenacity impresses me, reminiscent of a cornered mouse facing a much bigger foe. I like that in a man, Daniel. Uh, may I call you Daniel?"

"No."

"I see. Am I noting a bit of animosity carefully buried beneath that calm exterior?"

"Ah, my meal has arrived. Perhaps, Doctor, while you're analyzing, you'd like to tell me about my choice of breakfast repast?"

"Gray Wolf, you don't seem to realize the trouble you could be getting yourself into. What you're doing is blatantly in violation of medical ethics, not to mention most probably breaking a law or two."

"Observe how I set my fork squarely in the eggs, then use my knife to slice said eggs vertically and horizontally into perfect half-inch squares. I will admit, my ancestry shows through when it comes to bacon. I tend to eat it with my fingers. Is that a psychotic trait?"

"This is impossible! Gray Wolf, you're living outside reality; and when reality hits, you are going to be one surprised fellow."

"Actually, Nagel, I'm surprised you're still sitting here. Why are you visiting with a mere commoner when so many of the upper crust need your help? Why don't you try and put me out of business by doing your job properly?" Gray Wolf felt egg yoke trickle from the corner of his mouth, but decided to leave it for dramatic effect.

Edwin Nagel reddened from sheer exasperation. Fingers clutched into fists, then unclenched as he fought his emotions. Abruptly, the psychiatrist stood, bumping against the booth table in his haste to exit. Hulking over the still-seated Gray

Wolf, Nagel spoke in a volume more suitable for auditorium usage.

"I will personally see you defrocked of your illegal practice, sir! Once the AMA issues its ultimatum, I intend to have the local authorities look into this matter from a criminal standpoint." Nagel abruptly turned toward the cafe door.

"Doctor Nagel," Daniel called after the retreating figure. "Have a nice day."

This time, unlike the previous meeting's outcome, Gray Wolf ate his breakfast with gusto, relishing the greasy coating now firmly situated against the inside of his stomach. Something about Nagel's visit lit the fires, projected him into a good mood once again. Maybe it was the conflict; maybe it was seeing a pompous ass become irate. Dropping money on the table, Daniel sauntered outside into the early morning heat, whistling his favorite nameless tune.

Gray Wolf only spent two minutes chastising Jimbo Freeman about the previous night's faux pas. The ass chewing was friendly, brotherly, but the message was clear. Jimbo was to suggest no more dream referrals unless the afflicted was a mother, dad, or sibling. Freeman was horribly apologetic, not remembering his visit with Steve Abrams, or his running commentary on the virtues of soccer.

Driving home from the office, Daniel had his first twinge of bad mood since earlier in the day. Abrams would be coming to his home, replete with canine nightmare. *What is it about that boy that makes you uneasy, Gray Wolf? He's a transient, has a nightmare, and happens to run into a for-real Dream Catcher. Don't start thinking that destiny crap, kola.*

Still, not knowing anything about Abrams was disturbing. This would be his first session with a person no one knew. Daniel wasn't concerned for his safety. He didn't go to sleep until the client was in a deep slumber and he always emerged from a dream before the client woke. Maybe it was Abrams' nervousness. Maybe this guy needed professional help—someone like Nagel. *Yeah right, I can just see old Edwin thanking you for sending some business his way.*

Gray Wolf was still thinking about tonight's session as he pulled into his driveway. Still thinking about Abrams as he fixed a light supper. Only one bright light shown in the otherwise prospective dreary evening. He would be done with this guy after one session. After tonight, Steve Abrams would be just a dwindling unpleasant thought.

Daniel immersed himself in the evening news, enjoying the century-old anchorman on Channel Four. Bill Knutson had been with the station when it was running on kerosene. Knutson even had a brief flit with fame when his image flashed on the television screen momentarily during a scene from the movie, Thunderheart. Knutson offered the community a sense of steadiness, a sense of purpose, even in reporting the night's main topic of bingo abuse by unlicensed agencies.

The door chimes interrupted Knutson's dry editorial, pulling Gray Wolf from his sofa to the front door. He checked his watch—ten after ten—Abrams was only a few minutes late. Sighing, Daniel opened the door.

"Hello, Steve. Have any problems with the directions?" the Dream Catcher asked, looking first at his spectacled guest, then to the dark blue sedan parked in the drive.

"Not too much, thanks. I missed your exit the first time. Ended up at the Rapid Valley Speedway. Figured you didn't live there, so I backtracked, and here I am." Abrams entered as Daniel held the door open for him.

"Hey, you look kind of beat," Gray Wolf offered. "Guess you didn't get much sleep last night, but then you told me you wouldn't."

"Yeah, been up since yesterday morning. Hey, I want to thank you again for seeing me. I know this is sort of unusual."

"Forget it. Come on in and sit down. We'll talk for a few minutes about what's going to take place, then you'll hit the sack."

Comfortably situated in the living room, Gray Wolf explained the procedure to Abrams, careful not to omit anything even though he had given the same basic spiel a thousand times. Steve still appeared nervous, probably due to lack of sleep, Gray Wolf surmised.

"So, any questions before we make the trip?" Daniel asked.

"Um, why can't you just bomb the dogs, you know, nuke 'em? Maybe shoot 'em."

"Good question, Steve. See, early on I learned I couldn't use any force that might put the dreamer in jeopardy. Bombs would undoubtedly blow you up as well. No, don't worry, you wouldn't be killed in real life, but I could replace your original nightmare with a new one starring me. Now, how the hell would I fight myself?"

Gray Wolf grinned before concluding, "So, any other questions?"

"None that I can think of. I'm ready to begin, if that's the next step."

"That's the next step. Bathroom's on the right, bedroom's on the left. Use the bed closest to the window, okay? As I explained, I'll be in after you've gone to sleep, but before you start dreaming."

"Okay, Daniel, and thanks," Abrams said. "Oh, one thing. I didn't bring any pajamas; what do I sleep in?"

"Doesn't make any difference; sleep in your clothes,

underwear, or nude, I don't care," Gray Wolf replied with a smile. "I'm after your dreams, not your body."

Abrams stared at Daniel for a second before a brief smile of understanding crossed his face. "You're good with people, Daniel. You really know how to take the edge off."

"Good night, Steven. See you in your dreams."

Gray Wolf plopped back down on the couch as the younger man disappeared into the bedroom. He concentrated on the last five minutes of news, watching a would-be jock sportscaster rattle off baseball scores. As the local news ended, he picked up his L'Amour book, thumbing to where he'd left off during the Trina Ohlsen encounter. Glancing at his watch, Daniel figured he had at least an hour before his brand new best friend would be ready.

Fifty pages later, Gray Wolf set the book down and checked on his visitor. Steve Abrams lay sprawled across the far bed, snoring lightly. Though not a medical expert, Daniel knew from previous sessions that a person deprived of sleep usually achieved REM-stage more quickly. Abrams now displayed all the symptoms of entering that deep slumber level.

Shucking his tennis shoes, Gray Wolf settled onto the second bed. He glanced briefly at Abrams' flickering eyelids, then emptied his mind and fell asleep.

Daniel joined Abrams' dream in a narrow, dark alley. A distant street light cast guarded reflections at the mouth of the portal, illuminating the cobble stoned ground enough for him to make out puddles of water in the stony depressions. Gray Wolf hid behind an overflowing dumpster as Steve Abrams hurried into view, the portrait of a man pursued.

Abrams skidded to a halt at the alleyway, frantically looking over his shoulder before renewing the race against yet-unseen assailants. His mindless flight took him past Gray Wolf's hiding spot then deeper into the shadows.

Daniel saw Abrams' horrified expression as the man ran blindly toward the dead-end concrete wall hidden by darkness. He noted the glazed look in the dreamer's eyes, the open mouth uttering a silent scream. He sensed the sheer terror invading the man's dream thoughts, yet he remained still. The attackers, the dogs, had not yet come into view.

Seconds later, a pair of ferocious-looking dogs exploded into the darkened corridor, growling and snapping at their unseen quarry's scent. *Hey, this guy dreams in sound!* Daniel now understood Steve Abrams' horror. The canines were unlike anything he had seen or heard before. Guttural sounds emanated from the beasts' oversize mouths, exposed fangs glinting dully in the diminished light. Heads lowered, the hounds resembled Mastiffs on steroids; their gigantic front shoulder muscles bunching as they stalked their victim.

Dream beasts bothered Gray Wolf more than humans. More even than human-type creatures. Battle with a man-thing placed him at an advantage over the antagonist. Dream humans tended to display human traits, making them susceptible to Daniel's array of dream weaponry. Beasts were unreliable in their moves, harder to surprise because the dreamer tended to amplify the animals' already sharpened senses. Either way, his risk was not great; he could always remove himself from the dream by waking up. But chickening out from a nightmare didn't solve the dreamer's problem.

Gray Wolf squeezed further into the dumpster's shadow, allowing the dogs to slink by on their feral quest. *Okay, kola, how do you take care of this baby? There's two of them, and one of you.*

Steve Abrams' terrified screams interrupted Gray Wolf's tactical session. Jumping from his hiding spot, Daniel ran into the murky darkness toward the pitiful cries for help.

Only a few feet into the blackness, he saw the dogs, shoulder-to-shoulder, hackles raised, and poised to attack. *Think quick, Gray Wolf! You can't shoot 'em and you can't throw a spear into 'em. Abrams is in the line of fire. What can you throw?*

A split second decision made, Gray Wolf reared back and hurled a chunk of raw sirloin at the two dogs. The meat landed between the canines, smacking across their backs with a wet, sucking sound before sliding to the pavement. The reaction was immediate. Driven by the smell of blood, the hulking Mastiff-creatures tore into the lump of animal flesh, biting and snarling at each other for control of the prize.

Having guided their attention to the unresisting steak, Gray Wolf stealthily advanced toward the slavering animals, a lariat at the ready. He was hard pressed to choose which cur presented an easier target. Both creatures shook their obscene heads with equal vigor while attacking the meat. Daniel chose the animal on the right, looping the stiff hemp in front of the creature as it raised its head to warily glance in Abrams' direction. Dropping the rope around the massive upturned neck, he jerked backward, cinching the loop tight. A strangled yelp issued from the dog as Gray Wolf yanked the surprised creature back toward the dumpster. He quickly threaded the rope through an iron handle, drawing the struggling beast against the receptacle with this makeshift pulley.

Luck was with the Dream Catcher. The second brute ignored its mate's sudden upheaval in deference to ravaging the bloody hunk of meat. The unfettered creature did show signs of increased caution, alternately ripping great bites of meat and snarling in Abrams' direction.

Gray Wolf resumed his stalk, carefully sidestepping the restrained Mastiff beast to concentrate on the second misshaped creature. He had just extended the loop toward the cur's bloody snout when Steve Abrams broke his frozen crouch, shuffling deeper into the shadows to escape the horrible scene.

The dog's attention turned back to the initial prey. Its toenails clattering on the wet concrete, the dream creature leaped at Abrams' retreating form.

Caught off guard, Gray Wolf frantically threw the hemp loop in the Mastiff's direction. In mid-stride, the dog flipped as Daniel's rope cinched tightly around one extended leg. Enraged, the beast scrambled to its feet, gnashing at the taut fiber encircling its paw.

Gray Wolf knew he had only seconds before the creature noticed him. Tugging the rope harder, he kept the beast occupied with trying to free itself, while he searched his mind for a way out of the predicament. Realizing Abrams' was now out of the picture, Daniel produced a single-shot pistol. Still grasping the tether, he took wavering aim at the Mastiff creature and pulled the trigger. A light recoil, accompanied by the muted sound of compressed air, announced the discharge of the tranquilizer gun. The dog yelped as a dart penetrated its flank, turning its attention toward the feathered missile lodged in its side. Gray Wolf held the rope tight until the creature's struggles turned listless.

The Mastiff beast collapsed, victim of the powerful tranquilizing agent Daniel had summoned. Fight left the dog. Its paws ineffectually scraped and clatter against the pavement as the drug rendered it unconscious.

For good measure, Gray Wolf reloaded the pistol and shot the first beast still tethered against the dumpster. Within seconds, the alley was quiet, as both dogs fell into drug-induced slumber. Daniel quickly placed leather muzzles over the vicious mouths, then secured the creatures to the dumpster with chains.

Satisfied, the Dream Catcher withdrew, then woke.

Stretching lightly, Daniel looked across to where Abrams lay. *Yeah, kola, you sure picked some nasty-looking critters to haunt you. Things will be okay now, and you can go on your mysterious way.* The Dream Catcher was finished for the night, or so he thought. There was just something about this man ... this strange, nervous man.

Supporting himself on one arm, Gray Wolf stared at Steve Abrams' sleeping form. The man should have fallen into a deep sleep void of dreams. Instead, Abrams' flickering eyelids announced the presence of rapid eye movement associated with the dream stage.

"What's going on, Steve?" Daniel whispered, as much to himself as to the inert form on the next bed. "What're you dreaming about? Did the dogs get loose?"

Gray Wolf knew the last question was highly improbable. He was good at his job. Yet, in light of the ambiguity he now felt toward his forced dream catching profession, enough doubt existed to make him want to investigate. If the nightmare had reappeared, by remote chance, Daniel wanted to be done with it for good.

"Sorry, Stevie, but I'm comin' back. I just have to know." Resting back against the pillows, Gray Wolf emptied his mind and fell asleep.

Daniel joined Abrams in a residential neighborhood. A local neighborhood. He couldn't determine the exact location, other than it was on the more affluent west side of Rapid City. Gray Wolf watched Steve wander down the sloping walkway, casually browsing the moneyed lifestyle. *Looks normal so far. Maybe Abrams is thinking about settling down in Rapid and he's looking for a house, or something.*

It was the 'or something' that kept Daniel involved.

Under ordinary circumstances, he would have emerged from the dream. But Abrams was a strange bird, and Gray Wolf persisted in his voyeurism.

Steve Abrams approached a lone child, a pretty little blonde, playing in her front yard. Leaning down, he struck up a silent conversation with the preoccupied girl. Finally, she looked up and smiled tentatively at Abrams. He reached down and helped her to her feet, dusting the back of her dress off in a paternal manner. *You got family here, kola? Is this your little girl?*

Gray Wolf watched from his vantage point among a row of hedges, a slight unease building within him. *If you've got family here, why are you living in an efficiency apartment?*

Abrams snatched the little girl by the back of the dress, picked her up like a suitcase and raced down the street. He ran to an older, dark blue sedan, stopping long enough to hastily toss the squirming youngster through the open window, before turning back to look up the road. Apparently satisfied he had not been seen, Steve Abrams opened the driver's door and clambered in beside his captive.

Daniel crouched low in the hedges, not wanting Abrams to catch sight of him in this dream. *Whoa, shit! Time to back out, kola!* Gray Wolf dislodged himself from Abrams' nether world.

Sitting up abruptly, Gray Wolf looked at the supine Steve Abrams. The sleeping man's eyelids moved frantically, signifying he was still locked in a nightmare—or was it?

"You ain't nightmaring this one, Stevie. You're having fun, you prick," Daniel murmured, watching a light smile form on Abrams' placid face.

CHAPTER 7

So, why didn't you kill the dogs?" Steve Abrams asked. "I mean, I'm grateful for what you did and everything, but if the dogs aren't dead, can't they come back after me?"

Gray Wolf smiled in a friendly manner he didn't feel, "Well, Steve, I sorta have a thing for animals, you know? Monsters, that kind of stuff, I don't mind blowing away, but I got a soft spot in my heart for dogs.

"But hey," Daniel continued, "those dogs are well secured. They won't be bothering you anymore. Remember what I told you? No repeat customers."

"Well, okay. Thanks, Daniel, I appreciate your help."

"Okay, buddy, just go home and get a good night's sleep ... what's left of the night, anyway," Daniel said as Steve Abrams left the house.

Gray Wolf's smile faded the instant he closed the door. "I think you're a sick puppy, Steve Abrams. Really sick. Man, I hope your second dream brought you pleasure, you warped little son of a bitch."

For the first time in years, Daniel had trouble falling asleep. Tossing on the suddenly uncomfortable mattress, he kept re-visiting Abrams' little pleasure cruise into the world of abduction. Did the dream have any significance? Did Abrams have subconscious desires for such activity?

"Back off, *kola*," Gray Wolf warned himself. "Everybody has kinky dreams from time to time. Even your new friend is entitled, I guess. Hell, it's probably nothing. Guy doesn't remember dreaming it, most likely. He didn't ask me whether or not I was there."

Still unable to sleep, he glanced at the bedside alarm clock. "Twenty after five?" *Shit, boy, you might as well get into work early. That way you can leave early and drown your concerns in a couple of beers. But stay the hell away from the Casino Bar, okay?* Way too many weirdoes there.

Showered and shaved, Daniel felt almost ready to rejoin civilization. He decided against breakfasting at Tally's, on the off chance Edwin Nagel might be haunting the grounds again. Driving north toward town, Gray Wolf made an abrupt left turn onto St. Patrick Street, suddenly inspired to feast on the greasy goodness of Robbinsdale Bowling Alley's morning fare. The small breakfast nook in the bowling alley was one of only a few places open at 6:00 a.m., which further helped with the decision.

As always, the prospect of a hot morning meal elevated Gray Wolf's spirits. Whistling his favorite nameless tune, he sauntered into the icy interior. One thing to be said for the owners of Robbinsdale Lanes. They didn't skimp on the air conditioning. Being open twenty-one hours a day undoubtedly had something to do with the constant seventy-degree temperature refrigerating both occupants and equipment.

Daniel folded his frame into one of the six vacant booths. In total, there were seven cubicles; one other presently held a lone customer whose back was to him.

"Morning, Daniel," the waitress called from inside the kitchen. "Coffee's coming right up."

"Morning, Maggie," Gray Wolf called back. "Make sure it's hot and plentiful." Daniel buried his nose in the *Rapid City Journal* while he waited for the thick rich brew to appear.

Headlines blared out the latest Hills-wide news events: 'Young Miner Crushed to Death in Fluke Homestake Mine Cave-In; Mayor Haggerty Pushes for Higher Property Taxes to Offset Education Deficit; Camping Trio Found Safe After Spelunking Expedition Leads to Unexpected Overnight Stay'; the usual noteworthy local diatribe not likely to make it out on the AP lines. A very feminine clearing of the throat interrupted Gray Wolf's cursory expedition into Black Hills affairs.

Looking up, expecting Maggie to be standing at his table with coffee cup and pot in hand, Daniel stared into a face from the past.

"Daniel?" the pretty, dark-haired woman asked tentatively. "Is it really you?"

Open-mouthed, Gray Wolf only continued his stare.

"It's you all right. I'd recognize that look anywhere," the lady said with a slight chuckle. "But, it appears you don't remember me."

Gray Wolf finally found his voice, albeit not with a strong timbre. "Linda? Linda Pale Moon. My God, what are you doing here?"

Daniel jumped up, sliding the squeaking booth seat back in his exuberance. Tentatively, he put his arms out to hug her, hesitated briefly, then extended his hand instead.

"My God," he repeated, "It's been so long—what is it—eighteen, nineteen years?"

Ignoring his handshake offer, Linda flowed against him, at the same time wrapping her arms around his back. As she caught him in her warm embrace, long-dormant memories seeped into his mind. Self-consciously, he placed his arms around her, drawing her closer in a momentary hug. Resting his hands lightly on her shoulders, Daniel pulled himself away to better view the only woman he had ever loved. Plain English, let alone any witty repartee, deserted him.

"We look kind of silly, standing here in the middle of the restaurant," Linda said. "May I join you for coffee."

Flustered, Gray Wolf released the petite lady before making an exaggerated show of pulling the table out so she could be seated. Embarrassed by his schoolboy actions, Daniel slid the table back to its normal position before depositing himself in the other seat with a noticeable lack of grace.

Staring at her still-lovely face, Daniel uttered, "What are you doing in town? Gosh, I'd heard you moved to someplace east of the river."

"I did. Actually, I moved to Pierre, so I'm technically east of the Missouri ... by about one half mile," she replied with a smile. "As for what I'm doing here, my son is enrolled at South Dakota Tech, so I'm helping him move into the dorm for his freshman year."

"Your son? That means you're no longer Linda Pale Moon."

"No, I'm Linda Paxton now. Shortly after we ... graduated, I moved to Pierre, became a legal secretary and got a job at the big law firm in town. One of the brand new attorneys and I hit it off, dated for three months, then got married. It was all such a whirlwind and very hush-hush because of us working at the same firm."

The short update tugged at Gray Wolf's emotions. Linda Pale Moon and he had been steadies throughout high school. It was a foregone conclusion, at least in the eyes of their classmates, that they would marry. He was football captain. She was a cheerleader and homecoming queen. They had been virtually inseparable since their freshman year.

Now, Daniel realized, the emotion simmering just below the surface was jealousy. *Back off, Gray Wolf. You ditched her, remember? And she didn't even know why. How're you going to tell the only girl you ever loved you can't get married because you don't want kids? How do you explain why you don't want kids?*

"How about you, Daniel; are you married?"

"No, never did get married. I guess I got too caught up in my work. But, tell me more about yourself. Do you and your husband still work for the same law firm?"

"Umm, Allen, my husband, died five years ago."

"Geez, Linda, I'm sorry. I mean, I wouldn't have asked if I'd known."

"No, really, it's okay," Linda smiled that same smile Daniel remembered from almost twenty years ago. "Allen and I had a good life and we raised a fine boy. What more could I ask for?

"But, you haven't said much about yourself," she continued. "Tell me what you're doing."

Daniel related his career but didn't mention his Dream Catcher role. He was fairly sure Linda knew of his ability. It was hard not to know, growing up on the reservation as they had, but Gray Wolf had never spoken much about his legacy, even to the girl he loved.

"How long are you in town for, Linda?" Gray Wolf asked, eager to get the subject off himself.

"I took some vacation time from the firm; I'm a paralegal now, by the way. After getting David situated at Tech, I planned on hanging around for a few days, visiting some relatives and making sure my son doesn't flunk out after the first week."

She still has the same light sense of humor. You screwed up, old man.

Maggie, the waitress, interrupted Daniel's thoughts with two cups and a pot of coffee. "You two going to be sitting together?"

"Oh, yeah, just leave the pot, Maggie," Gray Wolf said. "Linda, did you want some breakfast?"

"No. Thanks, but I'm trying to watch my weight. I can't eat like I used to a few years ago."

Daniel quickly scrutinized the pretty lady. There wasn't a pound of misused flesh anywhere on her frame. He did notice Linda had filled out nicely since the last time he had seen her. He had seen that as they stood, had felt it as they shared a brief embrace.

"None for me either today," Gray Wolf murmured, not wanting to be the only one eating.

Wordless seconds passed as Daniel and Linda each worked on something to say. The company was pleasant, but the silence was embarrassing. Daniel tried to read his former girlfriend's expression and was frustrated he couldn't get any clear picture. *She's probably got a boyfriend, kola. Besides, she lives a hundred and fifty miles away. Lots of things have happened since she was your girl.*

Breaking the silence, Gray Wolf inanely asked, "So, what are your plans while you're here?"

Linda answered quickly, obviously glad to have the silence broken. "Actually, I'm going down to the reservation today. Mom and Dad still live in Pine Ridge, so I'll spend a couple of days with them, then come back up here for the weekend. I'll probably visit with my aunt and cousins for another couple of days, then head back to Pierre on Tuesday or Wednesday."

"Kinda hard to completely leave the old homestead," Gray Wolf said, nodding. "I go down to Badger every weekend to visit with Leo Red Hawk. Old Leo's been the closest thing to family since Mom died eight years ago."

"I remember hearing about your mother passing away," Linda offered in a subdued voice. "She was always such a sweet woman."

Gray Wolf nodded again, not able to find the right words.

Linda and his mother had been very close. He'd gotten into more than one heated discussion with Lorna Gray Wolf over his decision to stop seeing his long-time sweetheart.

"Well, it looks like we'll be passing each other on the road. Leo kind of expects me to show up every weekend. He's old and doesn't get out much."

"Does Leo still have the same idea about Ghost Dancing all the white men away so the buffalo will come back?" Linda asked, a light smile tugging at her lips.

Daniel laughed, relieved to be discussing a more neutral subject. "Oh, you know, he doesn't talk much about that any more, but he still keeps his dance gear stashed in his bedroom just in case."

"Give him my regards, Daniel. I haven't seen *Tunkasila* Red Hawk since we ... since I left the reservation.

"Goodness!" Linda continued, looking at her watch. "I'd better get on the road. Mom's preparing a big breakfast for when I get there. That's actually why I bowed out of your offer."

Gray Wolf rose as Linda Paxton slid from her seat. Emotions fluttered through his chest; a combination of relief because he didn't know what else to say, and disappointment because she was leaving so soon.

"Linda, I ... it's been really great seeing you again. I hope David does well in school and I hope you stay happy."

Daniel let himself be hugged again, relishing the brief squeeze and the light, perfumed scent of her hair.

"I wish you the same, Daniel," she replied, that beautiful smile on her lips as she looked up at him.

Is she happy to see you, kola? Her mouth smiles, but do her eyes?

"Well," Linda said, pulling away from Gray Wolf. "Take care of yourself, okay?"

Daniel watched her walk toward the exit, wanting to call after her, wanting to delay her leaving. Instead, he stood immobile as the pneumatic doors whisked shut behind her.

"Damn, Gray Wolf," he muttered to himself. "What's the matter with you anyhow?"

The remainder of the workday dragged by for Daniel Gray Wolf. Numerous times, he found himself stopping in mid-pencil stroke as a fresh image of Linda Pale Moon stopped by to visit. Each vision produced bittersweet emotions: The first date between a gangly, squeaky-voiced wannabe frosh jock and the blossoming rookie cheerleader; a first kiss two dates later, shared by tentative participants; then, their single, truly intimate moment after Senior Prom; and finally, four years of high school romance memories squelched by his sudden graduation night break-up from the only girl he had ever loved.

The following days were repeat performances, recollections only slightly diminished by the passing hours since Gray Wolf had seen Linda for the first time in nineteen years. Daniel was almost glad for the Friday morning call from a harried-sounding man named Rippey who had been referred to him. Could they meet this evening and take care of an ongoing nightmare? Yes, tonight would be fine. Thank you, Mr. Boyd Rippey; I needed that!

For some strange reason, the prospect of the evening's pending dream visit appealed to Gray Wolf. *Guess it's because you get to wallow in somebody else's problems for a while. Lets you forget about your own. Yeah, that's probably it.*

CHAPTER 8

I really appreciate you meeting with me on such short notice, Mr. Gray Wolf."

"Not a problem. And call me Daniel, please. C'mon in and sit down. We'll visit for a few minutes."

Boyd Rippey entered the house, nervously waiting in the foyer until Gray Wolf led him to the comfortable living room. Once seated, he appeared choked by the characteristic discomfort one experiences when visiting a doctor for the first time.

Daniel spoke first, easing the obvious strain. "I'd offer you something to drink, but I don't want any stimulant or depressant to interfere with your normal sleep pattern. Depending on how quickly we rid you of your problem dreams, a cup of coffee will be ready to help you make it home. So, tell me a little about yourself. You have a family?"

"Yes, I'm married to a really great gal. We have six kids, ranging from four to eighteen years old. We moved to Rapid City twenty years ago, just my wife and me obviously, and bought a big house because we expected to raise a family.

"But, don't we talk about—I mean—shouldn't I tell you about my nightmare?" Rippey continued.

"You can if you like, but it's not necessary. I get a chance to see it for myself, remember?" Gray Wolf said with a grin. "This really doesn't take long, and I'm pretty good about winging it."

"How did you get into this business? You know, what kind of qualifications do you have?"

Daniel saw the questions were well intended, abrupt only due to Rippey's nervousness, so he answered, "The only qualification I had was being a first-born son. The rest came naturally. You see, Boyd, this isn't a business, it's heritage. If I tried to make money out of this, then it would be a business, but our heritage and custom says the Dream Catcher should not profit from the gift he has been given."

Chatting for the next few minutes, Daniel explained the procedure that would be taking place. When he saw Rippey had no further questions, Gray Wolf said, "What you need to do now is get ready for sleep. Remember, your stay here is a short one—four hours at best—but you have to go to sleep. Don't lie there awake, expecting me to solve your troubles. I can only do it once you reach the dream stage. I'll be checking periodically until you've achieved the proper sleep level.

"So, anything else before we begin?" Daniel concluded.

"Well, if it's not too much bother, I'd like to give my wife a call. She's as concerned about this as I am. Just want to let her know everything's okay."

"Sure, go ahead. The phone's around the corner on the kitchen wall. I'm going to do some reading. You remember where everything is; bathroom's on the right, bedroom's on the left?"

Rippey nodded before walking into the kitchen. As Gray Wolf found his place in the tattered L'Amour novel, he vaguely heard a mumbled conversation taking place between Boyd and his wife. Snatches of "everything's fine" and "don't worry" drifted into earshot, a dedicated husband reassuring his wife. A light click signified Rippey had finished his call.

"Okay, all set, I guess," Boyd Rippey hemmed, standing in the kitchen doorway.

"Goodnight, Boyd, I'll be in shortly."

Gray Wolf engrossed himself in Louis L'Amour, reading swiftly as the western grasped his attention. He had stumbled across this western author quite by accident, not interested at first because of a misconception that L'Amour was just another cowboy and Indian writer. After realizing old Louie gave the red man a fair shake, Daniel had become a rabid fan.

Periodically, Daniel checked in on Boyd Rippey. Each time, he found the man either in a light doze or the earliest stage of sleep. It wasn't until almost three hours after their final 'good nights' that Gray Wolf noticed Rippey's eyelids flickering. Easing himself down on the adjoining bed for perhaps the thousandth time in his career, Daniel relaxed his muscles and fell asleep.

Gray Wolf entered a dreamscape of yellowed flatlands intermittently spotted with anemic, faded green trees. His gaze picked up only repetitive and boring plains that stretched peripherally to the horizon. *So, where's the problem, Boyd?* Glancing around, he saw a rocky bluff immediately behind him. The steep slope was a couple of hundred feet tall with pockets of boulders and rocks resting precariously in place. *Not a good time for an earthquake, kola. So, let's see what Mr. Rippey is up to.*

Gray Wolf strode across the dismal landscape toward a man-sized boulder laying at the foot of the cliff. Crouching behind it, Daniel waited for the man of the hour to appear. *Hell, for as long as it takes this guy to fall asleep, I could've brought my book with me to pass the time until ...*

Gray Wolf's thoughts were interrupted by Rippey's approach. The man had entered the barren plain from a thicket of scraggly trees fifty yards to the left. Rippey's destination appeared to be directly in front of the Dream Catcher's hiding spot. *What happens now, Boyd? What makes this a bad dream?*

Rippey looked around, but not with the intensity of a man searching for another person. His body movement and glances were more casual, more inquisitive, and reminiscent of a guy wondering what the hell he was doing in such a spot. Boyd stepped closer, still surveying the surroundings, a mild look of confusion on his face. He was now only a few feet from Gray Wolf's hiding place.

Apparently not finding anything to his liking or satisfaction, Rippey pivoted, retracing his path toward the thicket. He had taken only a few steps when the earth quietly split. The portion he stood on sank perceptibly below the ripped tundra in front of him. Rippey backed away, staring as the widening rend formed a semi-circle around him. Great columns of earth broke free, tumbling into a deepening chasm, until the terrified man stood on a mesa-like outcrop overlooking a bottomless canyon.

Rippey wheeled, seeking escape toward the bluffs. Toward Daniel. Again, the silent earth separated before him, dislocating the little plateau completely from the main land mass. Slowly, the breach widened. Rippey's disintegrating earthen platform separated further from the surrounding terrain. Two feet, then three. Shards of earth peeled loose and tumbled into the darkened void. Six feet of gap, now seven; an ever growing split yawed between the dream victim and safety.

That's it! Rippey dreams about falling. He's getting ready to jump, but he never makes it. Okay, Super Indian, time to do your thing.

Gray Wolf emerged from behind the boulder just as Rippey crouched to begin his spring toward solid land. "Boyd! Boyd, over here," he yelled, but no sound came from his mouth.

Despite the absolute silence, Rippey threw a frantic glance

Daniel's way, saw the Dream Catcher's extended hand, and leaped from his crumbling perch.

Gray Wolf spotted the problem right away. Rippey couldn't jump worth a shit. The man's feeble attempt left him hovering momentarily over the precipice, eyes bugged out in fear, before gravity caught up to him. Daniel would have laughed at the surprised 'O' puckering Boyd's mouth if this hadn't been the terrified man's nightmare, therefore serious business.

Balancing himself, Gray Wolf reached out and grabbed Rippey's extended hand in a steely grip. Momentum pulled him forward. He counteracted by flexing his right knee. Boyd Rippey banged against the vertical slope with a silent impact, jarring clods of dirt and rock loose to flutter down the yawning hole. But the Dream Catcher's hold was good and he pulled the squirming man back up to solid ground.

Rippey lay at Daniel's feet, sucking in huge gouts of oxygen. His fingers still held Gray Wolf's wrist in a death grip.

Hang on, kola. We saved you from the fall, but the nightmare ain't over yet.

Gray Wolf pried Rippey's fingers loose, then pulled the shaken man erect. With a series of hand gestures, he instructed Boyd to follow him. Not waiting for a return signal, Daniel began climbing the rock-strewn bluff behind them. Peripherally, he spotted Rippey clambering up the slope beside him.

Reaching the summit, Gray Wolf began pushing rocks and manageable-sized boulders over the edge. Rippey watched, curious at first, before finally catching on. Joining Daniel, he shoved stones and debris down the steep hillside. The joint effort had its desired effect. Tumbling rocks dislodged other rocks, which smashed into beds of precariously situated boulders. New slides fanned out to break loose further fragile outcroppings, until the entire hillside became an accelerating mass of falling earth. Silently, the earthen blanket gouged its way down hill.

Gray Wolf watched the avalanche spill into the chasm, thousands of tons of rock and dirt searching for a more stable resting place. As the side of the mountain shifted its geography, the gaping hole gradually filled. Heavy dust quickly settled, revealing a jagged scar of stone where a hole had once existed.

Noticing Rippey was engrossed in the man-made geological calamity, Daniel withdrew from the dream.

Gray Wolf stretched, yawning as he extended his arms. Looking across at the slumbering form of his recent dream partner, Daniel grinned. *Rest easy for a while, Boyd. This one was a piece of cake. Hell, I don't even have a headache.*

Lying on the bed, a few minutes' bonus for a job well done, Gray Wolf let his thoughts wander back to the chance meeting with Linda Paxton nee Pale Moon. Dormant memories of love and warmth had flooded him the instant she put her arms around him. There was no doubt he still felt something for this dark-haired Indian princess. There was also little doubt in his mind that Linda Paxton was over him and had been for quite some time. Hell, she had a kid, a son, who was now a freshman at South Dakota School of Mines and Technology. Pretty prestigious stuff, him going to this small school that had a national reputation for turning out some of the best engineers and scientists. And she was doing well, too, despite being widowed at what—thirty-three years old.

"Face it, hoss," he muttered. "She doesn't need an old warhorse who works at the steel mill. This lady's done all right for herself, has a real life, probably a nice house and a new car. Leave her alone and forget her."

The self-issued sage advice fell on deaf ears. Gray Wolf wanted to feel Linda's strength, wanted to hold her a little while longer and let the good memories flow between them.

Let it be, butthead. The woman doesn't fit into the picture you've drawn for yourself.

Sighing, Gray Wolf jostled his pillow into a more comfortable cradle, then fell asleep. A rare thing happened to the Dream Catcher. He had dreams of his own; nice dreams about high school days and about Linda.

CHAPTER 9

Boyd Rippey didn't leave Daniel's home until 7:30 A.M., and then amidst a flurry of apologies.

"Oh geez, I should have gotten up sooner. I'm sorry, I hope I didn't put you out or anything. It's just ... it's just ... well, it was so great to get a good night's sleep. Man, you were really there, weren't you—hey I gotta call my wife and let her know everything's okay—can I use your phone again, please?"

Rippey's exuberance was not uncommon. Freed of troubling dreams, he fell into the same 'everything's great with the world' routine of the truly unburdened.

"Sure, use the phone, use the john, have a cup of coffee if you like," Gray Wolf laughed, holding his hands out against the verbal barrage. "All I ask is you be ready to go home within a half hour. Hate to rush you, but I drive down to the reservation every weekend and I like to get an early start."

"Hey, sure! No problemo," Rippey answered, busily dialing the phone.

Daniel packed an overnighter with clean clothes for the weekend in Badger, listening with detached amusement as Boyd rambled on about how great a night's sleep he had. If Rippey's verbosity was any indicator, Mrs. Rippey probably wasn't saying much on the other end.

Yes, honey—that's great, honey—bring home a gallon of milk, honey. Hey, kola, who you poking fun at? At least he's got a wife and family to go home to.

Having suitably chastised himself, Gray Wolf zipped up the overnight bag, whistling softly under his breath. As much a routine as it had become, Daniel still looked forward to his visits with Leo Red Hawk. The drive was relatively quick and Leo's company was relaxing for the most part. Hell, even jawing with Mutt and Jeff on the Badger Liquor and Grocery Emporium front porch had its moments.

Carrying his bag into the living room, Gray Wolf caught the blissful tail end of Rippey's conversation.

"—love you too, baby doll. Don't worry, I won't forget the milk." Boyd hung up the phone, noting the wide grin on Daniel's face. "Did I miss something funny? You been watching cartoons, or something?"

"Naw, just a private joke. Listen, it sounds like you're all set. The dream's history, your wife and kids are waiting for you. Oh, don't forget the milk."

Rippey picked up his dop kit, checked to make sure the inventory was correct, then strode to the front door, stopping long enough to shake Gray Wolf's hand and offer one last profuse dialogue. "Thank you very, very much, Daniel. This was really getting to me, you know? It's such a relief to have that damned nightmare out of my system now, and I have you to thank for that, so -"

"You're welcome, now go take care of your hungry kids." Gray Wolf steered Rippey to the front door, prodding him on the back to make sure he left before another maelstrom of words could be uttered.

Relieved to be off dream watch for a while, Daniel quickly picked up the minor clutter in the living room. *Strip the spare bed when you get back. It'll give you something to do with your Sunday evening.* Right now, all he wanted was to be with friends.

Grabbing the sandwich he had prepared earlier, Gray

Wolf exited the house. Barring any obstacles, he would get to Badger only a half hour later than usual; not a big deal, considering Red Hawk was lousy company anyway when the Lone Ranger mysteriously appeared on his TV set.

The drive to Badger indeed went quickly as Gray Wolf passed the miles reminiscing about his high school sweetheart. He admitted, though Linda had faded from his active thoughts, she'd always been lodged somewhere deep and safe, immediately available when some external prompting made her visible. Now, after seeing her for the first time in almost twenty years, everything Daniel glanced at had Linda Pale Moon woven into the picture.

"Give it up, Gray Wolf, he scolded. "She isn't even Linda Pale Moon anymore; she's Linda Paxton now and she has a kid. No more cheerleader outfits, no more Homecoming dances."

The Badger Liquor and Grocery Emporium eased into sight, saving Daniel from further maudlin trips down memory lane. Pulling into the wide-open gravel parking lot, Gray Wolf produced a grin upon seeing the two cornerstones of humanity quietly rocking on the front porch.

"'Mornin', Daniel," Gilbert offered, holding out a gnarled hand.

"'Mornin' yourself, Mr. War Pony and Mr. Yellow Feather," he acknowledged, shaking hands with both gentlemen.

"Must be Saturday already, huh?" offered William Yellow Feather.

Gray Wolf chuckled, "Yeah, Dakota Steel wouldn't let me off on a weekday just to visit you old bucks."

"I seen Leo out and about this week," Gilbert War Pony said. "Probably gettin' supplies what with you comin' down for a visit."

"Gilbert, you old fart," Yellow Feather cackled. "Leo Red

Hawk waits for young Daniel here to bring him groceries. Why the hell would he go out and buy supplies if he knew this rich young brave was going to load him up?"

Keeping with tradition, War Pony ignored his friend and asked, "What's the word in the big city, Daniel?"

"Things don't change much. Mayor Haggerty grouses about there not being enough tourists to support all the businesses. Jumpin' Jack wants to raise the city sales tax. You know how it is."

War Pony and Yellow Feather chuckled. The ritual with Gray Wolf was a source of weekly amusement for the middle-aged men.

"Well, gents, I gotta see Mr. Trudeau inside and double the Badger economy," Daniel said, pulling open the screen door.

"Has that Coors been givin' you gas, William?" Gilbert War Pony asked his friend in a conversational tone, but loud enough for Gray Wolf's benefit. "Don't have the trouble with Budweiser like I do with Coors."

Gray Wolf grinned, making a mental note to 'surprise' the porch dwellers with a Budweiser.

"'Mornin', Mr. Trudeau."

The storeowner looked up from his magazine. "Hey, Daniel. Loaded up some stuff for Leo already. You're a little bit later than usual this weekend."

"Yeah, had some business to take care of before I could come down. So, what's Leo want as his surprise of the week, more fig newtons?"

"Naw, he says those bind him up. Hell, I told the old fart that wouldn't happen if he didn't eat the whole damn package at one sitting. Said this time he might want to try something more akin to soothing an old stomach, like artichoke hearts."

Gray Wolf laughed at the thought of Leo Red Hawk daintily pulling pickled artichoke hearts from a can. "You didn't happen to have any, did you?"

"Hell, man," Trudeau groused good-naturedly, "Does this look like a gourmet food shop to you? Don't have much call for that kind of stuff out here in the boonies. Thought I'd leave the surprise up to you this time. Let you piss the old buck off for not bringing the treat he wanted."

Daniel chuckled again as he looked around the cluttered food section of the Badger Liquor and Grocery Emporium. Ralph Trudeau packed a wide variety of groceries into a modicum of space. Most evident were staples, yet a respectable supply of convenience items occupied the two aisle platforms and back wall.

Wandering down the creaking uneven wood floor, Gray Wolf browsed through cans of corn, peas, soups, and six different kinds of beans, until he reached the canned meat section. Vienna sausage—yeah, Leo would like those, he thought. Scooping up five tins of the little delicacies, Daniel took his surprise to the counter and placed them beside the porch dwellers' ritual cans of Coors.

"This ought to tide him over for awhile," Daniel said, inspecting the bag of supplies while Trudeau rang up the additional items. "Oh, by the way, Gilbert mentioned he and William might like a Bud instead of the usual."

Trudeau exchanged two frosted bottles of St. Louis' best for the pale yellow cans. "That'll be twenty-four dollars and seventy-three cents, Daniel."

Gray Wolf plucked a twenty and a five from his wallet. Years of doing business with Ralph Trudeau had taught Daniel to trust the man. No need to inventory the bag for accuracy; if the storeowner ever made an error, it was in favor of the customer.

"See you next weekend, Daniel."

"Or maybe tomorrow," Gray Wolf said. "I'll probably spend the night at Leo's."

"Whew!" Trudeau sighed. "You got more courage than me, *kola washta*. I swear the only thing holding old Leo's shack together is his spirit ... that, and the handful of nails you pound into the walls every once in awhile."

"Hell, Ralph," Gray Wolf said, pushing his way through the screen door. "That house will still be standing when you and I are both residents of the Happy Hunting Ground. Leo will probably still be watching the Lone Ranger, too."

Stopping on the front landing, Daniel held out the bottles of beer to Gilbert and William. "Here you go, gents. Thought I'd mess with tradition and offer you something a little different."

"Well now, ain't this a pleasant change of pace," Gilbert War Pony said, accepting the cold brews. "Me and William was just talking about how a Budweiser would go down nice and smooth right about now. This is mighty kind of you, Daniel, but where's William's beer?"

"Real funny, Mr. Smart Ass," William Yellow Feather growled. "You better hand over one of them bottles before I'm forced to leave this rocker to find my skinnin' knife. Josey'd pitch one mean hissy fit, you comin' home all cut up and everything."

"No more'n Rosemary would, what with you slicin' your fingers off trying to get the blade outta the goddamned sheath," War Pony responded amicably, handing his partner the second beer.

"*Yaka kija.* You guys make my ears hurt with your tough language," Daniel laughed. "Do you ever say anything nice to each other?"

"Hell," Yellow Feather summed it up. "I'd say something nice if I thought this old son of a buck had any good qualities."

"Besides," War Pony added, "if we didn't have nothing to bitch about, conversation would lag after a bit."

Gray Wolf shook his head in mock exasperation as he walked to his pickup. Pushing the groceries inside, he called back to the loungers, "Good thing there aren't many cowboys left around here; you braves'd be fighting over their scalps."

"Bring 'em on down, Daniel," War Pony challenged, laconically raising his beer. "Hell, we'll sic the wives on 'em should you want to see how real scalpin's done."

Gray Wolf pulled out of the parking lot, leaving the two men to their good-natured bickering. In the distance, he saw Leo's house, a quarter of a mile and eighty years behind Trudeau's grocery store.

Leo Red Hawk was a dying breed, not unlike like his ramshackle house with the smoke curling from its chimney almost year around. The old Sioux heated his home and cooked his meals on a sturdy, cast iron, wood-burning stove. Cold artesian water flowed, courtesy of a hand pump situated in the twelve square foot area of the house recognized as kitchen. Electricity, Red Hawk's one grudging concession to technology, was installed only to power the ancient Sears color television.

Still a couple of hundred yards away, Daniel could make out the figure of Leo Red Hawk, shuffling from the outdoor john back toward the house. He watched the old man adjust his suspenders over the perennial flannel shirt and stuff the red plaid shirttail back into faded denims. Close enough now for Leo to see, Gray Wolf beeped his horn, waving out the window to his best friend in the world. Red Hawk returned the wave before ambling inside.

Daniel parked his truck and stepped out onto the dusty gravel of Leo's front yard. Hefting the grocery bag, he gazed about the landscape of his childhood, seeing freedom and openness, not the squalor.

"Are you coming inside, or are we going to have a picnic? Either way, I hope you brought some beer." Leo Red Hawk stood in the open doorway, watching Daniel with interest.

"Hold your horses, *Tunkasila*. I'm communing with the memories of my youth. Talking with nature."

"Yes, talking with nature is good, *Takoja*," agreed Red Hawk, "Especially nature in December, which will keep my beer cold. Nature in August tells me to drink before the chill leaves the can.

"Now, come and we'll speak of how Tonto saved Lone Ranger again," the old man meandered back inside toward his television, speaking to Daniel over his shoulder. "Did I tell you Tonto means 'stupid' in Spanish? I did tell you that … just last week, but you probably forgot."

Sipping one more breath of homeland, Gray Wolf turned and entered Leo's world of thirty-five year old Saturday morning kids' shows. Music blared. More sounds of whinnying and hoof beats, then the violins kicked in, obviously as the credits rolled across the screen. Daniel strained to remember the theme song booming from the abused speaker system.

Red Hawk provided Gray Wolf's 'name that tune' answer. "Fury. Yes, he's one smart horse. If we had a couple hundred war ponies like him, maybe Lakota would have been the national language. What do you think, Daniel?"

"I think your TV is haunted by *nagi*, by ghosts, Grandfather," Gray Wolf answered, handing an opened beer can to the old man.

"I don't care for Fury as much as I used to. This place he

lives on, this ranch, is a nice place but always in peril," Red Hawk philosophized. "If it wasn't for the damned horse, Joey, Pete and Jim would have been killed many times over. Of course, we must remember they are white men."

"*Tunkasila*, it's only movies. They're not real. It's all just for our entertainment."

"Something happened to make a man think of these stories," Leo replied doggedly. "What better way to tell of your experiences than to tell them on film? Yes, I think Fury's ranch is a dangerous place."

Gray Wolf shook his head. *How do you argue with logic like that?*

"So, Daniel, *Takoja*, are you married yet? Have you given us another *Ihanbla Gmunka*, a Dream Catcher?"

Gray Wolf sipped his beer, contemplating what to say to Red Hawk. He wanted to talk of meeting Linda Pale Moon, his mixed feelings over seeing her again, but that would only give the old man more ammunition. Instead, he spoke of dreams.

"Grandfather, something worries me. This week, I dreamed with a man who I believe has bad intentions."

"Tell me of this man, Daniel, then we will speak of intentions."

"This man is a stranger to Rapid City," Gray Wolf began. "He did not come to me by the normal method of referral, and it was not his nightmare that makes me concerned. He had dreams after I fixed his problem, after I made the nightmare go away -"

These are not your concern, *Takoja*," Red Hawk chastised. "This man you speak of is allowed the privacy of his thoughts. If he did not ask for your help, you should not have been in his head."

Daniel nodded, "I understand that, and I have never

before intruded where I was not invited. What I did, I did because I felt the nightmare might have returned. As I said, Grandfather, this man is strange, possibly *gnaskinyan*. You know, a little crazy."

"Daniel, you walk a special path. You supply a much-needed medicine that cures a problem. But, you are not *Wakan Tanka*, the Great Spirit, even though you have powers other men don't realize. I can only warn you on this. You must tread softly, my grandson. Do not think for this man—for any man—**ever!**"

Gray Wolf knew he was close, had been close, to violating the doctrine of his Dream Catcher legacy. What Red Hawk had just preached was straight party line, with no room for interpretation. In the thousand and some odd encounters since his coming of age, Daniel had never before re-entered a dream. Now, because of this unwelcome guest, Steve Abrams, he was very near to becoming a non-person within the Lakota.

"I will tell you something now, not to make your head swell, but to show you I understand why you say these things to me," Leo murmured. "What I tell you is the cause of many problems for the red man, white man ... all men. It is the time we live in—that is the problem."

When Daniel didn't respond, Red Hawk continued with more force. "You don't yet understand, do you? I have known five *Ihanbla Gmunka* in my life. Many more were known to me by legend. All of them, except for you, have a common thread."

"They all wanted to catch dreams. Is that what you're going to tell me?"

Red Hawk glared at Daniel with the intensity of one being forced to cope with a fool. "None of them ever 'dreamed' more than one hundred times. Your father was the only man to even come close to that number. And you have dreamed with how many ... a thousand people, maybe more? How many were Lakota, my grandson ... seventy, eighty at best?

"It is a sign of our time," the old man continued. "Today, bad dreams are more plentiful than the buffalo ever were. We talk, and you tell me who you dream with. You help the white man more than the red man because that is who needs the help. The Lakota have not changed much. They are still at peace with their nature. Now do you understand why being a *Ihanbla Gmunka* is important?"

Stunned, Gray Wolf tried to understand what Red Hawk was telling him. "But, my father was so weary, he was a beaten man because of this—this 'gift' of ours. And you're telling me he dreamed less than a hundred times?"

"Your father tried to play God, Daniel," Leo replied in a blunt tone. "He interfered with peoples' lives. Tried to mold them to a more peaceful existence. But your father did not have peace, so his way was a lie. He was the first to visit a white man's dreams and was not prepared for what met him. The *wasicun* have created their own nightmares. The white man's world is much more frightening than ours.

"*Tunkasila*, my ability is because I am Oglala Sioux," Daniel said, begging for comprehension. "You are right about how many of my red brothers I have dreamed with. But, I'm tired of helping everybod -"

Red Hawk cut Daniel off with a wave of his hand. "My son, I will put it to you straight. You have been chosen to help the white man."

"Chosen, by who?"

"Daniel, you make my head hurt," Leo said gently, shaking his mane of gray hair. "I believe I was right last week when I called you Tonto—stupid. I'm an old man who wanted the

Ghost Dance to work so the white man would go away and the *tatanka* would come back. I wish for the days of my forefathers. But I know of jet planes and televisions—white man things. The Ghost Dance did not work and the white man will not be going away, so we must live with them and help them when we can. It is our way. It is your way."

Daniel summed it up. "So, Gray Wolf gets to help everyone get rid of their nightmares, and then he has a kid, and his kid gets to help a whole new generation with even worse dreams. And I suppose I should feel guilty for not having a son to pass this on to?"

"You should, Tonto."

"Stop calling me that!"

"I only call you Tonto because I don't know the Spanish words for selfish shithead," Leo explained mildly. "I would like another beer now, if you are willing to share with me."

Gray Wolf opened another can and handed it to the old man. He then did something he had not felt the need for in ten years. Grabbing an open pack of Camels from the table, Daniel pulled two cigarettes free and stuck them in his mouth. Lighting them, he passed one to Leo Red Hawk.

"Why are you smoking?"

"Let's ... pretend it's a ... peace pipe," Gray Wolf coughed, waving the acrid smog out of his eyes.

The men smoked in silence, Red Hawk thoroughly enjoying the discomfort etched on Daniel's face; a result of nicotine bombardment after ten years' abstinence. Whether it was because he resolved an internal conflict, or due to cigarette-induced lightheadedness, Gray Wolf broke the solitude gridlock.

"Okay, you old coot. Why didn't you tell me this before?"

"There was no need; you had not tried to mold another person before."

"But that's just it, *Tunkasila*. I didn't try to interfere; I honestly thought Abrams was having another nightmare. That's why I dreamed with him a second time."

"And his second dream is the one you should not get involved in. You are a dream world *ukicita*, a soldier, not a doctor."

Daniel grinned, letting the tension ease away. "I guess this is why I picked you as my *Cannakseyuha*. You're my guardian, Leo," he explained unnecessarily.

Red Hawk smoked his cigarette and stared intently at Gray Wolf. "Yes, I was chosen to guide you, but you had nothing to do with the decision."

"I don't understand. If I didn't sort of migrate to you, how did we get together?"

The old Sioux pondered, deep in thought about whether to answer. Finally, Leo raised his eyes slowly to the ceiling and pointed a gnarled finger upward.

Gray Wolf laughed, but immediately stopped when he saw his ancient friend was serious. "You're telling me the Great Spirit, *Wakan Tanka*, told you? Now you're talking with the Big Man Himself?"

"I am ninety-eight years old and I talk to who I want," Red Hawk responded huffily. "But, if you must know, I speak with *Woniya*, the spirit guide. That is how you and I got together."

"Grandfather, do you realize how unbelievable this sounds. You converse with the great spirits?"

Leo Red Hawk's eyebrows rose. "*Takoja*, you walk in other men's dreams! Tell me which sounds more unbelievable."

Gray Wolf suddenly laughed, a great, deep belly laugh

that ended in a coughing spasm as he inadvertently sucked cigarette smoke deep into his ticklish lungs. Leaning against the kitchen table, he hacked and giggled until tears streamed from his eyes.

Puzzled, Red Hawk waited for his young friend to gain control before asking, "Did I say something funny, or are you trying to live up to the name Tonto?"

Daniel sat down before his knees gave out. Chuckling, he ground out his cigarette stub. "No, Grandfather, I was just thinking about how a noted psychiatrist acquaintance of mine would react if he had listened to this conversation."

"This psychiatrist, he is a white man?"

"Through and through."

"Then there is nothing to laugh at because he will never hear of what we speak."

Barely suppressing a fresh round of sniggers, Daniel said, "*Tunkasila*, you are a piece of work. How you can have that wry sense of humor one minute, then suddenly turn into a stone."

Red Hawk eased up from his shattered lounge chair and padded toward the door as Gray Wolf was speaking. Pausing at the entry, he declared, "I think you have brought some bad spirits with you this week and now they want to live in my house. We need to leave here now so they don't capture our souls."

"What—where are we supposed to go?"

"Take me to McDonald's restaurant in Pine Ridge. I'm hungry. The evil spirits will be gone by the time we get back."

During the half hour drive toward the reservation's largest town, Daniel told Red Hawk about meeting Linda Pale Moon again. The old man listened intently as the story of lost love unfolded. Gray Wolf left out nothing, sharing his deepest thoughts and concerns over seeing his former girlfriend.

When Gray Wolf finished, Leo said, "I remember this girl. Skinny little thing with big eyes. She always wore a red coat with white sleeves, even in the summer."

"That was my letter jacket, Grandfather," Daniel explained. "She wore it because we were going steady."

The old man nodded. "That is a relief to know. I was afraid her family was too poor to buy her the right size clothes. I could tell she would never grow into that coat."

"Well, she's not a skinny little thing anymore. Linda's a beautiful lady and she still has those big brown eyes that smile all the time."

"Can she still have children, *Takoja?*"

"Uh-uh, I know where you're going with this, you old fart," Gray Wolf grinned his answer. "I told you she already has a boy who will be in college this year. Linda's happy with her life. She has a good job and a nice house I'm sure. So, don't be looking to play cupid, okay?"

"Then, why did you tell me about her if you were not still interested? I think you should marry this girl. It is probably not too late for her to bear you a son."

"You know what I like about you, Leo? You make me laugh." And it was true. Despite the intensity of the morning's conversation, Daniel found solace in Red Hawk's simple but sharp humor.

"So now I am a source of amusement. I suppose you will just drop me off at McDonald's restaurant because you are ashamed to be around such a ridiculous old man."

"Thought about that, but if I wasn't with you, the manager would probably kick you out for flushing the toilets too many times just to watch the water swirl."

"I have seen flush toilets work before. I'm not impressed. Why waste good water when Mother Earth accepts what you offer to a hole in the ground?"

The town limit sign appeared, proudly declaring PINE RIDGE, pop. 2596. Daniel flipped the turn signal and prepared to cut across the two-lane highway into the restaurant parking area.

"Grandfather, do you want to eat inside, or go to the drive-in window?" Gray Wolf asked, searching for a parking spot in the crowded lot.

"We should go inside where the air conditioner will keep our drinks cool," the old man said philosophically.

"Okay, but remember, they don't serve beer with Happy Meals here."

"Then I will have a Big Mac and a beer."

CHAPTER 10

From the outside, the Pine Ridge McDonald's looked like a thousand other franchises in a thousand other towns. Wall-to-wall windows, red brick, and the universally recognized golden arches graced the intersection of the town's two major roads. Inside the burger haven, a visitor would have been equally comfortable ordering pizza or anything Italian. While recent national trends had been to employ an earth-toned Native American motif, this little outpost lived in Native Americana. Hence, Simon Dismounts Thrice, the owner, chose Italian decor. Framed Florentine prints, depicting gondolas on pristine canals, rested incongruously above the heads of the mostly Sioux clientele. Blaring orange Naugahyde booths, relics of a 1970's color craze, begged to be reupholstered in a more soothing color. However, there would be no mauves of the current faddish Southwestern theme. Southwestern meant Native American, and Pine Ridge had enough such ornamentation.

What else had not changed was the patented 'golden arch' flavor of hamburgers. Red Hawk sat in air-conditioned bliss, munching his third Big Mac while an awed Daniel still worked on his first.

"*Tunkasila*, where do you put it all?"

Gnawing another gouge from his dwindling burger, Leo answered, "Winter is coming early this year. All of the animals have begun storing up their fat."

"I suppose *Woniya* told you this ... about an early winter?" Shaking his head, the old man mumbled around the bun protruding from his mouth, "Spencer Christian on Good Morning America. I could drink another coke, please."

Chuckling at Red Hawk's gastronomical stamina, Gray Wolf headed toward the serving counter.

The cashier took his order for the third time, grinned and shook her head. "Somebody's got a tapeworm."

Daniel grinned back. "Somebody's got a ninety-eight year old grandfather who thinks he hasn't eaten in two weeks.

As he waited for Leo's coke, his attention was drawn to a young blonde girl's picture ensconced on the overhead television screen. A news report blared in accompaniment. *I've seen this girl before . But where? Oh, shit!*

"—details are sketchy but the Rapid City Police Department has confirmed Christine Hardesty, ten year old daughter of Congressman Randolph Hardesty, has been kidnapped. Our District of Columbia sister channel, WPOL, states Congressman Hardesty, a third-term West River Democrat, is presently en route to Rapid City to rejoin his family. The Federal Bureau of Investigation is now in charge of-"

Daniel broke free of the counter line and hurried back to where Leo Red Hawk was putting the finishing teeth marks into a handful of French fries. Tugging the old man's shirtsleeve, Gray Wolf said, "Grandfather, we have to leave right away! I must go back to Rapid City tonight."

Seeing the obvious distress in his young friend's eyes, Leo offered no resistance at being shuffled from the bustling noontime interior. Only after firmly latching himself into Gray Wolf's pickup seat did the old man speak.

"Something has troubled you, *Takoja*. Do we need to talk some more?"

"If we discuss it, we'll get into another argument, Grandfather," Gray Wolf said tersely.

"I believe I know what it is and I am sorry for upsetting you," Red Hawk murmured.

Busy checking for traffic before accelerating out of the parking lot onto the highway, Daniel barely paid attention to the old man's words. "What did you say, Grandfather? I was kind of caught up there for a minute."

"I apologized to you for being an old man with a young man's appetite. I should not have asked you for another coke in there; now you are upset with my greed."

Gray Wolf barked a short laugh, *"Tunkasila,* I'm not mad. This has nothing to do with you. I just can't talk about it right now, okay?"

They drove in silence with Daniel caught up in his growing concern over who might be involved in the Hardesty girl kidnapping. Leo contemplated whatever wise, ninety-eight year old men contemplated. Badger township came into sight before Red Hawk broke the burgeoning stillness.

"I will ask *Woniya* to guide you in your troubles, Daniel. You have chosen not to share your concern with me." There was no bitterness, no jealousy in Leo's words, but the message had an impact on Gray Wolf's conscience.

"Leo, you've been like my father for a long time, but there are some things a son can't talk about, even to his dad," he explained. "When the time is right, we will talk, but until then, I can't explain it to you if I don't know what I am going to do about this thing. It's just something I have to work out."

In his guarded way, Daniel was telling the old man

the truth. He had no idea what he could do about Christine Hardesty's abduction. All he knew was that young Christine had a starring role in Steve Abrams' dream, and Gray Wolf did not put much stock in coincidences. Abrams was involved somehow, but proving it was another matter.

Pulling into Leo's dusty driveway, Daniel didn't bother shutting the truck off. He looked across at his old friend, putting a false smile on for Red Hawk's sake. "I will be back next weekend, *Tunkasila*, and I will spend the night if you let me. As a matter of fact, I'll bring you a special surprise from Rapid City when I come back."

Fumbling with his seatbelt, the old man looked intently at Gray Wolf. "I would like to know what makes you run off, Daniel, but since you won't tell me, I will speak to *Woniya*. He thinks a lot about you, my son. I'll ask him to watch over you this week."

Red Hawk finally disengaged the harness from around his waist and opened the truck door. Early afternoon heat rolled into the cab as Leo clambered to his dusty yard. Shutting the door behind him, the old man peered in through the closed window, mouth forming silent words.

Daniel reached over and rolled the passenger window down. "I'm sorry, Grandfather, I couldn't hear what you said."

"I said, if you can not surprise me with a wife and new *Ihanbla Gmunka* by next weekend, then bring artichoke hearts." Red Hawk turned and began the slow journey to his house and an afternoon of enigmatic television programs.

Feeling guilty, but relieved to be alone, Gray Wolf backed out of the gravel drive, wheeling slowly so not to raise dust. *I should have told him. I should have let him know what's bothering me. Yeah, but if I did, old Leo would have hit me with 'this is not your concern. You are a soldier, not a doctor.'*

"So, who can I tell? Who's going to believe I know who the kidnapper is because I saw him do it in a dream?" Gray Wolf posed the rhetorical question to himself, already knowing the answer. He couldn't tell anyone until he had more proof.

"What if I'm wrong? What if ol' Stevie didn't have anything to do with the little girl's disappearance?" Daniel questioned further, then answered, "Hell, I'd be giving my paycheck to Mr. Abrams for the next hundred years or so, after he got done with me in court."

Fresh out of ideas, Gray Wolf turned the radio on. He punched the AM button, hoping to pick up KOTA out of Rapid City. The FM stations played practically non-stop music, only breaking for news in the event of a nuclear attack. KOTA, the radio affiliate of the city's anchor television station, was more likely to broadcast updates.

Amid a stream of distance-induced static, Daniel heard Chet Dunlap, the octogenarian KOTA disk jockey, rambling on about local weather patterns.

"—Hills are in need of the much-appreciated thundershowers now located over the Deadwood-Lead area. Local forecast calls for partly cloudy skies with a slight chance of afternoon or early evening thunderstorms. Let's hope the slight chance turns into reality this time, folks.

"Now, to repeat our feature news story, Christine Hardesty, daughter of Congressman Randolph Hardesty, was abducted from her West Rapid home this morning, some time between nine and ten o'clock. Local authorities will only confirm that a ransom note was found in the Hardesty front yard, wrapped in the ten-year old's doll blanket. Rapid City's field office of the Federal Bureau of Investigation is now at the scene, but refuses to give out any further details. The Congressman is scheduled to arrive at Rapid City Regional Airport within the hour amid, what local authorities say, is a shroud of extremely tight security.

"Christine Hardesty, youngest child of the charismatic West River Democrat, is a fourth grade student at Francis Howell Elementary School, in Washington, D.C. Rapid City Mayor, Jack Haggerty, has expressed the town's shock and dismay ... I'd like declare a side bar here, folks, just to add my own editorial. You know I've hopefully been a strong voice of the Black Hills for over fifty years and, never ever in my dreams would I have thought -"

Daniel Gray Wolf switched the radio off, not so much to avoid the dreary blathering of the ancient broadcaster, but because he needed to think about what Dunlap had just said. *Never ever in my dreams ... never in my dreams.*

"Holy shit!" Gray Wolf exclaimed as inspiration struck him. "I knew there was a reason I didn't kill those friggin' dogs."

Excited, and a little terrified, by the idea that burst into his head, Daniel spent the remaining drive home plotting how to bring off this highly abnormal plan. *What about it, hoss? Can you conjure up a nightmare you put to rest? Can you let the dogs loose so little Stevie Abrams gets scared shitless enough to call you back in?* To even think the words was chilling.

Gray Wolf had made up his mind, even though the variables, the unknowns, placed his chance for success at practically nil. He had to try, had to recreate the nightmare from where he left it. This was the only way it could be done. Directly contacting Abrams would arouse the man's suspicion and he'd be nervous enough as it was.

The other issue to consider was doctrine surrounding the Dream Catcher legacy. While there was no orthodox Lakota creed, spiritual beliefs were just as strong as any formalized religion. Though ambivalent toward his unique status among Native Americans, Gray Wolf would still not violate the dogma that prohibited entering another person's dreams unless invited.

"Technically, I haven't done anything against the Lakota ways," Daniel said out loud, rationalizing what he had done. "Abrams asked me to get rid of his nightmare and I did. He was still dreaming. I was concerned the nightmare had come back, so I re-entered.

"Now, I want to bring back his nightmare. I'll try to dream of the alleyway and the dogs, technically no longer part of little Stevie's mental make-up. Therefore, I won't actually be entering his dreams—it'll be my dream—technically. If this works, and the dogs become part of Abrams' night scene again, I won't go back in his head unless he asks me." *That is the big 'IF', kola. Abrams has to invite you back, otherwise you can't do shit.*

Gray Wolf felt justified in his logic. Boundaries were stretched perhaps, but the *Ihanbla Gmunka* doctrine was not breached. "Break one of the Ten Commandments, you go to hell; stretch a Commandment, and it's a venial sin. Sort of like heavy petting with your best friend's wife isn't really adultery ... technically. Yeah, what I'm doing is a venial sin, and I can live with that," he reasoned.

Approaching the turnoff for his home, Daniel opted to drive into Rapid City. It was only mid-afternoon, still plenty early to allow some cruising. He wanted to locate where Abrams lived, remembering the man had described his residence as a tiny efficiency apartment on Eighth Street.

Now all you have to do is check out a mile and a half of houses. See if you can spot a dark blue sedan with out-of-state plates.

Turning west on St. Patrick Street, Daniel drove the

four miles to Eighth, more popularly known as Rushmore Road. The busiest thoroughfare in Rapid City, Eighth Street ran north south with the southern route becoming Highway 16 that led to Mt. Rushmore. Summer time meant the road was even more heavily traveled as tourists rambled to and from their various Black Hills' destinations. Reaching the intersection, Gray Wolf headed north, avoiding the heavier commercial section of the road. If Abrams lived where he said he did, it would be on the more residential strip between St. Patrick and Kansas City Streets.

Daniel stayed in the far right lane, content to drive the speed limit as he searched the row of houses intermingled with gas stations and restaurants. Two parked cars stood out as potentially being Abrams'. At Kansas City, he turned left then pulled into the first driveway. Backing out, he reversed his direction, driving south on the road, searching for spots where Abrams might live. This side of Eighth Street netted him one additional dark blue auto.

"Well, this hasn't proved a whole lot, butthead," he berated himself. "You drive three miles and find three cars that could belong to this turd." Nonetheless, he mentally noted the location of each vehicle.

Time still on his hands, Gray Wolf decided to drive home, shower and relax with his Louis L'Amour fetish until sufficiently tired to attempt the big dream caper. Driving east, he switched the radio back on, hoping to catch an update on the Hardesty kidnap. Chet Dunlap's raspy voice greeted him through the twin speakers.

"—concludes our thirty minute song set featuring two pieces by the late, great Lawrence Welk. Ah one anna two ... sorry, folks, there's just something about Welk's music that brings out the nostalgia in me"

Gray Wolf snorted in reply, "Your whole world is nostalgia, Dunlap. Get on with the news."

"And now for a news update. Congressman Randolph Hardesty landed at Rapid City Regional Airport, surrounded by tight security. KOTA sources say the young representative appeared disheveled as he stepped from the private charter into a waiting limousine.

"Federal authorities are remaining tightlipped about details surrounding the abduction of Christine Hardesty, ten year old daughter of the charismatic congressman. Several attempts by our sister television station, KOTA Channel Four, to gain further information on the missing child's fate, were met by the standard 'no comment'.

"Interviews with neighbors of the Hardesty family provided no additional insight. There were no sightings of strange vehicles or people in the area about the time young Christine was taken from her loving family. When questioned about the ransom note attached to the child's doll blanket, no residents of the affluent west end neighborhood remember seeing the blanket, as it obviously was picked up by Mrs. Hardesty during her futile search -"

"Jesus, Chet," Gray Wolf groaned, shaking his head at the invisible radio announcer, "You guys still have summer interns write this stuff for you?"

"—additional item just in. President Clinton expressed his shock and concern upon being notified of the Hardesty kidnapping. The president vowed full government agency cooperation in locating the party, or parties, responsible for this heinous crime. Attorney General Richland has ordered in a crack team of FBI crisis specialists to assume command of the kidnap case. Richland assured the gathering crowd of reporters that the team being sent to Rapid City was of the highest caliber and had successfully negotiated several abduction incidents.

"Rapid City Mayor, Jack Haggerty, has pledged all available law enforcement personnel to assist the federal agents in any way. City police and county sheriff reserves have been called up, uniting this community's law agencies into a cohesive, manhunt-capable force.

"You'll forgive me, folks, but this whole scene is so unbelievable. A peaceful community of -"

Gray Wolf switched the radio off again, not wanting to listen to another maudlin editorial.

Lonely and disquieting thoughts ebbed through Daniel's mind as he drove down Rapid Valley Road toward his home. So far, only two people knew who the kidnapper was, and one of those wasn't totally sure. What the Hardesty girl must be going through, separated from family, scared, was beyond his comprehension at the moment. The thoughts did have their merit though. The vivid picture of Christine Hardesty strengthened his resolve to find a way back into Steve Abrams' head.

Entering the quiet house, Gray Wolf impatiently looked around for something to do, anything to wile away the hours until he could sleep. And dream. Louis L'Amour held little interest for him, the living room required no further pick up thanks to the habitual cleaning ceremony following last night's dream episode.

"Might as well watch the tube and see if anything's come up." Daniel punched the remote control, instantly bringing sound from the still-dark television.

As the picture brightened to life, Gray Wolf idly flicked through the channels, wondering if he could find Rin Tin Tin on his own set. Twenty-three stations viewed, and still no wonder dog. *How do you do it, Grandfather? Ah, hell with it ... one of the mysteries of the universe.*

Not because he wanted to, but because he had to pass the time somehow, Daniel picked up the western paperback that had been silently taunting him since his arrival. Propping his feet on the hassock, he sighed, "Okay, Louie, take me away for a few hours."

Shortly after eight o'clock in the evening, Slade killed the final outlaw and rode slowly into the sunset, a lonely but righteous cowboy. Gray Wolf flipped the exhausted novel onto the sofa beside him. He checked the wall clock. Eight twenty-three, it read.

"Close enough," Daniel murmured, rising from the couch to secure the house. Surprised, he found he really was tired. In his bedroom, he undressed quickly and slid between the cool sheets. A believer, but not overly religious, Gray Wolf found a prayer issuing from his lips, "Lord—or Woniya—help me with this, okay? An innocent child's life is at stake and I may hold the answer. I don't ask for much. Don't talk to you much, for that matter. But I really need you to understand why I'm doing this. I've been a good man and I'll take whatever path you decide for me. Just let me do what I need to tonight."

The Dream Catcher lay on his back and began to empty his mind—until a sensation of unfinished business crept into his thoughts. "Amen," he added almost apologetically.

His last thought before slumber was of a darkened alley and two Mastiff-type creatures.

Gray Wolf entered a dreamscape of haze and gloom, wet cobble stoned roads dimly reflecting the glow of distant streetlamps. Obliterating tendrils of cold mist swirled around him, hampering his efforts to gain bearing. *The alley's to the left, I think. At least it was to the left last time I was here.* Trusting his senses, the Dream Catcher moved against the yielding blanket of fog, feeling the icy touch of moisture against his outstretched hands.

There it is! Partially obscured by dense atmosphere, the blackened alleyway yawned at him from twenty feet away. Unexpected dread washed over Gray Wolf as he confronted the orifice. *Why am I afraid? Why do I feel threatened?*

The answer chilled him far more than the clammy mist ever could. *For the time being, Abrams is out of the picture. This is my show now!*

Heart pounding, Daniel stepped into the shadowed lane, away from the anemic friendliness of the dimmed streetlight. Each tentative step, each foot deeper into the black, brought fear closer. Darkness was virtually encompassing now. The feeble outside light barely touched the indistinguishable alley shapes and only painted things in different shades of ebony. Gray Wolf touched one of the nondescript shapes, cold, hard, and sharp-edged. The dumpster!

You're close now, kola. Time to conjure up a little light. Nothing happened. *Flashlight!* Nothing. *Candle!* Darkness.

Shit, Injun, this is a fine time to learn you can't Dream Catch your own nightmares!

Common sense told Daniel to get out of the alley but the nightmare proved a seductive mistress and whispered to proceed. He leaned forward, hand tracing the lip of the dumpster, searching for the chains that secured two very mean canines. His probing fingers touched the first link. Then the second. *Okay now, I left these creatures asleep. All things being equal, they should still be asleep.*

Tracing the first length of chain down to the shadowed form, Daniel was greeted by a low, ominous growl. *It's your nightmare now!* The Mastiff-beast was awake and not happy to see him. Mastiff number two uttered its own warning; deep, throaty, deadly. *Get your butt out of here. Forget this shit!*

Terrified Gray Wolf gingerly ran his hand across the freakish, misshaped head, searching for the muzzle clasp. Coarse hair bristled against his fingers in sharp contrast to the smooth-leathered muzzle strap. The Mastiff-beast didn't struggle, only waited with a deadly anticipation. Daniel found the buckle, cool against the growing heat of the creature. He tugged the leather strap, releasing it from the clasp. *I gotta set the second dog loose too.* Dream Catcher logic dueled with the nightmare-producing subconscious—and lost. The Mastiff, sensing freedom, pawed at the muzzle hanging loosely from its head.

Heart in his throat, Daniel ran from the alley as enraged howls signified the beast had freed itself. Throaty growls and clattering toenails on concrete announced the Mastiff's feral pursuit of its new quarry, one scared shitless Dream Catcher. Closer. The huffing and deep-throated growling was much closer now. Gray Wolf knew the oversized killer was only steps away. Blindly running through the grasping fog, he sensed the dog's attack. Felt the creature spring into the air mere feet behind him. Realized its gaping jaws were searching for his neck.

Wake up! Wake up! Jesus, please wake up!

"Mmmmshitmotherfuck!" Daniel screamed at the ceiling, bolting upright from his sweat-soaked bed.

CHAPTER 11

Excited, and a little scared, Steve Abrams tossed restlessly on his grimy bed sheets. Sleep, a scarce commodity until the Indian guy had put up the dogs, was going to be important now that Phase One was implemented.

"I did it. I actually pulled it off," he bragged to the walls of his tiny apartment.

No one would find the girl, at least not without his directions. Kidnapping Christine Hardesty proved the easy part. Hiding her took a little more energy, but the end result was well worth the effort.

Lying back, arms behind his head, Abrams quoted his favorite television hero. "I love it when a plan comes together." Smiling at how much he sounded like George Peppard, Steve thought about the events leading to today's success.

His arrival in Rapid City coincided with the Hardestys' last hectic two weeks prior to moving back to Washington for the fall term. Momma Hardesty was too busy packing the family valuables to be concerned for her children's whereabouts. Besides, this was Rapid City, the safe little town where nothing of this magnitude could ever happen.

He'd scouted the Hardesty residence, mostly with binoculars from the treed seclusion of Dinosaur Hill. Only once had he ventured onto West Penelope Street; only once prior to the kidnapping and that was on his first day in town. He figured it was safe. It was summer, and that meant vacation season in the Black Hills. Streets were littered with out-of-state license plates attached to every imaginable car and RV. Ah, tourist season. A tribute to the touring cousins glomming free room and board from the local cousins. No, he hadn't been noticed as he drove his three-year-old Dodge sedan, a respectable family car, past the Hardesty home. Hadn't been noticed taking pictures with his Polaroid so he could later identify the house from his vantage point on the nearby wooded hillside.

Finding a hiding spot for the girl had not been that tough either. Lightly populated, the Black Hills and surrounding areas offered an untold number of places where a kid could be stashed for a few days pending the ransom exchange. He'd needed a relatively flat area, a location not subject to high water tables or runoff. It also had to be secluded enough so he wouldn't be observed digging a five-foot-deep hole in the ground. These geological and geographical requirements had led him to the Badlands, forty miles southeast of Rapid City.

For a city boy like Abrams, the Badlands seemed aptly named. Several hundred square miles of flat-topped mesas, rock outcrops, mean sand and soft dirt conjured up nothing but desolate images. Two days of scouting the bleak area rewarded him with a perfect hiding niche. During his search, Steve had only seen one other car this far off the main road, an abandoned '57 Chrysler, rusted and riddled with bullet holes compliments of long-range target shooters. Absence of any tire marks on the dusty ground confirmed this was the ideal place. Besides, the old Chrysler made a good landmark to locate the kid after he'd buried her. He didn't want the Hardesty girl to die. At least not yet. All depended on how the ransom demands were met. If the esteemed congressman from South Dakota chose to play hardball via counseling from the feds, a simple plug in the air tube would convert Christine Hardesty's box into a coffin.

The toughest challenge had been excavating, then constructing the kid's new subterranean home, without being noticed. Abrams had pre-cut the plywood case, a simple five-foot long, by two-foot wide box, before leaving Indiana. A one-gallon collapsible water bottle, blanket, three quarter inch PVC pipe, shovel and cordless drill completed his kidnap kit. All components fit neatly into the trunk of his Dodge.

Physically, the hard work was over for Abrams. The hole was dug, box assembled and occupied, hole refilled, and the area swept back into obscurity. Poor, scared-shitless Christine Hardesty only fought when she realized where Abrams was going to put her. Her struggles aroused him, almost caused him to rape her, but self-control won out. What if he ruptured something and she slowly bled to death in her subterranean condo? No, he didn't want Christine dead. At least not yet.

Heavy-eyed with sleep, Steve Abrams smiled at the memories. "Yeah, I love it when a plan comes together."

Sleep, yeah, he couldn't get enough of it. What would this be the third—no, the fourth night now since Daniel what's-his-name had chained the nightmare dogs up.

"Fuckin' dogs," he mumbled, on the verge of slumber. "Never did like dogs."

Arms folded across his chest, legs out straight, Steve Abrams hazily wondered if young Christine Hardesty was lying in the same position. Smiling at the image, he fell asleep and dreamed of a dog.

It was Bowser all right, his childhood pet. Bowser, the dog of multiple lineage. Bowser the faithful follower of little Steven Abrams. In the dream, the dog was whole again, just like before Steven had begun satisfying his curiosity about Bowser's pain tolerance.

Abrams entered the picture, a nine year old already well on his way to psychosis, although he didn't know it then—or now, for that matter. Experiments in the name of juvenile science began.

Steven pumped his air rifle and shot Bowser in the flank again. Bright yelps of pain followed by canine whimpers, but no penetration. He marked his scorecard with a sixth notch. This won't do, so ... what else?

Bowser-in-a-bag; a test of animal strength versus industrial strength polyurethane garbage sacks. Steven stuffed the mutt in a translucent bag, tied the end and waited for the verdict. Death or Bowser. The dog won thanks to a frenzied effort of clawing. That won't do either.

Tag with the lawn mower. A new experiment pitting sinew against steel. Bowser might have won this round except he was still a little fuzzy from the bag trick. Cornered against the fence, a cowering Bowser disappeared beneath the power mower's raised front wheels. Lovely grinding sounds thumped beneath the chassis, followed by abrupt silence as the fur-tangled blade froze the engine. So much noise before and now silence slapped little Steve in the face.

No time to enter data in his ever present notebook. Steven hurriedly rubbed dirt into his eyes, a surefire tear maker, just as Mother stepped outside to check on the ruckus. An ecstatic, crying young Steven explained how Bowser had run in front of him. He couldn't stop in time and now his dog was so much fresh fertilizer. Covering his face and sobbing, the boy turned away from his mother so she couldn't see his grin. Or erection.

But, in the dream world, turning away didn't solve anything as it had in real life. Just as he swiveled from his mother, Steven the boy hunter became Steve the hunted adult. He realized that when he heard the first low, menacing growl.

Oh shit no no no! Not the dog again!

Abrams peered through his fingers into the fiery canine eyes of his nightmare hound.

No no no no—Gray Wolf—for chrissakes, help me!

CHAPTER 12

The wall clock read 1:37 A.M., Sunday morning. Daniel lounged on his couch, tired but too keyed up to sleep. A well-thumbed Louis L'Amour rested unopened on his lap.

Both pleased and terrified by his accomplishment, Daniel had released one hellhound, but at a cost. Unfamiliar with being on the receiving end of a nightmare, Gray Wolf flatly did not like the feeling, and vowed to never bring one on voluntarily again.

"Scary stuff when it's your dream, huh *kola?* Now, all you have to do is wait and see if little Stevie gets visited. And if he calls you again. Lots of ifs."

Deciding there was no use waiting for a phone call that might not happen, Gray Wolf picked up his dog-eared L'Amour novel. "Just you and me, Louie. Now, put me back to sleep."

Only three pages of the classic western were devoured before the telephone rang. *Bingo!* Resisting the urge to snatch the receiver off the hook, Daniel suffered the interminable seconds until two more rings had sounded.

Picking up the receiver, he sleepily husked, "Hello?"

"One of the bastards got loose. He almost got me this time!"

"Wha' ... who is this?" Gray Wolf stayed in his just-wakened role.

"Steve Abrams," came the near-hysterical reply. "I thought

you said I wouldn't be bothered by the fucking dogs again? Now one of 'em's back and I can't get any sleep because of the cock -"

"Steve?" Daniel interrupted, adding light sleep groans for authenticity. "Calm down now, pardner. What's this about one dog ? I thought there were two?"

"Only one's come back," Abrams replied, slightly more calm. "But it's the same sonofabitch that's been bothering me, Gray Wolf. The same sonofabitch!"

Daniel allowed his voice to sound more alert. "Geez, Steve, I didn't think this would happen. I mean, this is really unusual. Listen, we need to get together as quickly as possible. I feel responsible somehow for this nightmare reappearing."

"I need my sleep, Gray Wolf," Abrams persisted. "I've got important things to do and I need a clear head."

I know you do, my warped little friend. "Steve, when I said we need to get together quickly, I meant pronto. Like right now! My error has made you uncomfortable and I need to fix that. Look, I'll come to your place if you'll give me the address." *Come on, you son of a bitch. Let's see if you've got the little girl at your apartment.*

Silence greeted the Dream Catcher. *Oh, shit! Did I go and make him suspicious?*

Abrams finally replied, "I'm up now and probably won't be able to go back to sleep, but if you're free, can I come over tomorrow night—I mean, tonight—you know, Sunday?"

Gray Wolf breathed an inaudible sigh of relief. "Steven, I didn't want to tell you this before, but the dog getting loose could mean a potentially dangerous situation. See, dogs are tenacious and have a way of disobeying their masters if they set their minds to it. Same holds true for nightmare dogs. I'm afraid if we don't try and fix this thing now, well, I don't know what will happen."

"You mean, I'm in danger?"

"No! Yes. I don't know for sure. I do know we have to take care of this thing. My reputation as a Dream Catcher is at stake." *Careful, butthead. Don't lay it on too thick. Now, find out if he's got the girl at his place.*

"I can be there in fifteen minutes, twenty minutes tops," Gray Wolf said, a hint of pleading in his voice. "This is important for me as well as you, Steven."

More silence, then, "All right, but I don't have two beds like at your place."

"Give me the address and I'll bring my bedroll. That doesn't pose a problem. Your dog does."

"Well, okay. I live at 2734 Eighth Street, upstairs. It's a white two-story with green shutters. Outside stairway leads to my apartment."

"I'm on my way right -"

"Um, Daniel?" Abrams' tentative voice cut in. "What if I fall asleep while I'm waiting for you?"

"Don't! I'll be there in fifteen minutes." Gray Wolf hung up the phone. *Damn, the girl's not at his apartment. Not if he invited me there.*

Grabbing his sleeping bag from the hall closet, Daniel hurried outside, barely remembering to lock the front door behind him.

Ten minutes later, he turned onto Eighth Street. Heavy traffic, a combination of late night tourists and kids cruising, forced him to drive slower than he wanted. A sense of urgency filled Gray Wolf as he plodded at the thirty-five mile an hour speed limit.

"Come on, come on," he urged, uncharacteristically

beeping his horn at a slow-moving Pennsylvania car. "What the hell you gawkers doin' at two frigging o'clock in the morning? Get a move on, tourist! Shit, get a motel room."

Swerving into the left lane, Daniel gunned past the creeping auto, catching a glimpse of a middle finger extended in his direction.

"Same to ya, ass -" he retorted, but caught himself. "Calm down, *kola*. No use getting agitated before you need to. Save it for Stevie boy when the time's right."

Gray Wolf spotted Abrams' house, a cluttered, run-down affair near the corner of Eighth and Franklin. Steve's description of white with green shutters was a compliment compared to what actually met the eye. The house was probably white, but had not felt paint in at least two decades. Shutters, hanging listlessly from their brackets, were green by default, possibly with mold. Pallid light filtered through the cheap second floor curtains, a probable sign Abrams had heeded Daniel's words and not gone back to sleep. A blue Dodge sedan with Indiana plates rested in the parking lane. *OL3 dash 74M. Remember the tag number, kola.*

Gray Wolf wheeled his pickup into the gravel driveway and got out in time to hear the blaring challenge of Pennsylvania Tourist's horn. Waving a friendly greeting at the vehicle cruising by, he pivoted and trudged up the rickety steps to Abrams' apartment. The door sprang open before he reached the second floor landing and myopic Steve peered around the jam.

"Is that you, Daniel?"

"You expecting another Dream Catcher armed with a sleeping bag?" Yes, it's me." Gray Wolf stepped up onto the landing as Abrams held the door open.

Nervous, probably a little ashamed by the surroundings,

Abrams apologized, "Sorry about the mess. Can't seem to find the time to straighten things up."

Yeah, right, what with your kidnapping schedule and such. You able to tell me what you've been doing with your time, Stevie? "Hey, no sweat, pardner." Gray Wolf looked around the tiny, dismal apartment, trying to find something to compliment. He couldn't.

Steve Abrams wasn't through with the apologies. "Uh, Daniel, sorry about the way I spouted off to you on the phone. This dog thing just really ties me up in knots, you know?"

Waving his hand in dismissal, Gray Wolf said, "Forget about it. If I had done my job right the first time, you and I would both be sawing logs about now.

"And since I brought up the subject," he continued, "We need to sit down and talk for a couple of minutes before we put this thing to rest."

"Sure thing. Come on in the living room," Abrams offered.

Daniel watched from seven feet away as Steve feverishly dusted crumbs and bits of paper from the living room couch. Satisfied it was now decontaminated, Gray Wolf sat down on the complaining old sofa. Abrams straddled a hardback chair across the cramped room.

The Dream Catcher began, "I think I know what the problem is, Steve."

"Oh?"

"I don't think I had your trust that first time around. Don't get me wrong; it's probably my fault for not convincing you I could take care of the nightmare."

Abrams stared at Gray Wolf, a look of puzzlement on his face. "I trusted you enough to come out to your house. What's not to trust?"

Careful here, Gray Wolf. Don't go overboard with the mind games. "Before coming here to the Black Hills, had you ever heard of a Dream Catcher; ever heard of someone able to cure nightmares?"

"Well ... no."

"And when you talked with Jimbo Freeman at the bar, did you have your doubts about what he told you?"

"Yeah, kinda, because he had a few beers in him, but I decided to take a chance."

"Steve, I've never leveled with anyone like I'm going to do now. Maybe it's the circumstances. Maybe it's because you're an easy guy to talk to. *Yeah, right.* But you have a right to know. *Think of something quick, kola.* Um, what I'm trying to say is I've seen these dogs before. I've **met** these dogs before."

"You what? You met these dogs before. But where? Hey, Daniel, this isn't funny. I hope you're kidding just to cover up for your goof, but this is not one bit funny."

"Steve, dogs are symbolic in dreams. They stand for fear. Kind of like guardians of the unknown. Remember when I said I had a thing for animals; couldn't kill'em? Well, I was only partly telling the truth. These dogs cannot be killed. Believe me, I've tried before."

Distraught, Abrams concluded, "So, what you're telling me is you can't help me with these dogs. You go in and mess with my head, but you -"

"I didn't say that!" Gray Wolf interrupted sharply. "I'm telling you we can't kill your fear, but we can leash it. You told me only one dog came back. That means that we, you and I, were successful in harnessing part of your fears.

"That's where the trust part comes into play, Steve," he continued. "You're from out of state. You aren't as aware of these Native American mystical things as the folks around here. So naturally, there's some doubt as to whether I can help you."

"So, there is hope then?" Abrams asked.

"Of course there is. I wouldn't be here otherwise. The error was not in my dream catching ability, it was in my inability to verbally convince you to trust me. Your dog, your fear, is partially back because I couldn't gain your full confidence."

Staring at the floor, Abrams said to no one in particular, "I've got to get my sleep."

"Steve, we can lick this thing and hopefully tonight," Gray Wolf said, adding just enough fervent tremor to his voice. "What do you say, pardner? Trust me enough to tie this bastard up for good?"

Gray Wolf stood up and extended his hand, a gesture of impassioned goodwill. *Come on, Stevie boy, don't you feel the Mom, country, and apple pie oozing from my words?*

Abrams immediately rose from his chair and stepped across the room. Grasping Daniel's outstretched hand, he said, "Let's do it! Let's tie this bastard up for good."

"Good man," Gray Wolf said, patting the kidnapper's shoulder with his free hand. "We better get started. Show me where I should put my sleeping bag."

Not yet releasing Daniel's hand, Abrams repeated, "Let's really do it this time, okay? No more bullshit; no more lies."

Apprehension flared as Gray Wolf searched the man's eyes. Was that a warning? Did Steve's voice hold just a hint of malevolence? *You aren't cut out for this type work, kola. You're a Dream Catcher, not a cop. No more talk now. He's agreed to let you back in his dream. Do what you came for and get the hell out!* Disgusted by the physical contact with Abrams, Daniel pried his hand loose. He smiled at the man, hoping the sincerity didn't look forced. In response, Abrams turned and walked through the only other doorway in the apartment.

Gray Wolf took this as a sign to follow. Picking up the sleeping bag, he entered the dingy, unkempt bedroom. *Whew, what a pigsty!* He watched Abrams kick scraps of newspaper and clothing under the bed, obviously clearing a spot for Daniel to lay his bag. It was the first attempt at house cleaning Steve had done, Gray Wolf surmised, by the looks of the rest of the apartment.

At least Abrams looked apologetic. "There's not a whole lot of room. I can lend you a pillow."

Daniel glanced at the grimy, sweat-soaked bed linen before saying, "Thanks, but I'll be fine. We'll work this just like last time. I'll go out in the living room and read for a while until you fall asleep. Once you've started dreaming, I'll come in and join you. Okay?"

Nodding, Steve clambered onto the bed, anxious for the dream exorcism to begin. Tucked into his soiled surroundings, he looked over at the Dream Catcher. "Do you see any other dreams? You know, do you hang around after the nightmare's been solved?"

Better answer this one right, kola. "Nope, it's not in the Dream Catcher Book of Rules. Besides, once the nightmare is fixed, it's like I get pulled from the person's dream. My job's done, so the Great Spirit figures I don't need to be there anymore. Mystical stuff, you know?" *Good lie, Gray Wolf.*

Abrams rolled onto his side, satisfied anything else he might dream would not be shared. His stilted logic accepted Gray Wolf's answer, especially with the Great Spirit's name being mentioned. He might not know much about Indians, but he did know that if they referred to a higher being, they were dead serious.

Daniel retreated to the living room couch, in plain view of Abrams. *I'm gonna sit down here so you can see how sincere I am,*

Steve Abrams. I'll read my book, just like a good little Dream Catcher, until you go to sleep. Pulling L'Amour from his hip pocket, Gray Wolf turned his concentration to the fictionalized century-old struggle between cowboy and Indian. A smile tugged at his lips as he thought about the congruity between old Louis' plot and the very real situation of Daniel Gray Wolf, Oglala Sioux, and Steven Abrams, pretend cowboy.

Less than two hours later, Gray Wolf was lying on the floor beside Abrams' bed. He fell asleep, effortlessly emerging onto the dark, misty street of Steve's dreamscape. No fear this time—it was Abrams' nightmare again, not his.

Daniel made quick work of the demon Mastiff, tranquilizing, then muzzling the beast. He knew Abrams was cowering in the shadows. Watching. Normally, a quick, unnoticed exit from a cured dream was appropriate. This time, Gray Wolf made an obvious show of it He wanted Abrams to see him leaving. *All cured now, Stevie. And look, I'm leaving. Okay?* He left the dark dream world of Steve Abrams, woke up and stared at the sleeping kidnapper.

Thankfully, Daniel's sentry duty was a short one. Fifteen minutes after exiting the dog nightmare, he observed Abrams' fluttering lids, the involuntary response of sleeping eyes following a new dream sequence. "Let's hope this is the 'nightmare' I need to be in," Gray Wolf whispered to the supine form. Lying down on the sleeping bag, he drained his mind ...

***

... and entered a vaguely familiar landscape. Hidden behind a sandstone outcropping, Daniel viewed his surroundings. Rugged, nature-striped sandstone bluffs climbed on either side of the dirt and sand basin where he stood. Jutting rocks, similar to the one he hid behind, pushed through the crumbling soil, forming six-foot high sawtooths in a near-perfect semi-circle. Only two signs of mankind were present: a long-abandoned 1957 Chrysler, rusted tailfins pointing proudly to the southeast, and Abrams' dark blue sedan.

Movement near the sedan caught Gray Wolf's attention. From his vantage point fifty feet away, he watched Abrams struggle with a young, blonde girl. *That's Christine! Stevie boy, I could kiss you for your warped dreams. And right on schedule, too!*

Intent, Daniel viewed Abrams drag the Hardesty girl toward a pile of freshly dug earth. *You buried her, you sonofabitch! You killed Christine and buried her out here. Where the hell is here?* Unnerved by the dream spectacle, Gray Wolf forced himself to watch as Abrams resolutely picked the girl up, strode to the pile of dirt, then unceremoniously dumped her to the ground.

Abrams pointed at the hole, stridently gesturing as he uttered silent commands to the frightened child. Twice, the girl tried to crawl out. Each time the man pushed her back in place, shaking his fist and bawling mute orders. Abrams reached down and picked up a plywood sheet. Lowering the cover, he forced it in place, pushing against the struggling girl's up thrust arms. Kneeling on the lid, Steve grabbed a length of pipe and twisted it against the plywood until it stood upright.

That's an air hole! You didn't kill her—you buried her alive, you bastard. Relief flooded Gray Wolf, mingled with his revulsion at the dream enactment of Christine Hardesty's entombment. *Where is this place? It's the Badlands, but where? Remember the car, remember the outcroppings. You've got to find out where this spot is!* Not able to watch anymore, Daniel exited the dream as Abrams industriously piled dirt onto the living tomb.

Gray Wolf woke, trembling with emotion over what he had witnessed. Staring at Steve Abrams, he resisted the urge to choke the smiling, sleeping figure. *You fucker! I'm going to get you big time, Stevie.*

Abrams answered with a gentle snort, then languorously rubbed between his sheet-covered legs. Still caught in slumber, he clearly was enjoying the dream.

Daniel was torn between wanting to leave and knowing he needed to stay long enough to talk with the sleeping kidnapper. He tiptoed out of the bedroom, quietly setting up guard duty on the living room couch again. Looking at his watch, he murmured, "I'll give you two more hours, Abrams. You don't wake yourself up by six-thirty, I'll wake you up."

In the mean time, Gray Wolf decided he would not sit idle. There might be some clue in the apartment, something indicating where Abrams had hidden the little girl. Quietly, he searched through the mess of papers and trash decorating the living room. Nothing of interest appeared except for back issues of the 'Rapid City Daily Journal'. Daniel shuffled through the newspapers, hoping to find some hard evidence connecting Steve and the Hardesty child. Scraps of sheared leavings intermingled with sections of whole newspaper. He had all but dismissed the living room, except the remnants of paper bothered him. Why was the paper cut up? It wasn't like sections of Help Wanted ads had been separated. *Oh shit, he pasted together his ransom note from this stuff! Is that hard enough evidence to contact the police? No, not yet. There's got to be more. There's got to be something else that ties Stevie Boy in with Christine's abduction.*

Gray Wolf's search took him to the equally cluttered

kitchen area. A small mound of dirty eating paraphernalia dominated the sink. Plastic plates, grimy silverware, styrofoam throw-away containers that hadn't been thrown away, all were mixed together in a mini-landfill. He rifled the three sliding drawers, all mostly bare except for small pieces of debris. Working on the kitchen cupboards, Daniel spotted a plastic bottle of mucilage. *This is what he used to glue the ransom note together. I'll bet he -*

"What are you looking for, Daniel?"

Gray Wolf jumped at the sound of Abrams' voice, not tired-sounding, but a perfectly conscious voice with more than a hint of suspicion. "Oh shit, Steve! You spooked the hell out of me. Dream Catching's a thirsty business. I was looking for a glass to get a drink of water. Where the hell do you keep the glasses?" *That's right, kola, go on the offense.*

Abrams stood in the kitchen entry, looking at Gray Wolf for several seconds. Distrustful eyes softened a bit—just a bit—as he responded, "The next cupboard on your right. Should be some glasses in there."

Suddenly, Daniel was thirsty for real, the fright of having nearly been caught be Abrams parching his throat. Pulling out a plastic McDonald's drink cup, he made his voice casual. "Hey, didn't mean to look like I was snooping, but I didn't want to wake you up for something as simple as a drink.

"I think we put the dream to rest this time, Steve," Gray Wolf continued hurriedly. "That's one tough dog you have nightmares about, but I think we got him good this time. By the way, thanks for your help."

"My help?" A quizzical look attached itself to Abrams' face.

Keep the subject changed. Get his mind off you digging through his stuff. "Yeah, I could feel your trust a lot more. See, that's the kind of ammunition I need to put nightmares away for keeps. You watched what I did to the dog this time?"

Abrams nodded slowly.

"I tried to kill it, Steve, but there's some kind of block that won't let me do that. Every time I brought up a gun, it was only a tranquilizer. Hell, man, I thought of everything—forty-fours—thirty-eight calibers—but the nightmare wouldn't let me produce any one of those. But we still nailed him pretty good, Steve."

Relief wiped away all other looks from Abrams' face. "You think we got rid of them for good this time? Geez, I hope so!"

Gray Wolf studied the younger man, noting how quickly Abrams changed moods. For a moment, he almost felt sympathy for the kidnapper. Only for a moment, though, because he realized something in Steve's mental make up allowed these mood swings to happen. Something not quite normal. Distrust to doubt to hope in a matter of seconds. *You're programmable, Stevie Boy. The right person can manipulate you.*

"Me too!" Gray Wolf answered fervently. "You and I teamed up on those creatures, Mr. Abrams. We did indeed."

Abrams smiled, a delighted kid's smile, at the praise in Gray Wolf's voice. "Yeah, we bashed those fuckers big time, didn't we? Hell, I bet they're gone for good after the way you tied that sonofabitch up! Huh, don't you think?"

Despite wanting to rip Abrams' eyes out, Gray Wolf returned the grin. "Let's hope so, pardner, but remember what I said about dream dog's tenacity."

"Yep, we got 'em good this time. I just know we did." Hope, tinged with pleading, echoed in Abrams' reply.

"Steve, I need you to do me a favor—for my sake. Okay? I feel so darned bad about letting you down the first time, I want to make sure you'll be all right. Let's meet again this evening. That way I'll be around if the bastard shakes loose," Daniel said, and then added quickly. "Mind you, I don't think he'll get free, but I feel responsible, so I just want to make sure."

Abrams fixed Daniel with a look of resurged distrust. "What are you trying to tell me, Gray Wolf? Or, what is it you're not telling me. Why do you think it will be necessary for us to get together again?"

Be strong, but be careful, for chrissakes. Raising his hands, Daniel said, "Now don't go getting soft on me, Steve. I want this nightmare out of your system for good. Shit, man, what's one more night if it means these suckers are gone for good? I'm only asking for your sleep time. You have to sleep. Probably won't even be necessary, but my reputation's kind of at stake here."

Steve Abrams thought for a moment, the turmoil obvious as he drummed up everything Daniel had told him about dream dogs. He answered finally, "These bastards can really be dangerous you say?"

"Can be, yes," Gray Wolf concurred.

"All right, but only tonight. If these sonsabitches aren't gone by then, we part company, got that?"

"Amen, brother." *I'd like to part your frigging head with an axe, but you may show me more about the Hardesty girl, you prick.* "Well, you're going to be all right for the time being. I'm going home now and rack out for a few hours; catch some of my beauty sleep."

"Sure ... okay, Daniel. Ten o'clock tonight." Abrams' mind wasn't on Gray Wolf's departure.

Daniel exited the apartment quickly, gulping jolts of cool, pre-dawn air as he skittered down the rickety outdoor steps. Sleep, though a welcome prospect, was not foremost on his mind. *Poor little kid's buried in the Badlands. Where, though? Shit, there's several hundred square miles of Badlands. Probably one abandoned car per mile, too. What are you going to do, kola?* "It's time you talked with the police, Gray Wolf."

CHAPTER 13

Daniel Gray Wolf drove toward downtown, misgivings pulling at his thoughts. *Do I go to the FBI? No, I don't know those guys. Some dude walks in and says he knows where the Hardesty girl is hidden. Sort of. Feds will look at me like I'm some kind of wacko. Shit! Then they'd probably arrest me. Police Department? Badlands are in the county, not the city, so it's outside their jurisdiction.*

That leaves the Sheriff's Department, kola. Who do you know you can talk to? Tell them about this without getting laughed out of the building? You don't know Sheriff Robbins that well. Wait ... Ben Whitside. "Yeah, Ben, my brother Elk. You're a levelheaded guy. You'll listen to this."

Deputy Ben Whitside, Daniel decided, was the best possible choice. He remembered Whitside being involved in a major Native American issue just a couple of years ago. Very hush-hush stuff. Several unexplained deaths with lots of talk about ghost Indians being the cause. Even old Leo wouldn't talk about it.

"Let's see if you're on duty, Ben Whitside." Gray Wolf steered his truck east on Kansas City Street.

"Sorry, 'fraid Deputy Whitside's on day shift," the Sheriff's Department dispatcher said, eyeing Daniel suspiciously. The law enforcement office was not a hotbed of early morning activity. Pre-dawn visitors coming in and requesting a particular officer made for a chance to break the boredom. "Can the watch commander help you?"

"I guess not," Gray Wolf said. "I know Ben and needed to ask his advice on something."

"Is there something I can help you with?" A voice boomed out from a short distance away. "I'm Dick Perkins, watch commander."

Gray Wolf looked to his right, eyeing the thickset, red-faced man approaching from the office area. Feelings of being well outside his element pervaded. The officiousness of Officer Perkins did little to calm these feelings. "I ... uh ... I was looking for Deputy Whitside. Had something I needed to talk with him about. It'll wait, I guess, until he's on duty."

"Is this official business, Mister ... ?"

"Gray Wolf. Daniel Gray Wolf. Well, it could be official, but it's something I'd feel more comfortable discussing with Ben."

Perkins gazed at Daniel, no emotion reflected on his beefy face. "Have you been drinking, Mr. Gray Wolf?"

"What? Me? No, no, I haven't," Gray Wolf laughed nervously, but felt the anger beginning to burn his neck. *What the hell's wrong with you, kola? Why are you acting like a criminal around this guy? Tell the guy your suspicions.*

"If it's **possibly** official business, perhaps you'd like to share it with me in my office." It wasn't a request. Perkins held the half gate open for Gray Wolf.

Come on, butthead. These guys are trained to listen to far out stories. Perkins here isn't going to jail you. He's just doing his job. Daniel followed the watch commander through a myriad of desks, back to the far corner of the office. He sat down in the chair Perkins pointed at.

Uncomfortable moments of silence passed. Perkins stared at Daniel, chiseled jaw resting in the palms of both hands. "Okay, I'm all ears, Mr. Gray Wolf."

Just tell him, Gray Wolf. "I may have some information on Christine Hardesty's kidnapping," Daniel said more calmly than he felt.

Perkins' face remained stony, no emotions flitting across the fleshy features. "How did you come by this information?"

"It's a long story."

"I've got two hours to listen," Perkins responded, checking his watch in a business-like gesture. "Can you finish your story in that period of time?"

Gray Wolf's restrained anger bubbled out, "Possibly, Deputy, if you won't interrupt me anymore."

Dick Perkins' eyes widened ever so slightly, the sign of a man not used to being reprimanded. Yet, his voice displayed no animosity, or sincerity, as he said, "My apologies. You were saying something about the Hardesty girl?"

Confidence trickled back into Daniel's voice. He had gotten to this human monolith. "I might have some information about Christine Hardesty. But first I need to tell you a little about me; my background."

Gray Wolf spent the next twenty minutes explaining his heritage, his ability to cure nightmares, and his most recent dream catching client. He spoke in detail, omitting only Abrams' name. No need having the cops chasing the man just on the off chance he might be innocent. Daniel concluded by telling of his last visit, only forty minutes ago; the dream sequence, the cut up newspapers, the bottle of mucilage.

To his credit, Deputy Dick Perkins did not interrupt Gray Wolf during the twenty-minute monologue. Occasionally, he scratched a brief note on his desk blotter as Daniel spoke. Mostly, he stared at the Indian in front of him, practicing his stone-faced look. A full minute elapsed after Gray Wolf completed his story before Perkins spoke. His voice was soft, with no emotion.

"I'm supposed to believe this horseshit? I sit here and listen to some guy I don't know from Adam tell me he saw the Hardesty kid in his dreams, and I just fall all over myself following up on this ... this lead? Mr. Gray Wolf, I think you're either drunk, high, or crazy, possibly two or more of those conditions at the same time.

"I ought to run you in," he continued in a conversational tone. "We got a special FBI team in town, a full complement of field agents, the city police, and yours truly working this case, and you come in here telling me you know where the girl is. What's wrong with this picture?"

Gray Wolf stared back at the deputy, resentment building. "What's wrong with the picture is you haven't found Christine Hardesty. I've just told you more than all your combined manpower has been able to dig up."

"I don't have anything concrete to arrest you on, Gray Wolf," Perkins interrupted again. "But there are certain accuracies in what you describe. Probably a wild-assed guess on your part. So let's put it this way. I now know who you are and I'll be watching you. If I see your mug anywhere within fifty feet of an officer involved in this case, I'll throw your ass in jail for suspicion of being an accessory to a felony."

Gray Wolf rose, and then leaned across the desk, his voice duplicating the deputy's monotone. "Do me a favor, Perkins. Tell Whitside I was here. Show him the piddly-ass notes you took, and try to remember the rest of what I said so you can relay it to him with some small level of accuracy."

Dick Perkins grinned for the first time, but not in a friendly sort of way. "If you're involved in any way, you're going down. I'll see to it personally, Mr. Gray Wolf. Now, leave my office before I find something I might want to book you on. And remember ... I'm watching you, mister."

Daniel wheeled, his heart pounding more from anger than concern. Stalking past the dispatcher, he pushed through the twin doors and out into the gray light of approaching dawn. Deep breaths of cool morning air calmed him, cleared his head from the horrible mix-up of a meeting he'd just attended. *Forget Deputy Dawg in there, kola. The man is living proof that the Ghost Dance should have succeeded. Arrogant bastard!*

Dick Perkins rubbed his chin thoughtfully. Very strange man, he conceded as he picked up the phone. Dialing a string of well-memorized numbers, the deputy spoke into the receiver, "Hello, FBI? Give me the agent in charge of the Hardesty kidnapping."

Driving toward Rapid Valley, Gray Wolf collected his thoughts. *Sheriff's Department views you as a crackpot, headline-grabbing fool. Perkins wants the kidnapper bad. Anybody resembling a kidnapper, for that matter. It'd be good for his career. Another notch on his gun. What was that Perkins said ... 'certain accuracies in what you describe' ... ? Instead of helping, you may have set yourself up as a suspect.*

"If I can't talk to the law about this, who do I talk to?" Gray Wolf pondered, an unpalatable image of Edwin Nagel coming immediately to mind. "No! Not him!"

By the time Daniel reached his house, the idea of calling Doctor Edwin Nagel, noted local psychiatrist and dream therapist, had lost some of its shock. He worried whether the squinty-eyed, little bald guy would put aside past differences and speak with him from a professional standpoint. Nevertheless, he had to try. Someone had to listen to what he'd just experienced with Steve Abrams.

Out of habit, and a need to keep busy, Gray Wolf cleaned house for an hour and a half. Arranging the bookcase for the sixth time, he finally decided it was a decent enough hour to call the good doctor. After all, it was Sunday and Nagel probably had an early tee time. It was still with some hesitancy Daniel called the Nagel residence. A sleepy-sounding woman answered the phone on the third ring.

"Hello, Mrs. Nagel?" Gray Wolf asked, receiving a positive response. "Forgive me for calling so early, but I need to speak with Dr. Nagel. Is he there by chance?"

The sleepy voice responded, "You missed him by twenty minutes or so. He's golfing this morning out at the Elks Club. I could give you his beeper number, if this is an emergency."

"No, ma'am, that won't be necessary," Gray Wolf said quickly. "I'm very sorry to have disturbed you."

Hanging up, Daniel rushed into the bathroom to wash and run a brush through his unkempt hair. If he was going to meet Nagel at the Elks, he at least wanted to look less disheveled. He could almost imagine the psychiatrist's reaction if he showed up spouting his dream story and looking like a lunatic. The combined effect would probably justify landing him in a straight jacket.

Five minutes later, Gray Wolf pulled into the Elks Club parking lot, joining a dozen other cars proclaiming their owners' early morning golf, or breakfast, addiction. Nagel's Cadillac reigned prominent in the middle of the pack.

Rushing into the lobby, Daniel searched the dining area. At the far end, against the picture windows facing the first hole, he spotted Nagel sitting with two men. *No time to be shy, Gray Wolf. You've already been bashed once this morning.* Gray Wolf walked directly to the occupied table.

"Good morning, Dr. Nagel. Gentlemen," Daniel acknowledged the trio.

Nagel looked up, surprise registering on his goateed face. Placing his coffee cup back onto its saucer, he recovered nicely.

"Good morning, Mr. Gray Wolf. Is this a social call, or have you come to compare dream therapy methods?"

"I'm afraid it's not social, and I apologize to your friends. Could I speak to you in private for just a moment?"

Impatience sparked in the psychiatrist's eyes. "My colleagues and I were just about to have breakfast. By the way, Fred, Tom, this is the gentleman I was telling you about." Nagel's statement left little doubt whether or not he had put the dream catching topic to bed.

"Doctor, I need to speak to you about a confidential issue. Probably a medical issue, too."

To his credit, Edwin Nagel's professionalism superseded any personal quarrel he may have had. He knew Gray Wolf's make up, knew he wasn't devious. Just misguided. Rising from his seat, the psychiatrist touched a napkin to his lips. "If you'll excuse me for a moment, gentlemen." He followed Daniel out into the lobby.

"I hope you're being sincere, Mr. Gray Wolf," Nagel stated, leaning against the foyer telephone booth.

"Very. Differences aside, I need to see you, I guess as a patient. And as quickly as possible."

Interested, Nagel asked, "I gather this is something that can't wait until my normal practice hours?"

"Time is of essence, Doctor," Gray Wolf responded. "Without being melodramatic, we're talking life and death situation here. A period of hours, possibly minutes, could make the difference."

Nagel was intrigued. Despite what he thought of Gray Wolf's dream catching hobby, he harbored little doubt this man was completely sane. So, what kind of life or death conflict required immediate attention from a psychiatrist?

"Is this something that needs to be shared with the

authorities?" Nagel asked, only minutely concerned Gray Wolf might be involved in criminal activities.

"I tried." Daniel stared directly into the psychiatrist's eyes. "They didn't want to listen.

"Doctor Nagel, what do you have to lose, other than your tee time?" Gray Wolf continued, urgency creeping into his voice. "Worse case, you get to dig into a 'for real' Dream Catcher's head."

"And best case?" Nagel asked, already deciding today's golf match was history.

"We've got to go somewhere more private for me to tell you best case. Just let me say, if I can convince you what I tell you is true, you are going to be one astounded white man."

CHAPTER 14

I know who kidnapped Christine Hardesty." Daniel stated, leaning back in the cushy leather client's chair across from Nagel's desk.

"I see," Nagel said characteristically, not understanding how this required a meeting between the two men. "And how did you become privy to this information?"

Before Gray Wolf answered the question, he asked two of his own. "We understand that I'm here as a patient—a client. Is that correct? As such, I am entitled to the same courtesy and understanding you would display your other patients, correct again?"

"Yes, Mr. Gray Wolf, if that's the relationship you want."

Breathing deeply, Daniel said, "A man was referred to me because of his nightmares. While I was -"

Edwin Nagel blasted from his seat, forcing the chair against the credenza with a clatter. "Gray Wolf, I've really had enough of this dream catching malarkey! If this is some pitiful attempt to -"

"I'm paying you to listen, Doctor," Daniel interjected, voice steady. "Now before I file my own grievance with the AMA, I suggest you listen to what I have to say.

"A man was referred to me," Gray Wolf stated again, as Nagel sat back down. "He was plagued by dogs chasing him in his dreams. I dreamed with him, leashed the dogs, and then got out of his dream, as is the custom. I noticed this man still displayed rapid eye movement, so I thought he might be involved in another nightmare. Entering his dream, I saw him grab Christine Hardesty."

Nagel sat back down, waited several moments, making sure his client was done talking. "That's it? You 'dreamed with this man' and saw him abduct the Hardesty girl? Mr. Gray Wolf, do you have any idea how many people dreamed of this little girl because of the massive amount of publicity given the event? I would say literally hundreds, just in this city."

"This dream occurred last Tuesday. Christine Hardesty was kidnapped four days later on Saturday. But, there's more ... if you're willing to listen."

"I don't believe you, but at least you have my interest for another fifty-five minutes," Nagel conceded, checking his watch.

Unfazed, Daniel continued, "I had the same thought as you expressed. This guy appeared somewhat unstable and I figured it might just be a quirky dream he was having. But, when the news bulletin showed a picture of Christine, she was the same girl I saw in last Tuesday's dream episode."

"It's still not uncommon for a person to dream of a public figure or a celebrity. In this case, the daughter of a congressman," the psychiatrist reasoned. "Lord knows her picture has been in the local paper often enough."

Gray Wolf grimly smiled at the man. "We're not to the interesting part yet."

"I see. Then there's more?"

"Yes, much more. See, I'm taking this slow because you have a hard time believing my dream catching abilities. What I'm about to tell you will probably knock your argyle socks off, Doctor."

"I should remain seated then, so I don't collapse and hurt myself," Nagel droned, light sarcasm evident.

"I'd prefer that, yes. Besides, you're cutting into my time."

"Okay, Gray Wolf—excuse me—please proceed, **Mr.** Gray Wolf."

Daniel continued at a credible, even pace. "I felt the need to get back inside this man's dreams. I had to see if he was truly the kidnapper. Early last night, I conducted a little experiment. Something I'd never tried before. Alone, at my home, I put myself back in the dog dream. It really worked! Matter of fact, almost too well because it became my nightmare, not his. Anyhow, I released one of the creatures. A big Mastiff-like son of a gun. I didn't have the nerve to let both of them go. Remember, this was my nightmare now.

"I pulled myself out of the dream," Gray Wolf continued. "I knew I'd been successful in the first part of my experiment; what I didn't know is if this man would be hit with the same nightmare now that I'd released the dog. Since I wasn't sleepy anymore, I decided to sit up a bit. Read and wait, you know? Sure enough, about two hours later, I get a phone call from the guy, frantic as hell. The nightmare was back!"

Listening intently, Edwin Nagel appeared almost surprised when Gray Wolf stopped. He gathered his thoughts carefully before speaking. "You spin a good tale, Daniel, if I may call you that. But, you must realize what you're telling me sits a few yards outside normal medical boundaries. I can assign names, symptoms if you will, to what you think you believe. Delusion, *obscurum per obscurius*—explaining the obscure by means of the even more obscure, *cave canem*—beware the dogs, compulsive disorders bordering on sado masochism, and voyeurism. Should I go on?"

"I would believe the delusion bit, the Latin thingie meaning beware of dogs, and the masochistic tendencies for this guy."

"I was referring to you, Mr. Gray Wolf. Daniel, you're a very unique man, and I truthfully feel a series of treatments, coupled with a mild prescription of -"

"You still think I'm imagining these things, Doctor?" Gray Wolf asked, realization creeping in that Nagel thought the symptoms fit him. "But, let's look at the other side of the coin. Suppose I'm right. Suppose I have these abilities and did witness what I just described. It's either going to take a great act of faith on your part to believe me, or I have to prove myself to you.

"With a young girl's life at risk, you have to at least give me the benefit of the doubt. Now, do you believe me, or do you test my abilities?"

"You're very persistent, Daniel, and somewhat persuasive. But remember, my training is in dream therapy. All my years of studies, my scientific research, leads me to the same conclusion. What you proscribe is not possible in the known field of psychiatry. So, how would I test you on something that is not known?"

Gray Wolf stared at the man, weighing the ramifications of his next statement. "Let me dream with you."

Nagel laughed, a short barking sound. "Out of the question."

"What's the matter, Dr. Nagel, you afraid I may disprove years of work? Seems to me this would be the ultimate test. I do know some things about your profession—not much, mind you—but enough. For instance, I know, as a dream therapist you have probably trained yourself to be in control of your own dreams. You have developed the ability to plant subconscious, pre-sleep images, which you then dream about. You also can manipulate, to a minor extent, what happens during your REM-stage. Most important, you can control when you sleep."

"I see," Nagel said, relying on his habitual phrase to buy him a few seconds' thought gathering. Gray Wolf's assessment was correct. "When do you propose we conduct this experiment?"

"Christine Hardesty is buried alive somewhere in the Badlands. We don't have the luxury of setting an appointment for later in the week. I say you test me here, and now!"

"This is highly irregular and I think ... "

"Think about young Christine, and the off chance I know what I'm talking about," Daniel cut in. "If you're not comfortable with just the two of us, then call in a colleague, a controller. I noticed Doctor Munson's door open downstairs. He's a big guy, a chiropractor. If you're concerned I would try anything, he'd tie me in knots before you could say 'squat'."

"You peak my interest, Mr. Gray Wolf, and my competitive spirit," Nagel said with a smile, leaning back in his overstuffed chair. "And, despite my initial urge to run you through a series of competency tests, I believe you are as sane as I.

"Therefore," the psychiatrist continued, placing his hands behind his head, "I accept your challenge and offer you a small side bet."

"A bet? What kind of bet?"

"If you are not successful in entering my dream," Nagel paused, relishing Gray Wolf's curious look, "you will give up this illegal and immoral dream catching practice."

"And if I am successful?"

Leaning forward with a confident smirk, Nagel said, "I will share royalties with you, fifty-fifty, on what will be my best-seller depicting the biggest breakthrough in psychiatric dream therapy since Freud was a pup!"

Daniel leaned back in his own chair, astounded by Nagel's proposition. He needed the man's help, yet what the psychiatrist asked was no small wager. What if he lost? What if Nagel was so attuned with the dream world that he couldn't get in? The four hundred year old legacy hung in tenuous balance with Gray Wolf's next words.

"I accept. Do you want to call Dr. Munson in?" Daniel was too wrapped in the implications of accepting the bet to notice Nagel's confident smile falter.

CHAPTER 15

"How did you do that?" Nagel rubbed his temples, staring almost fearfully at Gray Wolf.

Daniel calmly sipped his coffee. The dream catching episode had gone badly at first, until he found his way through the ethereal maze the psychiatrist had set up. Once inside Nagel's dream, making positive contact proved relatively easy.

"I'm good at cross word puzzles," Daniel said, shrugging his shoulders.

"So, who won?" asked Dr. Bernard Munson, chiropractor and referee.

Dazed, Nagel pointed at Gray Wolf as he said, "This is incredible. I've got so many questions I have to ask you. How you are able ... how did you ... "

"I think Dr. Nagel's trying to say I was successful," Daniel said modestly. "Thank you for being here, Dr. Munson. It was kind of you to take time away from your practice."

"Okay, I'm outta here," Bernie Munson stated good-naturedly. "Besides, this little circus sure beat the hell out of polishing my bone-cracking table. Ed, my bill is in the mail."

Nagel didn't hear the man or see him leave. All his attention was focused on Daniel Gray Wolf. "But, this is so incredible! You have to tell me all about this ... this ability."

Gray Wolf nodded, "In due time, Doctor. Right now, you have to help me set this guy up. I've visited with him twice, have an appointment for this evening, but I'm a little concerned about his mood swings. One minute, he's scared, the next minute, he's suspicious of me. Then, all of a sudden, he's relying on me."

Turning on his cassette recorder, Nagel noticed Gray Wolf's reaction. "For my use only. Now, I want you to tell me anything and everything about this man—this kidnapper. We have to develop a strategy so you don't arouse too much suspicion."

For two hours, well past mid-morning; Daniel related what he knew of Abrams. Much of the dialogue was repetition of what he'd told Nagel earlier, but this time the psychiatrist listened intently.

Edwin Nagel interrupted periodically to ask specific questions. Gray Wolf answered, offering no lay interpretation, only facts surrounding his observations. Based on the information he was hearing, the psychiatrist was able to establish a preliminary conclusion.

"Daniel, my first hunch is we're dealing with a man plagued by character disorder, complete with sadistic and psychopathic-schizophrenic tendencies. Normally, I would not pronounce such a quick diagnosis, but as you say, we don't have the luxury of time for further evaluation. You're going to have to trust me on this assessment. That is, if you actually do plan on re-visiting the kidnapper."

Daniel nodded, "That's why I came to you, Doctor Nagel."

"All right," Nagel sighed. "Please remember, each piece of advice I give you is shadowed by a caveat, a disclaimer if you will. If this man reacts as you say, his schizophrenic disorder will allow for separation of incidents. He trusts your dream catching ability because it solves a problem for him. As long as you conduct your activities within that boundary, you should be on safe footing. Do not, I repeat, do not mention anything he could misinterpret. No casual comments about the abduction and certainly no allusions to mental disorders. He may have a paranoid trait I have not been made aware of and any such innocent statement could make him withdraw from you."

Disturbed by Nagel's intimations, Daniel asked, "So, I should proceed just as I have, play out another dream sequence?"

"I think so, yes," Nagel responded. "I would suggest you don't unleash the dog unless completely necessary. Just be there for him tonight. Show him you're a guardian, a friend. Obviously, you'll want to peek in when he attains REM-sleep."

"There's where I have a little problem. See, despite my overall feelings about the Dream Catcher tradition, there are certain rules I have to abide by. The main rule is to not poke my head where it doesn't belong. I've justified all the other things I told you, bending certain guidelines. But, if I don't let the dogs loose, I can't condone entering his dreams without being asked."

Nagel studied the man across the desk from him. A man torn by indecision about his ability, yet adamant in adhering to the tradition that caused his uncertainty. "Then we'll have to apply a different tactic.

"Daniel," he resolved, "you obviously have to unleash the dog again, some time today. This evening, when you visit with the kidnapper, it will be imperative you talk about dogs as much as possible. You need to plant a pre-somnolent suggestion, make sure he's thinking of the dog."

"Yeah," Gray Wolf agreed uncertainly. "I've got to unleash

that bastard into my own nightmare again. I swore I'd never mess with that."

"Would you feel better if I was present?" the psychiatrist offered. "You could sleep here, under my supervision."

Gray Wolf chuckled, "At a hundred fifty bucks an hour, I'd probably have a nightmare about your bill."

"You've given me a myriad of information to study. I can be doing some research while you sleep. This one's on the house, Daniel.

"Christ!" the doctor murmured, "I can't believe I just said that."

Fifteen minutes later, Gray Wolf entered the darkened dream alley a fourth time. Cloying fog swirled through the shadowy passage, chilling him as he inched toward the dumpster. *Maybe it won't be as bad this time. Maybe I'm building an immunity to these hounds.* An ominous growl, then another met his thoughts, as the second creature sensed his presence. The low-key sound turned into a threatening rumble as Daniel neared the trash bin. *Oh, shit, they remember me.*

He felt his way along the dim lane, fingers touching the moist, cool brick wall behind him. Each step was rewarded with renewed snarls from the beasts now eagerly awaiting him. *Can they remember?*

Focused more on the threatening sounds than where he was walking, Daniel's sidelong step jarred him against the dumpster's cold solidity. Vibrations and thrumming echoes reverberated the length of the metal receptacle. Crazed whines of anticipation roiled from the darkened area to the front of the bin. *Oh, damn! Oh, damn, damn!*

Gray Wolf produced the trusty tranquilizer gun, then stared in growing terror as the pistol melded into a leather halter loop. A powerful tug left no doubt what was attached at the hidden end. *Nooooo! This dream's getting out of control!* Quickly, he released the tether and produced the tranquilizer again. Immediately, the gun transformed into a leash, taut, demanding, straining as the Mastiff-creature pulled him toward darkness. *I can't ... hold ... this. Help me. Wake up, wake up, oh shit!*

Gray Wolf lost his balance as the beast jerked against the tether wrapped firmly around his hand. Falling to his knees, Daniel skidded partially into the shadows, inexorably pulled forward by the unseen hound. A final lurch, and he disappeared into the obsidian hellhole. *Wake up wake up wake up! Oh, Jesus, let me wake up!*

And the hounds attacked, tearing at him with their filthy ebony claws, butting him in raged frustration with muzzled jowls. Daniel pin wheeled across the rough cobblestones, helpless against the slavering Mastiffs' fury. Howls of victory ricocheted down the dismal corridor as the brutes shredded his shirt; gouged his flesh.

Gray Wolf weakened, felt the adrenalin seep from his system; or was it blood? *It's over. They've won and now I die. Noooo!* Fear, pure white-hot fear, coursed through his body. He grasped both hideous, swollen heads ramming at his face, searching for their throats. His fingers latched onto the restraining muzzles, burrowed into the coarse, saliva-soaked Mastiff hair. Dwindling energy reserves suddenly responded to the life-or-death ultimatum. He yanked against the tethers, freeing the creatures' horrible jaws. *Now!. Wake up wake up wake up -*

"Wake up, wake up. Goddammit, Gray Wolf, wake up!" Edwin Nagel screamed, slapping Daniel's face.

"Oh shit oo-no-no! Stop them, please! They're killing meee -"

"Daniel, you're awake. Snap out of it. You're awake, I said!"

"Wha' ... ?" Gray Wolf said dazedly, wincing as he rubbed at his bruised face.

"Jesus, man!" Nagel whispered. "Look at you."

Conscious, both of his surroundings and the pain, Daniel pulled trembling hands away from his face and stared at the ugly, livid welts coursing the length of his arms.

"Holy shit," the psychiatrist murmured, totally shocked out of character. "Hysterical conversion reaction. I see it, but ... holy shit!"

"Hysterical what?" Daniel asked groggily.

"Hysterical conversion reaction, dream-induced physical manifestations. You've got scratches and welts all over your arms. Shit! And your chest. Your shirt is ripped to shreds and how the hell did all this happen in your goddamned sleep?"

"I don't give a fuck if it's for the pope's daughter," Gray Wolf sobbed. "I'm never, never bringing on a nightmare again.

"Christ, Nagel," he said, now crying uncontrollably, "It, it was bad. I mean, it was really bad."

"But, it's over now. You won't have to do it again," Edwin soothed, gripping Daniel's shoulder.

Gray Wolf regained control, his sobs lessening as he glanced around the sterile, beautifully sunlit room. Doctor's decor had never looked so good. Leather, chrome, and glass. All man-made objects and very real, even in their austerity. Nagel's office was a happy place compared to hell.

"Are you going to be able to dream with your kidnapper tonight, after what you've experienced?" Nagel asked, very real concern in his voice.

Studying the abrasions on his arm, Daniel whispered,

"Yeah, tonight will be different. If I have to, I can kill those canine bastards. Shoot 'em, stab 'em, or bomb 'em, whichever comes first."

Comfortable that Gray Wolf appeared to be back in control, Nagel looked at his watch. "You should go home and clean up, get some real sleep, then give me a call later this afternoon. In the mean time, I'll be delving into the *aegri somnia* aspect of your friend."

"Agra what?" Daniel asked, trying to assemble his ripped shirt.

"*Aegri somnia*, sick man's dreams. In order for me to offer any further suggestions, I must research this phenomenon, confirm my initial diagnosis."

Gray Wolf stood at the doorway, unsure what to say. "Thanks again, Doctor Nagel, for finally believing. And just for being there when I needed you."

Nagel extended his hand. "Thanks for making me a believer, Daniel. I wish you luck on your encounter this evening. God, I'd love to be there!"

Exiting the psychiatrist's office, Gray Wolf shambled down the steps toward the ground floor. Dull throbbing pulsed through his muscles sending seismic aches that, by all rights, should not have been present. He passed by Munson's open chiropractic office door and heard a low whistle from within.

"Shit, man, I thought you said you won," commented the burly doctor, poking his head out the door. "If this is winning, old Edwin ought to be a real mess. Where did those abrasions come from?"

"Hysterical conversion reaction," Gray Wolf mumbled, spilling the full extent of his medical knowledge. "I dreamed them."

"Hey, remind me to never invite you to a slumber party."

Daniel shuffled outdoors, holding his arms tightly against his sides. He barely heard Bernie Munson's concerned follow up.

"Hey, Daniel, are you sure you're okay?"

Gray Wolf raised his arm in response, sharp pains shooting down his bruised sides at the effort. "Nothing a couple of baby aspirins and an ice bath won't fix." *Baby aspirins, my ass, kola. You better have a small mountain of extra strength stuff at home.*

By the time Daniel got his truck pointed toward home, the pain had receded to a dull, steady glow. Luckily, his head was clear, although the body would probably not have responded to any lightning-quick commands.

"One more night of this, Gray Wolf," he whispered to himself. "Give them one more night, and if you can't get the answers, leave it to the experts."

Pulling into his driveway, Daniel breathed a sigh of relief. The neat little bungalow not only promised an imminent hot shower and dreamless sleep, but sanctuary. *You've dreamed enough in the last ten hours to fill a month, kola. It's Sunday, the day of rest. Your rest.* Anxious to be inside, Gray Wolf didn't take notice of the nondescript brown sedan parked a hundred feet down the road. He therefore didn't see the two men sitting in the idling car, watching his entrance.

Cool air greeted Daniel and gently pushed him against the interior wall. Sighing, he closed his eyes. *It's noontime, yet all you can think about is bed. What about the girl? You think she's resting comfortably right about now?*

"Eat shit and die," he commanded his conscience. It didn't work.

Deciding he had a few ounces of reserve energy, Gray Wolf walked into the living room and snapped the television on. Maybe there was new information on the abduction. Eyes closed once again, he listened as the voices filtered in.

"—will neither confirm nor deny the authenticity of the ransom note found under the doorway of KOTA Channel Four Studio. Investigative reporter, Mark Lang, showed the note to the Federal Bureau of Investigation's local field agent, Dan Kingman, who immediately confiscated the paper.

"We're showing you viewers at home a photocopy of the ransom note. Not easily discerned in this copy is that the original was a plain white bond sheet of paper with newsprint letters and words pasted, or glued, to it. Channel Four, in an effort to keep the public informed of this unfolding tragedy, feels a responsibility to present all information as it sees fit ... "

Gray Wolf blotted out the remaining commercial drivel. His eyes were glued to the screened image of the ransom note, an eerie sight because he knew who had sent it. He scanned the warped poetry, lips moving as he memorized the lines:

Roses are red, Christine is blue.
If you were where she is, you would be too.
One million dollars, a number that's fair,
I need it by Tuesday, or she runs out of air.
The Feds are involved, my first note wasn't shared.
I'm dead serious and your bitch daughter is scared.
Pay me by Tuesday, I'll tell you the facts,
Mess with me, Daddy, and the girl gets the axe."

You're a sick puppy, Stevie. You didn't get enough attention so you had to write another note for the world to read. Gray Wolf tuned back in to the newscaster's report.

" ... Four has to assume the note is authentic and not a hoax. You, our viewers, had to be made aware a sick person is in our midst. "The FBI continues its mode of silence, only telling this station all possible manpower and efforts are being expended to bring about the safe release of Christine Hardesty.

"KOTA, Channel Four, will be broadcasting a news special tonight, preempting the regularly scheduled program. Please watch this live special, 'Christine Hardesty: A Ten-Year Old's Terror', tonight at eleven."

"Oh, Lord," Daniel groaned, shutting the television off. "What are these dipshits doing?" Long-simmering rage threatened to erupt.

Calming himself, Gray Wolf analyzed what he now knew. If the poetry lines could be believed, Christine Hardesty had at least enough water to last until Tuesday. The plastic pipe, he reasoned, would allow her unlimited air if it wasn't intentionally clogged.

The last thought forced a whole series of new concerns. What would a rainstorm do? Could enough water flow into the pipe to drown the girl? Worse yet, what about ground water? Or a windstorm. Would dust filter into Christine's tomb and choke her? How about insects? *Stop it! Stop working yourself up. It's not helping you find the girl.*

Gray Wolf was jarred from his horrible reverie by the jangling of the telephone. Picking up the receiver, he commanded, "Who is this?"

Moments of silence, then a woman's voice, "Um, Daniel? This is Linda, Linda Paxton. Did I call at a bad time?"

"Ohmigosh, Linda. No! Jeez, I'm sorry. No, you didn't call at a bad time," Daniel gushed. "I was just—I just walked in the door. How are you?"

"I'm fine, thanks." The voice tinkled with laughter. "Listen, I—well, I'm leaving for Pierre tomorrow. David's all situated at school and I was wondering if we could meet for supper tonight?"

"Tonight?" *You've got an appointment with a kidnapper tonight, kola.* "Oh, Linda, I've already made plans. I thought you would have been gone by now."

"I'm sorry, Daniel. Maybe next time I get to Rapid."

You don't meet Stevie until ten o'clock. Go ahead . Or are you afraid? "Listen, what time did you want to meet? I'm free until about nine-thirty, then I'd have to leave. It's not a date or anything." *Real swift, bonehead. What does she care if it's a date or not?*

"Please, don't let me interrupt anything. I just thought it would be nice to get together before I left. You know, talk over old times on the reservation."

Gray Wolf quickly answered, "It definitely would. Where are you staying and when should I pick you up?"

Laughter was back in her voice. "Why don't we just meet at The Embers, say about six-thirtyish?"

"I'll be there. And, Linda? Thanks for calling, I really appreciate it."

"See you tonight, Daniel."

Gray Wolf held the phone to his ear for several seconds, hoping Linda was still there. A dial tone announced her departure. Only then did he notice his hands were sweating. Reluctantly, he hung up the phone.

"Man, she still does it to you, doesn't she?" Suddenly, he wasn't so tired.

Abruptly, the phone rang again. Daniel whisked the receiver up, hoping to hear Linda's voice.

"Daniel, Ben Whitside here. How have you been?"

Whitside, calling me? "Fine, Ben. Haven't talked to you

in a coon's age. Matter of fact, I probably shouldn't be talking to you right now."

"I know," Whitside answered. "Dick Perkins told me about your visit this morning, and his warning. Understand, Dick's a good man, just a little over zealous. But, I know you, Daniel. I also know what you do behind the scenes if you catch my drift. So, I wanted to talk with you. Do you have a few minutes?"

"Sure, if you're willing to listen." Gray Wolf spent the next fifteen minutes telling Whitside what he knew and what he'd experienced. For some reason, he didn't include tonight's pending dream session.

Whitside offered an audible sigh, "Daniel, if anyone in this department believes you, it's me. I've gained a ton of respect for your Native American mysticism over the past couple of years. But, you won't tell me the guy's name or where he lives, and the most concrete thing I have to go on are your dreams.

"Let me offer you two pieces of advice, my friend," the deputy continued. "Number one, without going into details because I don't know any, the feds feel they're close to cracking this case. Number two, Perkins called the FBI after you left."

"So what does the second piece of advice mean, Ben?"

"It means the feds are following up on all leads given them by law enforcement officials. Chances are good you will be contacted.

"By the way, I could get shitcanned for mentioning advice number two, even though I've told you nothing specific. Let's just say this is some friendly talk between brother Elks, okay?"

Gray Wolf fought the sudden tickle in his stomach. "I understand, Ben, and thanks for the call."

"A last piece of advice, Daniel. There's a good chance your

guy is just another nutso with an overactive imagination. Stay clear of the investigation. Let the Washington boys take care of things."

"Yeah, thanks, Ben. I think I'll do exactly as you say." Gray Wolf hung up the phone after the second unexpected call in twenty minutes.

"Sorry, brother Elk," he whispered. "I've got to play this one out."

Gray Wolf checked his watch, noting it was just shy of twelve-thirty. "I need sleep more than anything right now. Sorry, Christine, but I'll be able to help you better if my mind's functioning properly."

Setting the alarm for five-thirty, Daniel Gray Wolf stretched out on the bed, cleared his mind of all thoughts except Linda, and fell asleep with a smile on his face.

Healing slumber gently gave way to the soft insistence of the alarm clock. Gray Wolf yawned, stretched, and examined his arms in the process. Pleasantly surprised, he saw the ugly welts had receded to faint red marks. Gratified by the quick healing, his spirits lifted considerably. Fifteen minutes under an alternating hot and cold shower added to his feeling of wholeness.

Whistling as he re-combed his hair for the third time, Daniel tilted his head to examine the image staring at him from the mirror. *Not too bad for a thirty-eight year old fart. Jeez, Gray Wolf, you're acting like a kid on his first date.* "Or going to the prom," he answered himself, remembering how Linda had looked that night twenty years ago.

Cleansing ministrations finished, he rummaged through his closet. "Where the hell are my gray slacks—and loafers— and that blue-striped shirt that shows off my eyes so well? Bit by bit, he located the items that were hidden behind a rack full of sport shirts and slacks.

"Let's see, we're meeting at The Embers, so I better take my blazer," he mumbled, then added with a groan, "and a tie. Damn ties. Some idiot invented them to hide missing buttons."

Despite grumbling, Gray Wolf was pleased with the finished product. Snugging the tie knot up against his neck, he struck several poses in front of the floor-length mirror. He flexed his right hand until the tendons stood out just right, then grasped the front of his jacket. Smiling at himself in the mirror, he murmured, "Just like in the Sears catalog, you good-lookin' hunk of red hot desire."

Finally satisfied he wasn't going to get any better looking, Daniel slipped his jacket off and headed to the front door. Whistling a new nameless tune for the occasion, he checked in at the foyer mirror. Nothing had faded, sagged or gotten dirty since his trek from the bedroom. He was ready.

Trying to appear casual, mostly for his own benefit, Daniel scanned his watch. *If I leave right now, I should have time to take the old truck through the carwash.*

Gray Wolf arrived at The Embers supper club with three minutes to spare. Ford pickup and owner shined like newly minted pennies as they pulled into a convenient spot near the entrance. Grabbing his jacket, Daniel literally trotted into the restaurant. He was looking across the wave of diners, hoping to spot Linda, when the maitre d' approached.

"Do you have a reservation, sir?"

Oh, shit, was I supposed to make reservations? "I—uh—I don't know for sure. Is there something listed for Gray Wolf or Paxton?"

"Yes indeed, Mr. Gray Wolf. The Paxton party is already seated, if you'd care to follow me."

Paxton party? How many people were sharing this intimate little dinner?

Daniel followed the maitre d', unnecessarily adjusting his tie. *Damn thing feels like a hangman's noose.* And then he was at her table, Linda rising to greet him while the second occupant remained seated.

"Daniel," Linda said, giving him a brief hug. "Right on time. My, you look handsome tonight."

Gray Wolf returned the brief embrace, but his eyes were on the boy-man sitting at the table. The lad was Native American, giving Daniel a brief start. In the fleeting seconds before Linda began introductions, he studied, and conjectured, about this third person. *Good-looking kid, but full blood. Didn't think Paxton was a Lakota name. Maybe it's her nephew. Shit, he's too young to be her boyfriend. Isn't he?*

"Daniel, this is my son, David. David, this is Daniel Gray Wolf."

The boy rose from the table and grasped Gray Wolf's hand in a firm shake. "A pleasure to meet you, Mr. Gray Wolf. My mother has spoken of you."

"Pleasure's mine, David, and please call me Daniel."

Eyes still on David, Daniel helped Linda to her seat. The boy was friendly enough, definitely courteous. He could now see the family resemblance. David had inherited his mother's classic features, but somehow stretched them over a six-foot frame. Only the eyes weren't Linda's—soft, yet guarded—not totally open for the world to see inside.

Linda's voice interrupted his assessment. "I hope you don't mind my bringing David along. I probably won't see him again until Christmas break."

"No, not at all," Gray Wolf answered, blindly seating himself while his eyes continued their exploration. *So, kola, what do you say to an eighteen year old chaperone?*

Not able to think of anything, Daniel turned his attention

back to Linda. *God, she's pretty!* "So, you're leaving for home tomorrow?"

"Yes, I'm leaving in the morning. I've got to be back at work on Tuesday. This way I'll have half a day to rest up before starting the grind all over again." Her bright brown eyes smiled as if this was the most important conversation of her life.

"You look very nice tonight, Linda." And she did. Long black hair flowed deliciously around her neck, hanging down in delightful contrast against a white silk blouse. Moderate red lipstick highlighted her full, smiling lips. Her manicured fingernails bore the same shade as her lips, nicely accenting the long slender fingers.

As much as you want to stare at this beautiful lady, don't ignore the boy, kola. Figure out something to say to him. "So, David, you're going to the School of Mines. Have you picked a major yet?"

David Paxton smiled, showing even white teeth. "Yes sir, I'm majoring in chemistry. If all goes well, I'd like to go on to medical school."

"Whew, chemistry," Daniel sighed. "I remember fighting through that in high school. Obviously, you found it easier than I did. What do you want to do with your degree?"

David's smile faltered momentarily. "I want to be involved in diabetes research. I'd like to be able to cut the mortality rate, at the very least extend the existing life span until a cure can be found."

"My husband—David's father—died from the disease," Linda added quietly.

"A noble cause, David. I wish you much success, and just a little advice. While you're studying to reach your goal, take time to enjoy yourself. Take time to look at the trees, watch a thunderstorm, feel the grass.

"What I'm trying to say," Gray Wolf continued, "is don't

become so all-consumed that you lose sight of who you are, or your relation with nature. Much can be learned from being attuned to your surroundings."

David's eyes widened as he looked first at Gray Wolf, then his mother. Daniel couldn't help but notice.

"I'm sorry," he offered. "That might have come out a little bit like a line from Kung Fu or something."

"No, Mr. Gray—uh, Daniel," the boy said. "It's just that Mom gave me pretty much the same advice. Is this like a heritage thing?"

Gray Wolf laughed because the kid sounded so sincere. "Yes, you might call it a heritage thing. Your mom and I grew up on the reservation during a time when that's about all we had. Our heritage, maybe a couple of cans of coke, and the stars providing the best drive-in movie you could imagine."

"I'll remember that, Daniel," David said. "My future plans are important to me. I'm afraid even to the point of not paying as much attention to who I am and what I presently have to offer our people."

"Would you care for something to drink, Daniel?" Linda offered, changing to subject abruptly as she beckoned a nearby waiter.

"I'd love to, but I'd better pass," Gray Wolf said, a tinge of regret in his voice. *Have to watch the stimulants and depressants before tonight's main bout, kola.* "Maybe a club soda with a twist of lime."

Daniel studied Linda as she prattled about trivial things, keeping a steady flow of discussion involving all of them. *She sounds happy, looks happy, but why is she directing conversation? Is it just me or did she steer us away from what David was saying? For that matter, what was David saying? Oh well, she's probably just as nervous as you are, kola.* David apparently did not share Gray

Wolf's introspection. He chatted in his friendly, intelligent manner.

Despite these thoughts, the evening was enjoyable and passed far too quickly for Gray Wolf. Supper had been delicious, what little he ate of it. Several times during the meal, and afterward as they sipped coffee, Linda touched his hand to emphasize a point in their talks. Each time her fingers made contact with his, a tingle of warm pleasure shot up his arm. If David noticed the touches, he made no comment.

Face it. She likes you, Gray Wolf, but as a friend. You had your chance twenty years ago and now you're two different people. She's going back to Pierre tomorrow and you won't see her for another twenty years.

The wall clock directly over Linda's shoulder raced toward nine-thirty. He tried to slow the timepiece, prayed for a sudden gift of psychic ability to stop time completely, yet the ornate hands swiveled in blissful unawareness of his silent pleas.

"Linda ... David ... this has been a wonderful evening for me," Gray Wolf said. "I—I really don't want it to end, but I have an appointment I must keep." He beckoned to their waiter.

"Daniel, let me," Linda said, touching his arm again. "I invited you, remember?"

"Absolutely not. This has been such a great evening, it's the least I can do." Gray Wolf handed a credit card to the server. "You can treat the next time. Then David. Then me again."

"Hey!" David laughed, holding up his hands. "I'm just an underpaid freshman. I've got a couple of years before my pride says I have to reciprocate.

"But, thank you for dinner, Daniel," the boy continued, extending his hand to Gray Wolf. "I'm glad I got to meet you."

"Same here, *kola washta*. Do well in school, and I hope you achieve your goals."

Signing the check, Daniel rose from the table, reluctant yet anxious to be on his way. Linda stood, then reached up and kissed him on the cheek.

"Still helping others with their dreams, Daniel?" she whispered in his ear. "I'll have to tell you mine some time."

Surprised, Gray Wolf knew his brown skin had just shaded a pleasant red. Hands lingering on Linda's arms, he looked into her smiling eyes. "I'd like that," he said huskily.

Releasing his old girlfriend, his love from a different life, Daniel turned his attention to David. "I'm in the phone book, my friend. Call me if you need anything while you're here."

Squeezing Linda's hand one last time, he turned away.

CHAPTER 16

Her light scent lingered on his jacket lapel, ample reminder of the all-too-brief meeting. *It was nice. No ... make that great, but put her out of your mind.* Gray Wolf reminded himself there were priorities, near term and long. Right now, breaking Abrams was top on the list. He would stick to the promise he made this morning. If he couldn't gain some clear-cut knowledge of the Hardesty girl's whereabouts tonight, the feds could have the case all to themselves.

"This is not my line of work," he reasoned. "I'm a Dream Catcher not part of a SWAT team." For some reason, the term Dream Catcher didn't stir the ambivalent seas as it had for the past several years.

The short drive on West Main Street took Gray Wolf past Baken Park, the first ever strip-shopping center in Rapid City. Continuing east, he navigated through the natural gap that unofficially marked the city's east-west boundaries. Entering the downtown district, nerves began toying with his stomach like a feather duster of soft tickles that couldn't be scratched.

"Getting close now, Injun," he murmured to help alleviate the light fingers of nervous reaction. "Only a few more blocks."

Turning south on Eighth Street, Daniel hurriedly glanced at his dashboard clock; nine forty-five showed on the LCD readout. Fifteen minutes to showtime. Getting to Abrams place too early might show anticipation, thus arousing suspicion. But, getting there later than the appointed time might smack of complacency, thus ... arousing suspicion.

Cruise for a few minutes, kola. Calm down, prepare yourself for putting on a good show, and get this thing over with. Gray Wolf drove past Abrams' apartment and craned his head out the window. Lights glaring from the second floor roused the ticklish fingers in his stomach again. *He's home. Hell, did you expect any different?* Daniel completed the route, driving south until Eighth Street ended and Highway 16 began its gradual six-mile climb into the Black Hills. He accelerated as the upward slope and gravity pulled at his speed.

"Why don't I just keep on driving? Maybe visit Mount Rushmore or take the scenic route to Leo's. What the hell, Gray Wolf, it sounds like a pretty good option." He whipped a u-turn at the Fairmont Boulevard intersection and coasted back toward the city lights of this solitary western tourist Mecca. Was it just his imagination or did the streetlights turn a shade colder?

Pulling into Abrams' driveway, Daniel noted the time. Nine fifty-seven. Close enough. Getting out of the pickup, he dragged the sleeping bag from the passenger seat behind him. *This is it! The last time you and I play dream tag, Stevie.*

Halfway up the outside stairs, Gray Wolf was greeted by Abrams flinging the screen door open. "Hey, Steve, you all set for our quality control check?"

Arms crossed, body resting slightly against the open door, Steve Abrams stared at the ascending figure. "I've been thinking, Daniel."

Uh oh. "Yeah, me too," Gray Wolf said, reaching the second floor landing. He stuck out his hand.

Abrams ignored the gesture, maintaining his crossed-arm

pose as he blocked the entry. "I don't think tonight's visit is going to be necessary."

"Oh, and why's that?"

"After you left last night—this morning—I went back to sleep and felt good. I mean real good, you know? I think your last session put the dogs away for keeps, so tonight would be a waste of time."

Gray Wolf frantically searched his mind for a response. "Well, have it your way, Steve. I could use a good night's sleep myself. It's just, well, I did some reading up on this stuff this afternoon. That's what I needed to talk to you about. But, heck, if you feel the situation's under control, I'll head on home." He turned and started down the steps, hoping Abrams would stop him.

"What stuff?"

Yes! "I'm sorry?"

"What stuff were you reading up on?"

Gray Wolf paused on the steps. "I checked up on some of my old Lakota writings about dog dreams. But heck, that stuff's a couple of hundred years old. Probably doesn't mean anything."

"What did it say?" A note of uncertainty crept back into Abrams' voice.

"It's pretty detailed on the status dogs have in dreams. Notes about some scary things my ancestors went through," Daniel lied easily. "But, shit, man, we're twentieth century guys. It probably doesn't mean anything."

"I guess I want to hear more."

"Well, do you invite me in, or do I get eaten alive by the mosquitoes out here?"

Abrams beckoned him upstairs. *Thank you, God— Woniya—whoever's looking out for me.*

Inside, Gray Wolf noticed Steve had forgotten to clean house again. If anything, more litter dominated the interior landscape.

"So, what about the dogs?" Steve asked, a note of demanding in his question.

"Like I said, it's probably nothing, okay? Words have a way of changing meanings after a hundred years or two. Maybe my translation was bad."

"Stop with the horseshit already!" Abrams yelled. "Just tell me what the fuck you read."

Okay, kola. Time to act a little hurt and outraged. "Hey, pardner, I didn't come here for my health, you know. I'm trying to help you get rid of nightmares that could kill you! There! Is that what you wanted to hear?"

"Oh damn!" Abrams moaned. "You're kidding me, right?"

"Dream Catchers don't kid about serious shit like this, Steve. I didn't want to have it come out like it did, but you kinda backed me into a corner."

"But—but, these dogs could really kill me?"

"Let me show you something," Daniel said, rolling up his sleeves. "Look at these marks.

"And these," he added, unbuttoning his shirt to expose the welts on his chest. "I got these from your canine friends because I was trying to help you."

Steve Abrams gawked at the abrasions and colored spots decorating Gray Wolf's upper body. His eyes widened behind their horn-rimmed spectacles. "This happened during my nightmare?"

"It sure as hell ain't war paint, pardner."

"Daniel, this has got me scared! Real scared."

Gray Wolf went for the kill. "Yeah, and it's not me they're after. It's you!"

The distress was obvious in Abrams' gestures. He sat down, rubbed his eyes behind their glasses, then abruptly stood up. Walking unsteadily to the kitchen sink, he drew a glass of water, but didn't drink from it. He dropped the glass in the sink, unmindful of the shattering sound, then faced Gray Wolf.

"I can't go to sleep!" he moaned. "If I go to sleep, the fucking dogs will get me for good."

"Not true!" Daniel countered, forcing himself to grip the kidnapper's shoulders.

Abrams was on the verge of crying. "Yeah? Look what they did to you. Hell, they don't even want you. It's me they're fuckin' after!"

"There's good news, Steve," Gray Wolf embellished, gently shaking the man's shoulders. "I learned something else from these writings. There's an old Lakota incantation I can use to put the dogs away forever."

"How do you know it will work?"

"Think about it. The Dream Catcher two hundred years ago must have survived if he was able to put this all in writing. And if I'm here, right?"

"Yeah, but what about the guy having the nightmare. Did he survive?"

Careful, Gray Wolf. Don't get too cute. "He made it, too. It was in the writing."

Daniel watched the relief spread across Abrams' face. For a second, just a second, he felt sympathy for the man. Then the image of an entombed Christine Hardesty washed away any soft feelings for this kidnapper. Let the son of a bitch squirm for what he's done.

"I suggest we get started, Steve," Daniel said, squeezing the man's arms for the sincerity effect.

"So, what are you going to do different? You said you learned an incantation. When do you say that?"

If this guy knows Lakota, I'm screwed. "When you lie down and get comfortable, I pass my hands above your body and say the magic words. You go to sleep, and if you dream of the dogs, they will be more receptive to my commands. Hey, remember, we may have put these creatures away for good last night. This might just be an insurance trip tonight."

"Yeah, but we can't take the chance, can we?" Steve asked, now sold on the idea.

This guy changes moods more often than you change socks, kola. Keep him receptive. "Now you're talking, Steve. Together, we'll lick these god-awful dogs. Get yourself ready for bed, then I'll start the prayer."

Abrams scurried into the bedroom with all the energy of a kid knowing Santa wouldn't come until he was asleep. Slipping under the covers, he called, "I'm ready."

Daniel quickly thought up some lines as he approached the grimy sleeping quarters. Standing over Abrams' reclined form, he raised his arms and began the chant,"*Waceunkiyapi kte.* (Let us pray.) *Wicasa kin he wahtani s'a ca slolwaye.* (I know this man is a sinner.) *Can wan bluha k'es, sintehla kin wakat'a tka.* (If I had a stick, I would kill this snake.) *Onnisike.*" (You are pitiful.) With a flourished wave, Gray Wolf completed the brand new ritual.

"What did you say?" Steve asked expectantly.

"I asked the Great Spirit to watch over you and to make the devil dogs go away from this earth, never to bother us again."

Steve's eyes sparkled with excitement. "Sort of like an Indian exorcism, huh?"

"Pardner, you hit the nail on the head," Daniel grinned.

"The spirit guide, Woniya, is in this room now. I can feel him."

Abrams drew the covers up to his chin and hastily glanced around the cesspool of a bedroom. "You know, I think I can feel his presence. That's good, isn't it?"

Gray Wolf stared down at the hopeful, receptive piece of garbage lying in the man-made filth. He had a difficult time masking his hatred. *Boy, you're going to lead me to Christine.* "Yup, that's real good. If you can feel it too, it means Woniya's here to watch over you while you dream. So, don't be afraid, okay?"

"How am I gonna get any sleep with you yammering on?"

It took Gray Wolf a few moments to realize Abrams meant that to be humorous. *Old zitface is excited about his big adventure. Okay, kola, let's give him an E-Ticket ride when the time comes.* "All right, all right, I'm outta here. I'll set up camp in your living room, just like before. When you're asleep, I'll lay my bag out and join you."

"Nighty-night, said the light. Don't let the bedbugs bite!"

Chills trickled down Gray Wolf's spine. Abrams' last repartee smacked of outright juvenile glee—and it rhymed— just like the ransom note. A very cogent thought lodged in his mind. Abrams was losing it; he was slipping. First the abrupt mood swings, now this.

Walking into the living room, Daniel recognized a sense of unease for his personal well being. Steve's impulsive transit between dispositions was beginning to scare him. Sordid questions blossomed, spread their roots, and then multiplied. *What's this guy capable of? You've never dealt with a crazy before, kola. Can he hurt you? Does he have a gun? Is he capable of waking up while you're still asleep?*

"This is the last time; the very last time," he said, repeating his earlier vow.

Daniel sat heavily on the couch and waited. He knew it would be at least two hours before Abrams was deep enough in slumber to start the dream cycle. His book, tucked into the bedroll, held no interest for him.

Gray Wolf attempted some mental gymnastics to wile away the time. Twenty years in the dream catching business; over one thousand dreams watched. Make it an even one thousand for easy math. At least two hours spent waiting with each person before the dream sequence started, so that's two thousand hours of lingering. Divide that by an eight-hour workday, that's almost two hundred and fifty days devoted to waiting. One full work year of waiting on people, not even counting the time actually spent in their dreams. The numbers staggered him.

Daniel stared at his watch. "Well, that little round of ciphering took all of three minutes. What do we do now for the next hour and fifty-seven minutes?" Giving up, he pulled the latest L'Amour paperback from his sleeping bag.

"Just you and me, Louie. Two hours to judgment," he mused. "Hell of a title for a book. Too bad you're not around to write any more."

***

Rawhide Higgins had just shot the third Skyler Ranch outlaw but had sustained a nasty stomach wound for his trouble, when Daniel heard moaning emanate from Abrams' bedroom. Quickly checking his watch, he mumbled, "It's only been a half hour. You can't be dreaming already."

Steve Abrams whined, mired in the sticky clutches of REM-sleep. Although his body was in repose, Abrams' eyelids flickered wildly from the intense combat taking place in his mind.

"Strange stuff," Gray Wolf muttered as he hurriedly rolled out his sleeping bag. "You shouldn't be anywhere near deep sleep yet, Stevie." *Has to have something to do with his mind frame. Shit, I wish I could call Nagel about this, but there's no time.*

Stretching out on the bedroll, Daniel tried to clear his mind. Abrams' muffled cries, combined with his own concerns in dealing with this unpredictable man, would not let sleep overtake him immediately. Raising up on one elbow, the Dream Catcher studied the passive-yet-agitated kidnapper's form.

Stunned, Gray Wolf looked on as four ugly welts puffed up on Abrams' arm. *Shit! Claw marks. The friggin' dogs are attacking him*! A second group of scratches materialized, longer and more swollen than the first, running from shoulder to elbow. The vicious parallel lines reddened then seeped blood. *Oh shit, they're going to kill him*!

Unnerved by the psychosomatic display, Daniel forced himself to recline. *Empty it! Drain the mind. Christ, you've got to get in there*! Precious seconds passed while he calmed his heart rate—steadied his breathing. A half-minute later, he walked into Abrams' life-or-death nightmare.

Horrifying sounds of struggle poured from the pitch-black alley. Snarls and barely-human screams reverberated into the misty dimness of the open street where Gray Wolf stood. The enraged dogs were winning. Producing a flashlight in one hand and heavy machete in the other, he stormed the alleyway.

Daniel's spotlight cast its shallow beam down the bricked expanse, illuminating a confusing mass of writhing bodies. Only as he ran closer, could he make out the Mastiff-creatures' complete dominance of Steve Abrams.

One beast straddled the man's prone form, its snapping teeth only inches away from Abrams' exposed throat. The second hulk furiously mauled at his leg, alternately scratching and biting the torn flesh. Abrams was fading fast, his strength all but depleted from holding the slobbering jaws short of his neck. Steve screamed, an ululating warble of fright and rage as the Mastiff broke free from his grip. Drooling fangs pushed closer, nipping at his throat. The teeth snapped shut, but ripped air instead of flesh, as Gray Wolf's whistling blade severed the monstrous head from its body.

Daniel turned his attention to the second Mastiff-creature just as it released its hold on Abrams and launched at him. Machete only half raised, he fell back under the onslaught of two hundred pounds of airborne fury. A strangled yelp issued from the creature's gaping mouth as it struck him. Momentum shoved Daniel against the unyielding dumpster. His head crashed into the cold steel. Brilliant sparks of white flashed. A thunderclap of pain dulled him to near senselessness. Now the creature was on Gray Wolf's chest, fanged jowls lined up with his throat.

Semi-conscious, Gray Wolf waited for the beast to finish him. Waited. Waited. Why didn't the creature kill him? His vision gradually sharpened although white patches of lightning still flitted on the peripheral edges. The swollen, obscene Mastiff face lay inches from his, yet made no move to rip his neck apart. In fact, the creature made no move at all. Then Daniel understood.

Pushing mightily at the bristled head, Gray Wolf dislodged the creature. The Mastiff flopped loosely onto the damp cobbles, exposing the machete firmly embedded in its massive chest. Only the wooden handle and two inches of blade protruded from the bloody, matted breast. Gray Wolf withdrew from the dream and allowed himself to cry.

In the relative safety of Abrams' bedroom, his injured sobs eventually turned to tears of frustration. *Shit damn piss! After what's just happened to Stevie—the trauma—his injuries, I won't find out more about the Hardesty girl. He's gonna wake up and be either scared out of his wits or pissed.*

For the third time that evening, Daniel waited; waited, this time, for Abrams to rouse from the horrible nightmare and begin some kind of tirade. He lay on his bedroll, sure that the kidnapper would snuffle and snort himself awake momentarily, yet all remained still.

Carefully, Gray Wolf raised himself until he could look at Abrams' face. The kidnapper's eyes, weak and bare looking without the horn-rimmed spectacles, twitched and flitted beneath their pale lids. *Good Lord, he's dreaming again! By all rights, my perverted little friend, you should be wide-awake by now, nursing your injuries and babbling about the dog attack.*

Gray Wolf had to go back in, had to see if this second dream was about Christine Hardesty. "I hope you haven't conjured up some other crazy nightmare, Stevie," he whispered.

Settling back down, cushioning his aching head as best he could, Daniel relaxed and slipped into Steve Abrams' dream world for a second time.

He found himself behind a familiar outcropping of rock. *Yes! The Badlands.* Hidden, he watched Abrams' dark blue sedan slough to a stop beside the abandoned Chrysler. Apprehensive, he decided to let the dream fully run its course before he would withdraw this time. And so, he gazed out onto the dreamscape.

Steve Abrams exited the car like a man on a mission. Deliberate steps took him to the upright pipe protruding from the ground. First tapping the plastic tube with his keys, the kidnapper bent over and cupped his hands around the opening.

He lowered his mouth in the valley formed by his fingers, and spoke a silent message into the pipe. Next, he leaned his head against the tube, obviously listening to the muted response. A malicious grin split his face, testimony that he had heard the screams or cries the young girl undoubtedly uttered.

Almost casually, Abrams glanced around the site. He bent, then cupped a handful of loose dirt between his palms. Rising slowly, spiteful grin still plastered on his lips, the kidnapper let the soil trickle between his fingers into the pipe opening. Hands emptied, he quickly placed his ear against the tube. Malevolent joy forced his grin even wider. The dirt must have evoked a proper response from his captive.

Abrams scooped another handful of dirt, this time not as casually as the first. The horrible grin was still evident, but his eyes had hardened into obsidian pools magnified behind their spectacles. He poured the soil, then grabbed another handful; then another; and another; each time dribbling the dirt and dust into the receptive air pipe.

You sick bastard! Gray Wolf couldn't watch any more. *Remember, this is a dream. Christine's not feeling this ... unless this is something Abrams has already done. Concentrate on the area, find landmarks, more information. You need more to locate the poor girl.*

He forced his gaze onto the surroundings. Same as before, thank God. Saw-tooth ridges, six to seven feet high, jutted in a semi-circle from the loose soil. The nearby multi-colored sandstone mesa, rose a hundred feet before flattening off like the deck of an aircraft carrier. And the abandoned car, the Chrysler, pointed its butt leisurely toward a distant valley surrounded by sage and sandstone formations. *OK, kola, remember the valley off to the left, the direction shithead drove in from.*

Suddenly, it was dark—not just nightfall-type dark, but all encompassing, total black. Gray Wolf strained, searching the void with blind eyes and flailing hands. All sense of direction, of balance, eluded him. *What's going on? Where the hell am I?*

Noise to his right, a tittering laugh, gave Daniel his first sensory jolt. More noise, this time to his left, an answering snigger, suggestive and evil. Yet, the blackness prevailed, brilliant in its lack of shade or form. Absolute nothingness cloaked him. *It's a dream, another goddamned warpo dream!* A caress of moving air, currents produced by a body fleeting past him, roiled the atmosphere. The void moved, shifting slightly to accommodate whatever had breezed near him. And then he saw.

It was a woman—at least the hazy shape resembled that of a woman. Bloated, naked breasts flopped in slow motion, grayed fleshy thighs jiggled as she padded across the blackness. Another wisp of current, more filtered movement, then a naked Steve Abrams appeared, chasing the gelatinous mass of femininity. Abrams, equally blurry against the complete gloom, appeared physically normal until he veered sideways in his pursuit. Only then was his obscene, gigantic erection apparent. Steve's sexual member jutted out at least two feet from his pubic area. *Holy shit, kola, you'd do Trigger proud! Okay, boy, I'm outta here.*

Gray Wolf woke to darkness, but at least a natural darkness he could see through. Passing headlights reflected against the grimy bedroom window, accompanied by the comforting sounds of real, moving cars. He breathed an audible sigh of relief. *I'm back from the crapper Abrams calls a mind. What the hell was that last episode anyway, Disney Does Dallas?*

A poignant need to be away from the soiled bedroom and its diseased occupant coursed through Daniel. Too much contact, too often, with this vicious little shit placed a weight on him far heavier than he was willing to bear. *Do I wake him up and tell him I'm leaving, or do I just get the heck out of Dodge?*

"St ʒve. Steven, wake up," Gray Wolf urged, shaking the man from his otic dream. "Wake up, dammit!"

/ ram ʒed on his side, hazy remembrance of the mega-sex ʃantasʹ a half-smile from his thin lips. Only when full coʳ ˍess washed over him did he realize his body hu· ˌne reality of why he hurt exacerbated the pain.

Jh, shit, Gray Wolf," Abrams groaned. "Where the fuck were you when the dogs attacked?

"God! Look at my arms," he screamed, noticing the physical proof of his ordeal. "Those bastards clawed me up. One was at my throat. Shit, another one chewing on my leg. OWW, my leg! Gray Wolf, you sonofabitch, you let them do this to me. You let them get -"

"Shut up, you whining little shit!" Daniel growled. Anger overruled logic; he had been pushed and bullied by this prick once too often. "Don't you ever blame me for your nightmares or what happens to you in them. You saw the marks on my arms and chest. Do you think I enjoy getting shredded in your dreams then yelled at when you wake your pitiful ass up?"

Abrams shut up as told, his raging eyes transposing into ones filled with fear. "Hey, Daniel, I didn't mean it. Okay? Oooh, Christ, I hurt!"

Alarms jangled in Gray Wolf's head. That quick mood swing again. *This boy's losing it!*

"Steve," Daniel said calmly. "Did you see what I did to the dogs?"

Abrams nodded slowly, afraid to open his mouth.

"I got rid of those bastards, Steve," he continued, deceitful fervor creeping into his voice. "I killed them, cut their heads off, slashed their hearts out ... I killed them, Steve." *I also got all I'm ever going to get out of you, you worthless turd.*

"They—they're gone for good?" Abrams asked in a small voice.

Play up to him, Gray Wolf. "Yes, they're gone for good. You're free, Steve."

Excitement filled the kidnapper, animated his speech and movement. "I'm really free? No more dogs? Hot shit! Damn oh damn!" he screeched, bouncing on his bed like a three year old.

"We're both free, my friend," Gray Wolf stated dramatically. "Free from the devil curs that sought first you, then me." *Really thick stuff, kola, but Stevie appears to be lapping it up.*

"It was that incantation thing, wasn't it? Your two hundred year old prayer worked its magic."

Gray Wolf nodded, hoping the gesture looked modest.

"Wow, damn it to shit! We need to celebrate, you and me, Daniel. I am one psyched mother. I feel so alive! And hey, I'm not tired at all anymore," Abrams rambled. "So, how about it? You up to a little celebration?"

"Man, I'd love to, but I gotta be at work in eight hours. I need to get home, clean out my underwear, then hit the sack."

Steve didn't comprehend at first, then a glow of understanding lit his face. He giggled, "Clean out your underwear; yeah, I like that. But, I'm still stoked, man!"

An idea welled in Daniel's mind, just a tiny seeping of a plan. "Well, unstoke yourself, pardner. Why don't you read a book, take a walk. Better yet, take a drive. Yeah, take a drive with your window down. Blow all those cobwebs and evil dog spirits out of you once and for all." *Yeah, take a nice long drive and show me where Christine is buried.*

"As for me," he added, sidling toward the living room, "I'm going home and rack out."

"Geez, you deserve it, Daniel," Abrams gushed, full of brotherhood and fellowship now that he was rid of the beasts. "Damn, you were magnificent tonight. Killed those suckers dead!" The kidnapper slid off his bed and followed Gray Wolf into the dingy living room.

Plant the seed deeper and get out of here. "Yeah, here you go, getting ready to take a victory lap in that car of yours, and I gotta get my beauty sleep so I can go to work. It's a tough life, Steve, you on vacation and me slogging away at the steel mill." *Take a drive, butthead. Go out and brag to Christine how you're free and on top of the world. Lead me to her, then you and I will have a real honest-to-goodness showdown.*

"Hey, Daniel," Abrams said, holding the screen door open. "This weekend it's my treat, okay? I'm getting some money, umm, sent from home you know? We paint the town this weekend, on me."

"Sounds good, pardner," Gray Wolf replied, sidling past Abrams and onto the outside landing.

"And, Daniel," Steve said huskily, extending his hand. "Thanks again for what you did. I mean that."

Hiding his disgust, the Dream Catcher clasped Abrams' hand. "Forget about -" His words were interrupted as Steve impulsively hugged him. *Oh, shit! I'm gonna puke.*

Breaking free, Daniel offered a quick wave over his shoulder as he hurried down the steps. He opened the truck door then looked up. Abrams stood on the landing, silhouetted against the porch light, arm raised in farewell. *You follow my subliminal messages, Stevie, and I'll see you a helluva lot quicker than you think.* Starting the truck, he backed into the parking lane before smoothly joining the late-night traffic flow.

Gray Wolf drove two blocks north, just to make sure he was out of Abrams' sight, before turning right onto a side street. Accelerating, he turned again at the first intersection, then right again, ending up facing Eighth Street. Slowing, he pulled against the shadowed curbside, fifty feet off the major drag. He hopped out of the pickup and walked back toward Abrams' apartment. *Betcha a dollar he heads this way in less than five minutes.*

Daniel was wrong by twenty-five minutes. Half an hour after his own departure, he saw the lights flick out in the second story apartment. Abrams emerged from the outside door and scurried down the steps. Gray Wolf watched the kidnapper circle behind the blue sedan and enter it with all the casualness of a man going to the convenience store for a pack of smokes. He slid into the shadows of a hedgerow as Abrams wheeled the auto out of the driveway and pointed its big nose north. *That's my boy.*

Daniel waited until the blue sedan had accelerated past him before running to his truck. Hopping in, he pulled to the mouth of Eighth Street, peering right to make sure of Abrams' location. Joining traffic, he maintained his surveillance from three cars back. The pickup's added height offered him an advantageous view of the sedan.

"Let's go find Christine, Stevie," he muttered, carefully keeping a hundred yards between the kidnapper and him.

Light traffic spattered the eastbound lanes of Interstate 90 this time of the evening. Sunday night, one week before Labor Day weekend, even the tourists were tucked safely in bed. The flow consisted basically of rural locals heading home from a visit, airmen returning to Ellsworth Air Force Base after a night of girl chasing, or truckers bent on logging a few extra non-authorized hours. Daniel had no trouble keeping track of Abrams' sedan. He memorized the taillight shape, the cant of the vehicle, everything he needed to know to follow this particular 1990 Dodge sedan. Even the occasional lane cutter posed no problem. Gray Wolf knew there were very few exits to the Badlands, knew Abrams wouldn't be making a sudden turn for at least the next thirty miles. It was a game of patience, cat and mouse, with the cat tailing his prey toward the bait.

As he stalked Abrams, Daniel mentally reviewed the ransom note. He needed to be objective, to erase the disturbing thoughts about Christine's terror and discomfort. *If what Stevie writes is true, she's got water and food to last her until Tuesday. You have to forget what she's going through right now and concentrate on finding her in time.*

It happened around Wasta, thirty-five miles east of Rapid City and a good ten miles west of the first probable exit into the Badlands. A loud thump, followed by a wildly gyrating steering wheel informed Gray Wolf of a blowout.

"Shit! Just what I needed," Daniel groaned, fighting to maintain control of the bucking vehicle.

Easing his foot from the accelerator, Gray Wolf allowed the pickup to coast to a stop in the breakdown lane. Out of the truck, and with the door properly slammed in disgust, he automatically looked into the distance. A trail of reddened taillights, now all looking the same, receded from view across the rolling landscape.

"Damn damn damn!" he raged, walking around the pickup until he spotted the offending right front tire. "I'll never catch up."

He knew continuing the chase would prove fruitless. Five, maybe six minutes were needed to change the tire; far too long a head start for Abrams. Quietly, he put the spare on, not once exposing the storm of emotions ripping at him. *It wasn't meant to be, kola. You weren't destined for a big showdown with Stevie, boy.*

He retraced his route, pulling a careful u-turn across the shallow median before connecting with the westbound lanes of Interstate 90. Driving toward home, he weighed the options. Go to the cops again? No, he didn't have anything more substantial. Go directly to the FBI? Absolutely not! He'd be detained for God knows how long while they questioned him.

"Who can I tell?" he mused out loud. "Who might know where this place is ...

"Yes! Leo Red Hawk! Why didn't you think of him before, you chowder head?" Leo knew the Badlands better than most cartographers.

Ten minutes later, he exited the interstate highway at New Underwood, a sleepy community of five hundred and fifty-three souls, mostly military. Driving south past the two bars that comprised downtown, Daniel was soon out into the moonlit rolling plains. At one-thirty in the morning, he had the road to himself, although calling it a road certainly was an undeserved compliment. A myriad of strategically placed holes chattered the pickup across the asphalt road surface. *Careful, Gray Wolf; you don't have a spare tire anymore.* The back road shortcut might save him forty miles, but no vehicle was going to make it on three-or-less wheels. Gray Wolf slowed to forty-five and maneuvered around the worst of the ruts.

***

Safely parked on Leo Red Hawk's gravel lawn, Daniel released a tired sigh. The back road trip had taken fifty minutes of fighting a washboard trail, but truck and tires had withstood the beating. Leaning back against the headrest, he surveyed the darkened hut in front of him. *Do I wake him up now, or do I let both of us sleep for a few hours?*

An image of Christine Hardesty, cold and frightened,

lying in an underground box, gave him his answer. Heaving another tired sigh, he dismounted the sturdy pickup. Outside, the chilled early morning air kissed his exposed skin. Gray Wolf shuddered lightly as mild wind currents played against his sweat-soaked back.

Knocking on Red Hawk's door elicited no response. He knocked harder, rattling the glass panes in the peeling door. Muffled snorts emanated from within. Daniel tested the doorknob and pushed open into Leo's superheated kitchen. For a moment, he savored the penetrating warmth.

"Who is there?" inquired a sleepy voice. "Has Woniya taken to entering through doorways now?"

"It's me ... Daniel, *Tunkasila*. I knocked but you wouldn't get up."

"The sun is sleeping, the animals are sleeping; I should be sleeping, too. Why are you here? It is not Saturday, is it?"

Gray Wolf moved into the tiny living quarters; saw the old man half-rising from his bed. "I need to speak to you about a very important thing, Grandfather. I know the hour is late, but a little girl's life may depend on your knowledge."

Springs creaked an ancient, disconsolate lament, as Red Hawk slipped off the bed. Shuffling, barefoot sounds emerged from the pygmy-sized bedroom, followed shortly by the shadowed outline of the old man.

"You not only disturb a warrior's slumber, but place a guilt trip on him in the same breath," Leo groused. "Did you bring some artichoke hearts? Probably not, I think. You're here to question your grandfather, not feed him."

"*Tunkasila*, if you can help me, I will buy you two cases of artichoke hearts, two cases of Vienna sausages, and two cases of ice cold beer to wash them down."

Leo Red Hawk eased into his dilapidated lounger,

nodding sagely as he descended. "So, you have hurt a little girl and now need some place to hide from the police. Am I close to the truth?"

Exasperated, Gray Wolf said, "Grandfather, I have never hurt anyone, but I will consider it if you don't stop with these silly questions."

"Now he threatens an old man," Red Hawk yawned, obviously not feeling threatened. "So, before you piss in your britches, sit down and tell me what bothers you, my night owl."

Gray Wolf grabbed the only other chair in the cluttered interior. Throwing his leg over the rickety kitchen chair, he faced Leo Red Hawk. "I need your help in finding a certain spot in the Badlands. I know what it looks like, but I don't know where it is."

Red Hawk snorted, "You talk in riddles, *Takoja*. If you know what this place looks like, why is it you don't know where it is?"

"I—I dreamed of the place," Daniel said in a faltering voice.

"This dream, it was with the man you were telling me about earlier? How did you come by this dream? Was it within your boundaries as *Ihanbla Gmunka*?"

Gray Wolf hesitated, "Technically, yes, I was invited to dream with the man."

"Daniel," the old man said gravely, "You talk like a white man now. When you use big words with me, I think you are telling me half truths."

"Grandfather," Gray Wolf persisted. "That's not what is important right now. This man is very sick in the head. He has kidnapped a little girl and buried her alive somewhere in the Badlands. I have seen where he buried her. I can describe the spot to you."

The old man stared at Gray Wolf through the darkness. Daniel felt the eyes burning into his soul.

"But it *is* important, *Takoja*," Red Hawk finally said. "What you haven't told me is what I must hear. Yet, I am afraid to hear it. This is not the doddering old man talking to you now; this is the wise old Lakota; the one who knows of our ways. If you have strayed from the path set for you, I cannot help you. The old ways cannot be changed. Ack, I might as well die now."

"Grandfather, we're talking about whether a little girl lives or dies here, not curing someone's nightmare!"

"Have you gone against the pact of the *Ihanbla Gmunka*?" Red Hawk asked.

"*Tunkasila*, when we last visited, you told me I was chosen to help the white man. You said Woniya was looking after me because I had a special mission. Does that not represent change? Four hundred years, we keep this a secret among the Sioux Nation. Then, my father tries to help a few white men but fails. I have helped many men, red and white. Tell me, is that not a change of the old ways?"

Red Hawk stubbornly declared, "It is written -"

"Nothing is written!" Gray Wolf interrupted vehemently. "I am *Ihanbla Gmunka*. I would know what is written. The story was passed to me from my father, and to him by his father. Do you think *Woniya* or *Wakan Tanka*, the Great Spirit, is upset with me? I don't!"

"I will ask him, Daniel," the old man said quietly. "What you say holds some truth. My heart hears your heart and I am not feeling so much like dying now."

"One other thing," Gray Wolf pushed. "If you are, as you say, one of the last true Lakota, why do you wear cowboy boots and why do you have a television set? Does that not represent a change? Did your father watch cartoons on Saturday morning, or the Lone Ranger, or Rin Tin Tin? I don't think so."

"So, now it has come to making fun of an old man. First, this young pup threatens to hurt me, and now teases about one of my few means of relaxation."

"Come off it, Grandfather. You can't have it both ways. Quit making up new rules for an old game. Who was it that said, 'you can't bullshit a bullshitter?'"

"Sitting Bull, I think, but not in those words," Leo answered, pushing himself out of the lounge chair. "But, I must sleep on this. I will talk with Woniya and then we will decide. In the morning.

"You can sleep here if you like," the old man said over his shoulder as he shuffled into the bedroom. "We will talk more after the spirit guides me."

"Why can't Woniya talk to you now; why can't he give you guidance?"

"He is guiding me," came the sleepy reply. "He says, 'Red Hawk, you must get some sleep and not bother with this crazy man until the morning.'"

Disgruntled, Gray Wolf eased into the lounger, pushing it back into a precarious horizontal position. *It's only about four hours, kola. Go easy on the old man. Hell, he was close to disowning you.*

***

"Wake up, Tonto. I have been told to speak with you about the girl."

Daniel roused slightly, then sought an impossible comfortable position on the rickety lounge chair. The incessant prodding at his boot, combined with a pungent burning aroma, drove away any remaining hope for sleep.

"Get up, lazy," Red Hawk admonished. "The sun greets us and I have even made coffee."

"I was wondering what that smell was," Gray Wolf mumbled. "Thought you might have taken to burning tires in your stove."

"Join me at the table. We will drink coffee and speak of the little girl." The old man turned away and ambled three feet into the kitchen area.

Wide awake now, Daniel pushed out of the chair, wincing as the muscles in his back threatened to backlash into tiny knots. Stretching only produced a groan of pain instead of the intended relief. "Whew, it looks like I'm going to have to buy you a new lounge chair. This one and I don't seem to agree with each other."

"Buy one if you like for your use while you are here," Red Hawk said. "That chair and I have come to an agreement. I don't say bad things about it and it doesn't try to hurt me."

Gray Wolf fixed a baleful stare on the old man. "You speak to the chair spirits as well, I suppose?"

Red Hawk shrugged. "Maybe you should try it some time. You are the one with the backache, not me."

Daniel edged off the lounger and made his way into the kitchen. He picked up a steaming, cracked ceramic mug and studied the contents. Murky brown liquid, bearing the faintest tint of oily green, stared back at him from the depths of the cup. Intrigued, he gingerly dipped his forefinger into the brew. In the split second it took his mind to register searing heat, the oily green had collected around his boiled digit.

"Ow, damn!" Gray Wolf groaned, popping the injured finger into his mouth. Just as hastily, he spit out the inflamed member. "What the heck did you put in the coffee, or is your pump acting up again?"

"You just drank the liniment for my rheumatism," Red Hawk intoned, then pointed at the counter. "Your coffee is over here."

Daniel picked the real coffee cup up with his left hand, still nursing the throbbing finger. "You were going to let me drink that crap? Damn, this is going to blister."

"Children learn by doing," Leo said, nodding his head sagely. "The good thing is you will never have rheumatism in your finger." He sat down on the lone kitchen chair, then added as an afterthought, "Tonto."

Rebuffed, Daniel sipped at his coffee, finding it only slightly more palatable than the liniment. He grimaced at the bitter taste.

Leo watched the pantomime with light amusement. "Better drink up. If we are to find your young girl, you will need some energy. This is my special warrior's blend. Very strong medicine."

"What did you put in it?" Gray Wolf asked, experimenting with another swallow. Fifteen seconds of aging had not tempered the potent elixir.

"A little ground hair from *tatanka*, some bitter root, part of a blue jay's nest. You know, the usual mystical stuff laying around in my medicine bag."

"God, *Tunkasila*, you're kidding. Right? Please say you're kidding."

"I see you are in no mood for humor this morning," Red Hawk muttered. "It is yesterday's grounds, mellowed with a can of Coors and touch of Tabasco."

"Yesterday's grounds mixed with what?"

Defensive, Leo answered, "I would have used fresh grounds but you didn't drink the coffee I made two days ago. Do I look like a rich man, one that can throw his food around?

"Are we to speak of the girl," he added, building an offensive attack, "or do you wish to continue finding things wrong with the way this old man lives?"

"Woniya says it's okay to speak with me?" Gray Wolf asked. "He's not upset with me for stretching my powers?"

The old man answered in a serious voice. "He understands why you did what you did. But, he is upset with me for not being a better guide. I will visit the sweat lodge this afternoon to atone for my sin. Now tell me of the girl."

Gray Wolf studied the old man's face momentarily before beginning. He told Leo Red Hawk everything, from his first meeting with Steve Abrams, through last night's aborted drive toward the Badlands. Particular attention was given to the dreamscape where Daniel believed Christine lay hidden. Closing his eyes, he relayed the details as they flashed into his mind.

" ... and there's a rusted old fifty-seven Chrysler sitting in the middle of this circle of rock outcroppings. The car's tail end points toward a valley. I don't know what direction it runs. Southeast, I think. I just know this valley has sandstone spires and lots of sagebrush running on either side of it." Daniel let the final sentence trail off. He had given Red Hawk all the particulars he had seen.

After only a slight pause, Leo said, "I know of this place. It is an old Lakota ceremonial site, but it hasn't been used for almost thirty years."

Joyful anticipation perked Gray Wolf like a cold shower. This was what he had hoped for; Red Hawk knew the spot where Christine Hardesty was buried.

"It is Thomas Red Shirt's Chrysler," Leo continued. "I drove with him to the place, then his car gave up its spirit. We figured *Wakan Tanka* wanted it, so we left it there. Ceremony didn't go good that time. The car must have been full of evil spirits. We haven't used that site since then."

"You can show me how to get there?" Daniel asked, excitement rising in his voice. "Is it far?"

"I did not count the miles," Red Hawk said. "But I know the way. We should go now and free this young girl."

Gray Wolf needed no further prompting. Helping the old man from the chair, he literally pulled Leo toward the front door. "Come on, Grandfather. We can pick up some doughnuts and coffee along the way. I'll need a shovel from your storage shed. And could you grab some blankets?"

Red Hawk trundled back into the bedroom to search for extra blankets while Gray Wolf quickly washed out the coffee cups. Wiping the mugs dry, Daniel pushed open the back door and trotted toward the ramshackle storage shed. Just inside the shack's doorway, he found a rusty spade, hefted it, and then checked to make sure the handle was sturdy enough. Satisfied, he walked around the house intent on depositing the tool in his pickup.

"Mr. Gray Wolf? Daniel Gray Wolf?" A middle-aged, sturdily built man called to him from Red Hawk's front stoop.

Daniel eyed the suited man. "Yes?"

"Freeman Togweiler, Federal Bureau of Investigation," the man replied, brandishing his credentials. "The gentleman now behind you is Special Agent William Anderson."

Gray Wolf turned briefly, catching a glimpse of the second individual walking toward him.

"I'm in kind of a hurry, guys. What can I do for you?"

Togweiler stepped down from Red Hawk's rickety porch, then placed himself three feet in front of Gray Wolf. "We'd like to ask you some questions about Christine Hardesty's abduction."

CHAPTER 17

"A m I under arrest?"

Togweiler, not quite friendly, but thoroughly professional, answered, "Agent Anderson and I are tasked with following up on any information given us by the Pennington County Sheriff's Department. We were told you visited the department early yesterday morning."

Super Cop Perkins sicced the feds on me, Gray Wolf thought. Good old Dick Perkins.

"Am I under arrest?" Daniel repeated, sensing Agent Anderson closing on him from behind.

"We'd just like to ask some questions, Mr. Gray Wolf. Back in Rapid City, if you don't mind. This can be done on a voluntary basis, or we can legally detain you if it becomes necessary."

Impulsively, Daniel blurted, "I—I know where the Hardesty girl is hidden. We—I was just going out to find her."

Anderson spoke for the first time. "Who are you visiting here, Mr. Gray Wolf?"

Nerves tingling, Daniel said, "Leo Red Hawk, an old friend of mine."

"Is Mr. Red Hawk presently here?"

"I am here. What are you doing on my property?" Leo said from the doorway. The old man stood, holding two blankets, while he glared at the federal officers.

"Mr. Red Hawk, we're with the Federal Bureau of -"

"I heard who you were," Leo interrupted. "You still have not answered my question. What are you doing on my property?"

Somewhat flustered, Togweiler responded, "We're just asking Mr. Gray Wolf some questions about -"

"Did you bring any tobacco?"

"Pardon me?"

"I asked if you brought any tobacco with you. It is the polite thing to do when visiting one of the tribal elders."

"I'm afraid neither Agent Anderson nor I smoke, Mr. Red Hawk." Togweiler's rosy complexion darkened a shade.

Leo pushed, obviously enjoying himself. "The tobacco is not for you, Agent Rotweiler. It is for me. Any time a *wasicun*, a white man, comes to my house, he must bring tobacco. I like Camels. Daniel here, he brings me tobacco all the time and he does not have any white blood in him. That means he is a good man, and now you are trying to arrest him."

Of the two perplexed men, Agent Anderson found his voice first. "We're not here to arrest anyone, Mr. Red Hawk. We simply want to ask Mr. Gray Wolf some questions."

"Yes, I heard that," Red Hawk said, nodding his head. "I also heard you say you could legally detain my young friend if necessary. Even to this old Indian, that sounds like you want to arrest Daniel."

Gray Wolf decided Leo had helped enough. "*Tunkasila*, these men are trying to find out about Christine Hardesty, the young girl I told you about."

Red Hawk was on a roll. "Did you two know my grandson is a *Ihanbla Gmunka*, a Dream Catcher? He knows where this little girl is because of his dreams. Woniya told me it was okay for Daniel to do what he's doing."

"Grandfather, enough!" Gray Wolf commanded, embarrassed because of the looks Anderson and Togweiler were exchanging.

"That's all very interesting, Mr. Red Hawk," Togweiler said. "I'm sure we'll discuss this man's, um, abilities when we get to Rapid City.

"Now, Mr. Gray Wolf," the agent continued, "perhaps if you'd put that shovel aside, we could be on our way."

Daniel suddenly realized why the second agent, Anderson, had stayed behind him. He still held the shovel in a vaguely threatening port arms position. Carefully, he leaned the tool against a straggly scrub oak.

"How long have you been following me?" Gray Wolf asked.

"Mr. Gray Wolf," Togweiler said patiently. "It would really be better if we discussed things back in Rapid."

"You should either answer his questions here, or arrest him, *wasicun*," Red Hawk interjected. "Daniel knows his rights."

Daniel groaned at the amount of help he was getting from the old man.

Togweiler sighed, looked at his partner for support, before reciting, "The Sheriff's Department called us early yesterday morning, shortly after you visited them. Because of the national attention on this case, we have to follow any leads. Agent Anderson and I proceeded to your house about eight-thirty, watched you arrive at approximately noontime, then maintained surveillance until you left at approximately six o'clock that evening. We continued our watch at the supper club, and then followed you to a house on Rushmore Road. We passed you after your flat tire near Wasta, then waited until you put on the spare and headed here."

Goosebumps sprinkled across Gray Wolf's arms. They'd been tailing him since yesterday at noon. They'd seen him at Abrams' apartment. His chilling thoughts were broken by Red Hawk's question.

"That is a lot of trailing. When do you go to the toilet?"

Anderson harrumphed an embarrassed reply, "We relieve each other ... what I mean ... when possible, we work in shifts. But -"

"How is it your suits aren't wrinkled; why don't you need a shave?" the old man persisted. "I would like clothes like these."

Gray Wolf warned again. "Grandfather, back off!

"You'll have to excuse Leo, gentlemen," he continued, addressing the agents. "So, why did you contact me now?"

Togweiler answered, "You appear to be an inordinately busy man, Mr. Gray Wolf. The number of trips and stops are hard not to notice. After your drive to the reservation early this morning, we felt it best to visit with you."

"Kinda suspicious, huh?" Daniel asked lamely, though his mind was working furiously.

"Let's just say our curiosity is perked."

Red Hawk butted in. "All this talk makes my head hurt. I am also hungry. But, there are more important tasks at hand than filling an old man's belly. Instead of driving back to Rapid City, maybe you two would like to join us. Daniel has dreamed where this young girl is buried."

"Buried?" echoed the agents, looking at each other.

Thanks, Leo. "Christine's still alive," Gray Wolf added hastily. "But her time is running out. The kidnapper vented her tomb, left enough water for her to survive until tomorrow."

Agent Togweiler's glance at his partner apparently gave him the impetus he needed. "Daniel Gray Wolf, you're under arrest for the kidnapping of Christine Hardesty. You have the right to remain silent. You have the right … "

As Togweiler droned the Miranda Rights, Anderson grasped Daniel's hands, expertly slipping the handcuffs around the stunned man's wrists.

"What the hell's going on?" Gray Wolf demanded. "Why am I being arrested when I just told you I know where the girl is buried?"

Anderson cinched the cuffs a little tighter. "The public is not aware Christine Hardesty is buried. Only the congressman's family, and the FBI were privy to that information. Oh, and the kidnapper, of course."

"But, but the ransom note on television?"

"Made no mention of the girl being entombed," Togweiler finished Gray Wolf's sentence. "Do we bring the old man in?" Anderson asked.

"We don't have anything on him," Togweiler said, dismissing Leo Red Hawk like he wasn't present. "Besides, at his age, he won't wander far away."

Gray Wolf pleaded, "We're wasting valuable time. I'm not the guy you're looking for. Hell, I was down here on the reservation with Leo when the girl was abducted."

Togweiler studied Gray Wolf then Leo Red Hawk. "If we can corroborate your story, you will be released. Until then, we must take all necessary precautions.

"Agent Anderson," Togweiler continued, turning toward his partner, "would you please escort Mr. Gray Wolf to the car while I speak with Mr. Red Hawk for a moment?"

Leo turned his stony gaze fully onto Freeman Togweiler. The agent grew uncomfortable under the old man's scrutiny.

"Mr. Red Hawk, it probably would be helpful if you joined us. This is strictly an invitation, mind you. Daniel Gray

Wolf is now considered a suspect because of his statement to the Sheriff's Department, his unusual nocturnal habits, and the privileged information just divulged to us."

"Are you going to handcuff me and rough me up, too?"

Exasperated, Togweiler said, "No one is roughing up your friend—or grandson—whichever he is. Mr. Gray Wolf could be in serious trouble. Anything you can do on his behalf will only help him. As I said, I'm inviting you to join us—for Daniel's sake. It's your option."

Red Hawk thought for a moment before responding. "I will come for Daniel's sake. But, you better not try any funny stuff. I have many friends here and they do not like nosy white men. They would enjoy showing off your curly scalp at the sweat lodge."

"I'll keep that in mind, sir," Togweiler answered dryly. "Do you need to bring anything; medication, personal items?"

"I suppose you would not allow me to bring a beer. Driving is thirsty business, you know."

A faint smile tugged at the agent's lips. "Sorry, it's against regulations."

"Then, I am ready. Are you going to use your siren? I have never driven in a car with a siren before."

Togweiler escorted the old man to the idling sedan. Opening the front door, he helped Red Hawk into the passenger seat. With a practiced motion, he slid into the rear seat beside Daniel, smoothing nonexistent wrinkles from his suit pants in the process.

"Call in our location, Bill."

Anderson carefully backed the auto out of Red Hawk's dirt and gravel front yard. Wheeling onto the main road, he toggled the microphone. "Base, this is Car Seven, Agents Anderson and Togweiler. We're proceeding through Badger on the Pine Ridge Reservation. We have taken a Daniel Gray Wolf into custody on suspicion of kidnapping. Also with us, but not under arrest, is one Leo Red Hawk, an acquaintance of Mr. Gray Wolf's. ETA of ninety minutes."

A static-filled response burst from the radio speaker. "Ten four, Car Seven. ETA of ninety minutes." More noise filtered through the interior as the remote unseen dispatcher signed off.

Gray Wolf squirmed in his seat, searching for a more comfortable position. Leaning back against the seat sent needles of pain coursing through his arms as the blood supply slowed. Wriggling again, he leaned against the junction of the seat and car door, finding temporary relief from the prickling numbness.

"Are the cuffs really necessary, Agent Togweiler?" Daniel asked. "They're cutting off my circulation."

"Sorry, standard procedure."

Leo Red Hawk turned slightly and looked back at his friend. "Woniya told me you would be tested, *Takoja*. He said you would overcome these obstacles and become stronger for it."

"Thanks, Grandfather, but that doesn't help right now," Gray Wolf replied, grimacing as the restrictive metal bands cut into his wrists.

Red Hawk shifted his gaze to Togweiler. "You are the one who seems to be in charge. Why is it you won't listen to what we have to say? Daniel told you he was here on the reservation when the young girl was kidnapped. Is it because I am an old man, or do you just not like Native Americans?"

Togweiler visibly stiffened. "Mr. Red Hawk, this has nothing to do with age or race. A child has been abducted and it's our job to find her and the perpetrator."

"What tribe are you?"

"Pardon me?"

"I asked what tribe you belong to," Leo repeated. "I can tell you have some of the blood in you."

Togweiler stared at the old man before replying, "I have some Ojibwa blood."

Red Hawk leaned back in his seat, a smug look crossing his lined face. "Then that explains it."

"Explains what?"

"The Ojibwa and Lakota were not on friendly terms. Your people pushed mine from our hunting grounds east of here many years ago. We grew strong, yet we did not seek revenge. So, why is it you still carry this grudge?"

Despite his discomfort, Gray Wolf was enjoying Leo's barbecue of the federal agent. The old man had a perfectly cognizant way of clouding an issue, baiting a person into a heated discussion before lambasting them with logic. He waited for the final blow.

"Do you know much about your heritage, Agent Rotweiler?" Red Hawk pushed.

"That's Togweiler ... and yes, I have some familiarity with that part of my background."

"Did you know the Ojibwa put much faith in their visions? They had a dream society not unlike our own. These men of vision told their people where to hunt, make camp, even when to make war. They did this because they could see things other people did not.

"Daniel here," the old man nodded toward his friend, "is the last of the *Ihanbla Gmunka*, the Lakota Dream Catcher. He has the special power to see into other men's dreams. That is how he knows of this girl."

Togweiler wasn't convinced. "That's an interesting story,

Mr. Red Hawk. I know a little about the Ojibwa dreaming societies and I don't recall hearing of anyone being able to see into other people's dreams."

"Possibly this is the reason we do not hear of the Ojibwa much anymore," Leo offered. "In the Lakota tribes, a Dream Catcher is a very important man, one to be listened to. Maybe if your tribe had paid more attention to learning of visions instead of kicking us out of our hunting grounds, you would be stronger today."

Gray Wolf felt Red Hawk's emotional words, knew they had not been said in a humorous vein, knew even more so the words were addressed to him as well as Togweiler.

Daniel needed to speak. "Leo speaks the truth, Agent Togweiler. There are things happening you apparently are not aware of, even with your Native American heritage. Things such as why I know where the girl is buried.

"So, it comes down to what is most important ... catching a kidnapper ... or finding Christine Hardesty alive. I think even you know the answer."

Freeman Togweiler looked across at Gray Wolf, contemplated what had just been said. Carefully, he replied, "You realize by leading us to wherever the Hardesty girl is, you could be further implicating yourself. Not only you, but Mr. Red Hawk as well."

"I am not concerned for myself. I know things will work out," Leo interjected. "But, there is a little girl out in the Badlands who does not know how things are going. Daniel has told me she has very little time left. And we are wasting that time driving into Rapid City."

"You're fully aware I've read you your rights?" Togweiler asked Gray Wolf. "What you say and do is now on the record.

"Sir," the agent said, turning toward Red Hawk, "we

haven't advised you of your rights because you haven't been charged with any crime. I hope you realize you could be considered an accessory to kidnapping."

Red Hawk nodded, "I understand what you say. Woniya watches out for old men and fools. I believe Daniel and I are both covered by these categories.

"If you wish to find the little girl, you should turn right at the next road," Leo added softly.

Agent Anderson, quiet until now, asked his partner, "What do you think, Freeman?"

"How far is it from here?" Togweiler asked Red Hawk.

"I do not know the miles, but we are now three beers away. Perhaps thirty-five or forty minutes."

"Does this place have a name? Can we call it in?" Anderson questioned.

"The Lakota call it *Mnikaoskokpa mayasleca*. The white man may know it as Coyote Canyon."

Anderson picked the car microphone up. "Base, this is Car Seven, Anderson and Togweiler again. Uh, there's been a slight change of plans. We are diverting to the Badlands, a place possibly called Coyote Canyon. The suspects insist Christine Hardesty is at that location. Have one of our folks scan a geodetic map of the Badlands for this site and have a chopper on standby."

Togweiler quickly lifted the microphone and added, "Just in case."

Gray Wolf noticed how the federal agent emphasized the word 'suspects'. *Shit, I'm sorry, Leo. Looks like I've gone and got you involved. All because I wanted to play detective and stretch my abilities a little to see if I still wanted to be a Dream Catcher.* One thing Daniel realized. He wanted to stay a Dream Catcher. Maybe it was what the old man had said just a few moments ago. Maybe it was the tenuous situation, the uncertainty surrounding his immediate future. Whatever it was, Gray Wolf knew he couldn't give up this ability.

"Turn right on the next road." Red Hawk's voice pulled Daniel back to reality.

The scenery changed subtly, rolling plains melding with slabs of painted dirt rising from the green-carpeted landscape. Distant spires of sandstone, sharpened by wind and rain, pointed their crooked fingers skyward.

Coming to the Badlands always brought a feeling of melancholy to Gray Wolf. The land held a desolate beauty, hundreds of millions of years in the making, yet virtually uninhabited by man. Despite barren appearances, the land teemed with animal and plant life. Late summer sunflowers stood lonely vigil along the deserted road. Clumps of sweet grass, used in Native American rituals, sporadically poked through the heartier, more-plentiful wild clover. All this land, all the spires, gullies, and drying fields, once belonged to the red man. Now it was national park ground, grudgingly made available to the Lakota for their infrequent off-reservation ceremonies. And now it was the unwanted home of Christine Hardesty.

Thinking of the girl deepened Gray Wolf's pensiveness. *Has she been able to cope? Does she have a strong will? Is she still alive?* No matter how hard he tried to detach himself, Daniel was involved. He felt her terror, her inability to shift to a more comfortable position; felt the closeness of the tomb. *We're coming to get you out, little girl. First we save you, and then Leo and I figure how to clear ourselves.*

"Looks like the road ends up ahead," Anderson said.

Red Hawk peered at the surroundings. "The pavement stops, but you will bear off to the left. There is a dirt trail that will lead us to the place."

Daniel suddenly remembered, "We didn't bring a shovel. How are we going to be able free her without a shovel?"

"There's one in the trunk," Togweiler said, then added for Leo's benefit, "along with changes of clothes in the event we have to perform lengthy surveillance."

Red Hawk looked back at the agent, sizing up the wrinkle-free suit. Togweiler noticed the scrutiny.

"Sorry to burst your bubble, Mr. Red Hawk," he explained. "Believe it or not, we federal agents are human and tend to get our clothing dirty just like other mere mortals."

Had the tension, the officiousness, lifted somewhat? Was this man actually making conversation? Daniel took the less strained atmosphere as a good sign. *Togweiler's just doing his job. I bet he doesn't really believe we're the bad guys. Maybe Leo's little Indian brotherhood and fellowship speech did some good.*

With the handcuffs still constraining him, it was obvious to Gray Wolf that Togweiler hadn't completely swayed.

"Turn right at this fork," Red Hawk instructed. "Those rocks on the horizon are where we want to be."

Daniel's stomach tickled, a brief flare of anticipatory nerves. *Just a couple more minutes, Christine! We'll have you out and on your way back to Mom and Dad.* He squinted through the dirty windshield, noting the vague familiarity of the area. Sagebrush and occasional croppings of spires dominated his view. *Yes! We're on the road I saw last time I was in Abrams' dream. We get around this bend and I'll bet I can see the old Chrysler.*

"There's the car! There's the old junker I told you about!" Gray Wolf shouted at Red Hawk.

"That is Thomas Dismounts' car," Leo confirmed. "I see the spirits chose to leave it here. I do not blame them. It was an evil piece of machinery anyway."

Anderson wheeled the sedan into the circle of spires. Even at a sedate speed, the auto raised billowing clouds of dust.

"Be careful around here!" Daniel ordered, forgetting his present incarcerated status. "You don't want to run over where Christine is."

"Where exactly is she, Mr. Gray Wolf?" Togweiler asked quietly.

Gray Wolf didn't hear the suspicion in the agent's voice. His agitation was too great. "Over there; in front of the car somewhere. Look for a piece of PVC sticking out of the ground."

"Got it!" Anderson exclaimed, unable to hide his excitement behind the professional veneer. He braked the car to a halt twenty feet from a dull white pipe protruding between two melon-sized stones. William Anderson exited the sedan before Togweiler could unfasten his seatbelt.

Togweiler assisted Gray Wolf from the auto as his partner rummaged through the trunk. "I'm sure I can count on your cooperation while we search the area," he said, looking Daniel in the eye.

"If you had an extra shovel, I'd help you." Gray Wolf returned the agent's gaze.

Anderson, armed with a shovel, trotted to the burial site. Obvious efforts had been made to smooth out the area, yet freshly-dug soil lay mounded in a rough perimeter about the rock-supported tube. Leaning down, he placed his mouth near the pipe. "Christine? Christine, can you hear me?" He rested a cupped ear against the tube. Looking up at Togweiler, he shook his head. "Nothing." Carefully, he began spading loose dirt from around the rocks.

"Don't knock the pipe loose," Daniel warned unnecessarily. His caution elicited a brief scowling glance from the agent.

Leo Red Hawk joined his friend, watching the excavation with interest. His comment caught Gray Wolf off guard. "Your dreams are good ones, Daniel. I think it is right you made the decision to bother this kidnapper for more detail. Woniya will be happy with what you did."

Eyes never leaving the living grave, Daniel said sourly, "Yeah, maybe I can Dream Catch for all the rest of the convicts in the penitentiary."

"You knew there would be ruts in this trail you chose. Have some faith. The spirit guide watches over you. I watch over you."

"Thanks, *Tunkasila*." Daniel looked up briefly and smiled. "I need a little guidance just about now."

"You have chosen to stay our *Ihanbla Gmunka*," Red Hawk said, catching Gray Wolf off guard. "Do not look surprised. I heard it in your voice. When this is all over and the little girl is back with her family, you will have to get busy and produce a son. I'm ninety-eight years old and I grow tired of watching out for you."

Their conversation dwindled as they watched the progress William Anderson's shovel made. A hole three feet in diameter by twelve inches deep now circled the white plastic air tube. Each spade full of dirt brought Christine Hardesty closer to freedom.

"Got it!" Anderson shouted, his shovel tapping against a wooden obstruction.

Casting a final warning glance at Gray Wolf, Freeman Togweiler crouched beside his partner. Using only his hands, the agent scooped crumbling lumps of earth away, slowly exposing a plywood surface.

Anderson experimented with the shovel, poking its blade into the soil until he determined what direction the box laid. Dirt spattered onto the adjacent hard packed ground as he quickly troweled a rough clearing. Slowly, an outline of the grim container appeared.

Kneeling, both agents pried around the edges, cracking the lid slightly. The cover grated noisily against the rough plywood edges, sliding on a thin coat of dirt granules. A final tug, and the lid popped off, sliding to an upright position between the coffin and hole.

Their view blocked by the lid, Gray Wolf and Red Hawk scoured the agents' faces for a reaction. They were not rewarded with looks of relief. Instead, Anderson quickly extracted a handkerchief and covered his nose and mouth. Togweiler bent down, reaching inside the box. Anderson, his face still covered, leaned over his partner and looked at the same hidden secret that held Togweiler's attention.

"What the hell's going on?" Daniel asked. "Is the girl all right? Somebody tell me what's happening!"

Togweiler straightened up, still partially concealed by the protruding lid. He looked in Gray Wolf's direction then back down.

"Oh shit!" Daniel moaned. "Are we too late?"

"Come over here, Mr. Gray Wolf." Togweiler's statement was not a request.

Daniel shambled across the uneven surface, a precarious walk without the use of his arms. He neared the excavation, not wanting to see what was inside the box, yet needing to know the outcome.

"Is she dead?"

"She's not here," Anderson replied. "But maybe you already knew that, Gray Wolf."

"Not here? But this is the site! This is the area I saw. There's the box with the air pipe." Words rushed from Daniel's mouth as he peered over the rim.

Except for a soiled blanket and lumps of smeared fecal matter, the plywood coffin was empty. The stench emanating from inside was what caused Anderson to cover his nose and mouth.

Gray Wolf was at a loss. "I don't understand. He must have moved her."

"Who is this 'he' you're talking about, Mr. Gray Wolf?" Togweiler asked. "You say you're not the kidnapper, yet you haven't told us who is."

"He's a transient. Guy by the name of Steven Abrams. At least, that's the name he gave me. I didn't say his name before because I was afraid of wrongly accusing someone if I was mistaken about where the girl was located."

"It's pretty obvious the girl isn't here, Mr. Gray Wolf," Anderson commented with some rancor.

"But the hole is; the coffin with the air pipe; just like I saw it in his dreams," Daniel countered. "There's no doubt in my mind anymore."

Pointing to the hole, Togweiler said, "You'll excuse us if we still harbor some doubt. This proves nothing except that you are aware of a hole in the ground adorned with some human waste, a dirty blanket ... and this." The agent gently pushed a sheet of paper into Gray Wolf's view. "Read, but don't touch!"

Prickly fingers of anxiety grabbed the Dream Catcher's stomach as he read the note. The prose, the glued-on newspaper print; was definitely directed at Gray Wolf.

I Moved the One you are seeking
And you know why—I saw you peeking.
It's not polite to stay in dreams
When you're not invited so, it seems,
The little girl suffers for your sin
The horror she knew, she'll know again

"Shit!" Daniel muttered. Abrams had caught him lurking, had seen him visit the other dreams. But when? How long ago? How long had Christine been moved?

"You want to tell me about this?" Togweiler asked, waving an accusatory finger at the paper then at Gray Wolf. "What does it mean?"

"It means Abrams spotted me when I entered his dream about the girl. I just don't know when. I visited with him three times. The first time was before he kidnapped Christine, so that probably doesn't count. He had to move the girl some time after either the second or third visit. My guess is last night because I felt his presence around me as I experienced one of his weird dreams."

Togweiler eyed Gray Wolf. "So, this Abrams is the guy you visited last night. Is he the man you followed out on the interstate?"

"You were trailing me," Daniel answered hotly. "What do you think?"

The agent looked uncomfortable for a moment before saying, "We lost track of you for a little while after you left this guy's apartment. You cut off Rushmore Road and took a side street. We were in another lane and couldn't catch up to you."

"So, how did you happen to pick me up again?"

"Pure luck," Togweiler said. "We cruised on Rushmore Road and about half an hour later, you popped up again. That's when we followed you out onto the interstate and eventually to the reservation."

For the first time in many hours, Gray Wolf thought only of himself. He said suddenly, "What time was Christine kidnapped?"

Togweiler started the typical bureaucratic diatribe. "I can't discuss that information. It's confidential and -"

"I'm a suspect in this thing, Togweiler, so fuck your confidentiality! What time was Christine Hardesty kidnapped?" Gray Wolf demanded.

"She was last seen at approximately ten-twenty in the morning," the agent sighed.

Daniel smiled, not out of happiness, but triumph. "Use your portable phone there and call the Badger Liquor and Grocery Emporium. Ralph Trudeau's the owner. Ask him what time I stopped by to pick up groceries for Leo Red Hawk. If Trudeau's not enough of an alibi, ask for either Mr. Yellow Feather or Mr. War Pony. They'll be sitting outside on the rockers. They all commented on me being a little later than my usual ten o'clock ... say around ten-thirty.

"Now," Gray Wolf continued, "if I was the kidnapper, that means I made it from Rapid City to Badger—a distance of a little over eighty miles—in ten minutes. I drive fast, but not that damned fast."

"Okay, okay," Togweiler relented, holding up his hands. "I'll call these guys. If your story checks, I'll release you."

"Bill," the agent added, "call in about the note, the site. Everything we see here. I want a forensics team sent pronto to check the box contents, tire marks, etcetera. While you're at it, have base contact our reservation team—I think it's Goodman and Schmidt. Ask for them to speak with a Ralph Trudeau at the Badger Liquor and Grocery Store. They need to find out when Mr. Gray Wolf showed up there on Saturday. If Trudeau's not available, have them check with ... "

"Gilbert War Pony or William Yellow Feather," Daniel clarified. "They'll be sitting on the store's front porch."

As Anderson walked toward the sedan, Togweiler said to Gray Wolf, "I can't take the cuffs of yet, you realize, but I hope your story corroborates. In the mean time, I think I'll have the

Rapid City field office check up on Mr. Abrams' whereabouts. See if he's still at the same apartment."

"Ten to one says he's not there," Gray Wolf declared. "Your boys will find an empty apartment, littered with two weeks' worth of dirty everything."

Leo Red Hawk, silent up to this point, said, "My work is through here. I am tired and hungry. If I am not under arrest, will you take this old man home? If I am under arrest, take me to Rapid City and feed me."

"Sorry, Mr. Red Hawk," Togweiler said, smiling. "We've got to hang around until the chopper gets here. I do have some MRE's in the trunk, if you're interested."

Leo nodded sagely. "Of course, I am interested. Is it something to eat?"

For the next thirty-five minutes, Red Hawk contentedly munched his way through two unpalatable Meals Ready to Eat packages. While he smacked his lips, or belched at the preserved delicacies, Gray Wolf and the FBI agents impatiently waited for the forensics chopper.

A distant, but unmistakable thwacking sound of rotor blades signified the approach of the helicopter. Togweiler had laid two orange strips of polyurethane down, marking a landing site well away from the vacant grave and any possible evidence. As the aircraft's thrumming drew closer, the car radio crackled to life. Freeman Togweiler hopped into the sedan to answer the call.

"Base to Car Seven. Agent Goodman confirms one Daniel Gray Wolf was present at the Badger Liquor and Grocery Emporium, Saturday, at approximately ten twenty-five. Misters Trudeau, Yellow Feather, and War Pony all agree on the time. Goodman found all the guys there, just like the suspect—uh—former suspect said."

Smiling for the first time that morning, Togweiler acknowledged, "Uh, roger, Base. We are releasing Mr. Gray Wolf."

Beneath the increasing volume of helicopter sounds, Daniel heard enough of the conversation to realize he was a free man. Smiling despite the discomfort in his hands and shoulders, he waited, deciding to make Togweiler come to him to undo the cuffs.

"Sorry about all this," Freeman said, unlocking the steel manacles. "There were a lot of fingers pointing in your direction for awhile."

Rubbing his wrists to wake the sluggish circulation, Daniel smiled in relief. "I'm just glad you guys were able to make contact with the Bureau down on the reservation."

Togweiler glanced at Gray Wolf. "You're taking this quite graciously for a man who was handcuffed for several hours."

The Dream Catcher shrugged. "Maybe I'll be pissed later, but right now, I'm just glad to see my hands again. "Besides," he admitted, "I'm sure my actions did seem a little peculiar."

"Speaking of peculiar," Togweiler said, "can we talk about your psychic abilities a little? Maybe on the drive back to the reservation? Also, I'm going to want a description on this Steven Abrams."

"I'm not psychic -"

Remaining conversation was drowned out by the sounds of the helicopter flaring to a soft landing. Even from fifty yards away, dust swirled around Gray Wolf and Togweiler as the rotors' downwash fanned dried soil and debris in all directions. Two men hopped off the craft, duck walking below the spinning blades even before the engine had spooled down. Freeman Togweiler trotted over to meet the forensics team. Crouched against the decreasing maelstrom, he carried on an animated conversation with the men, gesturing periodically in Gray Wolf's direction. The three men emerged from under the whirling rotors and strode toward the Dream Catcher.

Togweiler led the forensics men to Daniel. "This is Mr. Gray Wolf. He's the one who found the site."

A youngish agent, clad in light chinos and FBI-issue windbreaker, studied Daniel momentarily. His watery blue eyes took in the whole picture. "Agent Togweiler tells me you dreamed about this area. What was it, some sort of vision?"

Gray Wolf detected no sarcasm in the man's voice, yet he looked at Togweiler for a reaction. Seeing none, he answered, "Not a vision. I'm a Dream Catcher. I saw this place when I visited the kidnapper's dream."

The forensics agent's eyes widened.

Oh shit, here we go again.

"You're *Ihanbla Gmunka?*" the agent asked, incredulity filling his keen eyes. "I've heard about you."

It was Gray Wolf's turn to show disbelief. Not only had the agent called him by the Lakota name, he had pronounced it correctly as well.

"You know about this mystical stuff?" Togweiler asked the forensics man.

"Yeah, I've always been fascinated by how the Native Americans stayed in touch with their cabalistic side where us white guys kind of lost out over the years," the agent replied, then turned back to Daniel. "So, you dreamed the location? How did you get the kidnapper to invite you in?"

Surprised at the depth of the man's knowledge, Daniel was about to answer when Red Hawk spoke from behind him. "What Daniel did was a little bit wrong, but Woniya has granted that it was for a good cause."

"I was asked to cure a nightmare," Gray Wolf explained

hurriedly. "When I was finished, the guy still displayed signs of dreaming so I went back in. That's when I saw this area the first time. After that, I justified the need to find out more detail."

"I am his earthly guardian," Leo added proudly. "Daniel is the last of his kind and the gift will end unless he hurries up and produces a son."

"*Tunkasila!*" Gray Wolf warned. "You already know my intentions."

"Yes," the old man nodded. "But I also know it takes nine moons to produce a child; a new *Ihanbla Gmunka*. I do not know if these old bones can last that long."

"Bob," Togweiler addressed the forensics agent. "We'll let you get on with your work. You know the routine. I'd like a DNA match up on all evidence you find. I'm sure the congressman's family has a locket of Christine's hair you can compare it to. Also, there's some fecal matter. I need it age checked. It might give us some clue to how long the girl's been gone from here."

"We'll take care of it," the agent answered before turning back to Daniel. "I'd like to talk with you more about your ability, Mr. Gray Wolf. Here's my card. I'd really appreciate a call when you have some spare time."

"Is this professional or personal curiosity?" Daniel asked.

"Both. The Bureau regularly uses a psychic to help on cases. Maybe we can discuss you employing your dream catching prowess to help out if needed."

"Perhaps," Gray Wolf answered, knowing he couldn't accept such a proposal. He led Red Hawk back toward the agents' sedan.

"Don't even say it, Grandfather," Daniel admonished. "I have no intentions of using my ability for personal gain, or for invading other people's dreams. At least not after this is all over."

"Perhaps your conscience is bothering you a little, *Takoja*," Red Hawk said with a slight smile.

"My conscience is bothering me a lot, but mainly because I couldn't get to Abrams in time," Gray Wolf admitted. "Although, I did something else I've never done before. Never even knew I could do for that matter."

"And that was to make up a dream to get back in the man's head," Red Hawk finished.

"Did I tell you about that this morning? I honestly don't remember saying anything about that."

"You told me, or Woniya told me," the old man said. "It makes no difference because you say it to me now."

Daniel helped Leo into the back seat of the auto. Walking around to other side, he slid in beside the old man.

"It—it scared me to recreate the dream, *Tunkasila*," Gray Wolf said. "I did it twice. Each time it was a little worse experience for me. I was afraid I would be killed."

"It is good you were scared by this, Daniel. It takes powerful medicine to do what you did, but even more powerful knowledge is needed to control such a thing. Very few men in the history of the entire Seven Tribes of the Council fire managed to bring dreams to life."

"Well," Gray Wolf said, "you don't have to worry about me trying it again. From now on, I'm just a plain old ordinary Dream Catcher."

Discussions completed with the forensics team, agents Togweiler and Anderson climbed back into the auto. Freeman Togweiler turned to look at Gray Wolf. "The Hardestys received another ransom note this morning, some time after we arrived out here. The forensics boys brought me a copy."

Daniel replied, "Why are you telling me this? Are you going to show me the note, or is this just an FYI?"

"That depends," Togweiler answered, studying the Dream Catcher for a reaction.

"Depends on what?"

The agent sighed, then rubbed the weariness from his face. "Bob Talmedge, the forensics agent you spoke to, places a lot of faith in what you do. He's kind of the field office's resident Native American expert. Talmedge thinks you can help us locate this guy. So, I show you the note if you offer to help us."

"Thanks, but I think I'll pass," Gray Wolf said. "The FBI has a ton of agents, including a special team from Washington, working on this kidnapping. Hell, you might be part of that team for all I know. You men are trained for this kind of problem. I just dream with people to solve your everyday garden-variety nightmare."

Togweiler shrugged. "Suit yourself. You've certainly done enough already. At least we think we know who we're looking for now."

Gray Wolf stared out the window, absently watching the terrain pass by. *What did I hear in Togweiler's voice? Was it relief, or is he trying to play on my conscience? Skip it, kola. Like the man said, you've done enough.*

Turning away from the window, Daniel looked at Leo Red Hawk. The old man's eyes were closed and he appeared to be napping. *A big day for you, Grandfather. Your belly's full and now you deserve to rest. Hell, I might just take a nap myself.*

Leaning back against the seat, Gray Wolf closed his eyes. But sleep, the one commodity he was expert in, would not come. He rested his head against the padded window frame, hoping a change of position would cure the brief spurt of insomnia. A gentle nudge dissolved any prospect of slumber. Opening his eyes, Daniel peeked in Red Hawk's direction. The old man gestured for him to draw close.

"I've just visited with Woniya," Leo murmured in Lakota, evidently wanting the conversation to be private. "He thinks you need to help find the girl."

Gray Wolf answered in the dialect, "I thought Woniya was every Lakota's spirit guide. How is it you get to talk to him so much?"

Red Hawk shook his head. "Maybe the guide has time to listen to those who have something important to say. I am only telling you what has been told me. Woniya believes you are responsible for finding this child. He approves of your way of doing things; says you have strong medicine and can handle the danger."

"I promised myself I wasn't going to create dreams anymore, Grandfather. I still have marks on my body from the last time—very real marks made by a dream dog. It's time I looked out for myself."

"By staying a Dream Catcher, your right to comfort comes second, my grandson. I have faith in your ability. Woniya has the same faith."

Still in Lakota, Daniel argued, "What about the tradition? If I go back and make the dogs appear to Abrams, I will be breaking the code."

Red Hawk laughed softly. "You and I have much to learn about the Other Plain, Grandson. Things are not much different there than here. There are no rules that cannot be changed, so I am told. Decisions are made, destinies are altered. Nothing remains the same, even in the Land of Fallen Warriors."

Engrossed in their conversation, Daniel and Leo didn't

notice the curious looks from Togweiler. The communication in an unfamiliar tongue had caught his interest.

William Anderson, carefully watching the road, only cast occasional glances in the rear view mirror at the rear seat occupants. "What the hell do you figure they're talking about?" the driver asked in a low tone.

"Beats me," Togweiler replied in an equally guarded voice. "But it must be important NA stuff. The old man's got Gray Wolf's attention about something."

"Why do you suppose Talmedge wanted you to make the offer to Gray Wolf," Anderson asked. "And, what's your feelings on the subject? Hell, you're in charge. Talmedge's a forensics guy."

"I don't know," Togweiler murmured. "It might have something to do with us not knowing jack shit about the kidnapper ... even with all our Washington firepower. Gray Wolf here has given us more to go on than the twenty Pentagon pukes they sent. Besides, Talmedge puts a lot of credence in this mystical stuff. Psychics, seers, now Dream Catchers."

"Could be why he's still an evidence hound instead of a field agent." Anderson offered.

"Talmedge likes what he does. He's good at it. No, make that an expert at it. He's passed up three open slots for field assignments."

"No shit!"

The agents were suddenly, and acutely, aware the rear seat conversation had ceased. Togweiler turned to see Gray Wolf and Red Hawk watching with interest.

"Sorry, gentlemen," Freeman Togweiler offered. "We don't have the luxury of lapsing into a second tongue."

"Mr. Togweiler," Daniel said, "will you share the ransom note with me?"

"Does this mean you're thinking of helping the Bureau?"

Gray Wolf cast a glance at his mentor. "Let's say I was convinced it was the right thing to do."

❝ ... suspect has light brown, thinning hair, and wears round tortoise-shell glasses. He stands approximately five feet nine inches and weighs one hundred and forty-five pounds. Abrams drives a nineteen eighty-nine or ninety, dark blue Dodge four door with out-of-state plates; possibly Indiana. It is unknown whether he is armed, but Steven Abrams should be considered dangerous.

"Put out the APB," Togweiler continued, holding the microphone a Bureau-standard two inches from his mouth. "Mr. Gray Wolf will talk with our artist when we get back from the reservation. Seven out."

"Base copies," came the static-filled reply. "APB will be issued ASAP."

"M-N-L-O-P," Red Hawk intoned.

"Pardon?" Togweiler asked, distracted by the old man's meandering.

Leo smiled at the agent. "The white man's world is one of letters and numbers, not words anymore. Nineteen, eighty-nine, ninety, A-S-A-P. Is this what they teach in the white schools now ... letters and numbers?"

"Don't listen to him, Agent Togweiler," Gray Wolf muttered. "I think Leo's having a sugar attack. He's just using his mouth because he doesn't have anything to put in it."

"You *wasicun* have lost the art of language," Red Hawk goaded. "You either say too many words, or use letters and numbers. It is a poor way to visit between men."

Anderson grumbled over his shoulder, "I notice you speak English, old man."

"That is because the *wasicun* will not learn the simplicity of Lakota. In my language, this conversation would be five words long. Yes, to speak with the white man takes patience, but it makes my head hurt. I am also thirsty."

"Probably because of the MRE's you—uh—because of the dried meals you ate, Mr. Red Hawk," Togweiler said, correcting his acronym to avoid a further lecture. "I hope you can wait until we get you home. It's only another twenty minutes or so."

Leo was about to retort when Gray Wolf quieted him with a restraining arm. "*Tunkasila*, stop yanking the man's chain. You're just pissed off because you can't watch television right now. When we get back, I'll stop at Mr. Trudeau's and pick up some beer for you before I head to Rapid."

"Lone Ranger will be over by then," Red Hawk grumbled. "It is probably an exciting episode I have not yet seen either."

"But, you'll still get Rin Tin Tin this afternoon," Daniel reminded him. "Besides, you've seen these shows a hundred times."

"Hey, I remember those from when I was a kid," Anderson said, a smile playing on his lips as he reminisced. " ... and let us ride back to yesteryear with the masked man and his faithful Indian companion, Tonto ... "

"Hell," the agent continued, "I thought those shows were long gone."

"Did you know Tonto means 'stupid' in Spanish?" Red Hawk asked the agent.

"Is he always this cantankerous?" Togweiler asked Daniel.

"Only after I have eaten some of *wasicun* M-N-L-O-P's,"

Red Hawk answered. "Your food has made me thirsty and I will have to shit when I get home, thank you very much."

Gray Wolf hammered the old man with a fierce look. Lapsing into their native tongue, he asked, "Grandfather, what has gotten into you? Why do you whine like a coyote at these men?"

"It is a test," Leo answered simply.

"What kind of test?"

"I am guardian to the Dream Catcher. If you are to help, I must make sure this Rotweiler is stable and will not fly off like a drunken hummingbird."

"I think they are questioning your stability right now. And, I think you are being a little Tonto."

"I am an elder of the Oglala Sioux. Everyone else believes what I say is wise."

"Wise ass maybe," Gray Wolf broke into English, not finding suitable Indian dialect to express his feelings.

"You will some day learn my words have deeper meaning," Leo continued modestly in Lakota. "This is not all idle talk of an old man. There are many strong thoughts stored underneath these gray hairs. I am tired now. These men will not stop to let me get a drink, so I will rest and put all of you out of my misery." Apparently feeling vindicated, Red Hawk lowered his head and dozed.

Gray Wolf used the respite from Leo's rambling to study the ransom note Togweiler had shared with him earlier. Though it was a facsimile, touching the copy chilled Daniel because he knew the source. Meandering lines of newspaper print stared back at him, another kinky poem from the disturbed kidnapper.

Ring around The rosEy,
Someone's gotten nosy.
Give me the bread,
or The girl is dead
You still have Until Tuesday
A tiSket, a taskET,
An IndiaN found the CaskEt
I moved the kid,
She'S Now well Hid
Mess With me, she GeTs her ass kicked

Thankfully, Leo slept the remaining miles back to Badger. Daniel needed the time to concentrate on what he could do to help locate the missing girl. He loved Red Hawk dearly, but the man sometimes constituted a walking cluster fuck.

Frankly, he had no idea why they needed him, other than to offer details for a composite sketch. The note held no clues he could discern, no hint to Christine's whereabouts.

Togweiler interrupted his thoughts. "Can you determine anything from the note, Mr. Gray Wolf? Does this give you any ideas where the little girl might be?"

"I started to tell you before; I'm not psychic. I can't read minds or see into the future. You know, none of that metaphysical stuff. I fight nightmares, pure and simple, Agent Togweiler."

"Uh-huh," the agent intoned noncommittally. "If it's not too big of an imposition, might I ride back to Rapid with you? That'll give us a couple of hours to talk over some issues.

"As you may realize," Togweiler continued, "I don't have a real comfort level with this Dream Catching scenario yet. I'd like to learn more about it. Of course, that is if you don't mind the company."

Gray Wolf shook his head. "No, that'd be fine. I'm just trying to figure out what it is the FBI needs me for."

"Mr. Gray Wolf," Togweiler began, "I'm a meat and potatoes kind of guy. I was taught in the old school that there's a plausible answer for everything. Now, I may have read more into your abilities—suggesting you might have extra sensory capability—but, dammed if you didn't lead us to the burial site. The result of a dream, no less. I'm looking for anything, and I do mean anything, to help us locate this Mr. Abrams for questioning."

"OL3-74M," Daniel suddenly blurted. "Damn, I just remembered! Abrams' Indiana tag number is OL3-74M."

"You're sure it's Indiana?" The agent jotted the numbers on a tiny notepad, then held it near sighted close while he called in the additional information.

Amidst waves of humid air waltzing across the asphalt, the two stores and eight houses comprising metropolitan Badger appeared on the horizon. Late morning heat shimmered the length of road, distorting the distant buildings into mirage-like images.

Daniel surveyed the countryside, comparing how the heated air clouded Red Hawk's home town while allowing the stark, flat-topped buttes to appear crystal clear. The dichotomy of the area played in his thoughts. *Old Leo sees the heat as solace, warmth for his bones. And what do you see, kola? A need for air conditioning to fight off the August sun.* Had he copped out, forsaken his heritage for the freon-induced creature comforts of the white mans' world?

And what about the girl? What about Christine? Was she now in some place less stifling, or was she buried again in the baked soil? Gray Wolf fervently hoped her new prison didn't surround her with the same terror.

William Anderson slowed as he approached the approximate city limits of Badger. Good citizen that he was, Anderson carried an ingrained deference to the laws of larger communities, perhaps a safeguard against the chance presence of playing children. Cruising south past the commercial center, he slowed even further, searching for Red Hawk's nondescript driveway.

Leo woke with a slight jump, yawned, then stretched in the confines of the back seat. "Did we pick up some beer?"

"I'll stop back by the store while you go speak with the toilet spirits, *Tunkasila*," Gray Wolf said. "The agents are busy men and don't have time to make a beer run."

"I've been thinking."

"You were sleeping," Daniel corrected.

"Some of us can do both, *Takoja*," Red Hawk chastised. "As I said, I've been thinking, Woniya and me, about this little girl."

"Who's this 'woh-ni-yuh' guy you keep talking about?" Anderson asked, phonetically pronouncing the foreign-sounding name.

Red Hawk rolled his eyes as if he were dealing with a child. "An old friend. These eyes cannot see the things they did seventy or eighty years ago. Woniya looks for me, then talks to me and guides me."

"So, we're talking spirits here," Anderson said noncommittally.

"Let it rest, Bill," Togweiler warned before turning toward the old man. "I'd be interested in hearing what this friend has to say."

Looking smugly at Daniel, Leo Red Hawk continued, "Woniya believes my grandson here is your only hope in finding the young girl. He tells me Daniel has the medicine to get this child back safely. Without *Takoja's* help, you will be—how do you say it—pissing in the wind."

"What am I supposed to do, Grandfather?" Gray Wolf asked, already knowing the answer.

"What is it this kidnapper fears more than anything?"

"He's scared of his dream dogs, but I already said I wasn't -"

Red Hawk raised his hand, silencing Daniel. "I know what you are going to say, but think hard about this. A little girl, a small child with many years of happiness ahead of her, needs your help. If you are to call yourself the *Ihanbla Gmunka*, then it is your duty to find this girl. Woniya has said so."

Gray Wolf didn't speak until Anderson pulled up in front of the ramshackle house. When he did, the words poured out with a tinge of sarcasm. He had automatically lapsed into Lakota, only spicing it up with English swear words. "It seems so goddamned convenient, Woniya talking to you any time you want something to go your way. First, you tell me the 'great spirit guide' is pissed because I meddled in this guy's dreams. Now you tell me he wants me to bring the dogs back so I can get back in Abrams' head. Is there a chance we're getting what Woniya and you want mixed up a little? Is there just a slight chance our beloved spirit doesn't talk to you as much as you say? How about I get a chance to council with Woniya. I've got a few things I'd like to say to him!"

Red Hawk's reply was simple, with no bitterness. "You are not yet ready to speak with Woniya. I have been your earthly guide since you were a pup. The spirit sees fit to contact you through me because I have not been poisoned by the white man ways. You cannot blame Woniya if I have failed you. I am an old man and maybe some things get hazy. But I tell you this, when the spirit guide visits me, it is with the clarity of a young man's first kiss."

A chastened Gray Wolf got out of the sedan and walked around to help Leo. As he opened the old man's door, he said, "I apologize, Grandfather. I was ... I'm just scared to go back into that dream, so I took it out on you. I didn't mean those things I said."

"Only a fool confronts danger without fear, Daniel. You are right to be afraid. That means you will be careful.

"Now," Red Hawk concluded, turning toward his house, "I will be thirsty by the time I get out of the toilet. Are you going to get me some beer?"

Daniel smiled, knowing he had been forgiven.

CHAPTER 19

In a very un-agentlike display of relaxation, Freeman Togweiler leaned back and loosened his tie. The monotony of the drive, coupled with several days of interrupted sleep, had lowered the man's reserve. Gray Wolf's careful driving habits lulled the agent further into a civilian mode.

"So, Mr. Gray Wolf, how does one become a Dream Catcher?"

Daniel glanced briefly at Togweiler. "You send five Rice Krispie box tops along with a coded application to the Kellogg folks. In six to eight weeks, they send you your dream catching kit."

Freeman smiled at the answer. "I enjoy the humor, but I was actually asking a serious question. Despite my mixed heritage, I'm not familiar with much of the Native American ways. I'm hoping to see some way your ability can benefit us in this kidnapping case."

"Okay," Gray Wolf said. "Let's start over here. First, I'd appreciate it if your training allowed you to call me Daniel. I'm not much on protocol when it comes to being addressed."

"Okay yourself, **Daniel**," Togweiler emphasized the first name. "My family calls me Butch. Feel free to use the name when we're alone. Call me that around any of the other agents and I'll be forced to kill you."

"Gotcha," Daniel grinned. "Butch the Fed. Yeah, I can see why you'd show extreme prejudice against someone calling you that in a more formal surrounding.

"As far as how I became a Dream Catcher," he continued, "it's an inherited trait. Being's as how we're becoming familiar with each other, I'll show you a little something."

Gray Wolf brushed the hair back from his right temple. "See that birthmark in the shape of a spider? That's *Wakta Iktomi,* the mark of the Dream Catcher. *Iktomi* was—is—a mischievous group of spirits, usually well intentioned in their deeds, but sometimes a little misguided. Legend says the spider people were responsible for what dreams got through to my people. Some days, good dreams were allowed. Other days, nightmares. Kinda like an arachnid with PMS, you get what I mean? Anyhow, only the first son of the Dream Catcher is blessed ... or cursed ... with this symbol."

Togweiler studied Gray Wolf for a moment before replying. "I couldn't help but overhear some of your conversation with Mr. Red Hawk. Seems you've got mixed emotions about this—this ability."

"Well, Butch, let's put it this way. Since I was sixteen years old, I've been on call. Someone has a bad dream, and Gray Wolf has a movie date that same night, guess who gets the pleasure of my company? It ain't the chick."

"I can imagine that it's tough on the social life. I understand you're not married. Is this due to, or in spite of, your gift?"

Daniel chuckled before answering. "Up until a couple of days ago I had decided to deprive the entire Lakota Nation of future Dream Catchers. Selfish motives probably. But I didn't want a kid of mine growing up with the responsibility and pain that comes with the position. Not after what I've seen."

Togweiler was intrigued by this personal drama. "So, Daniel, how do you solve these nightmares?

"There are some rules to the game," Gray Wolf began.

"First, the person must be suffering from recurring bad dreams. Second, this person has to be referred by a mutual acquaintance; someone who knows both them and me well. By the way, Abrams was an exception to this rule. A buddy of mine from work sent him my way while in a drunken stupor."

Daniel suddenly veered the pickup to the left, then back into the proper lane.

"What the hell was that all about?" Togweiler asked after regaining his seat.

"Sorry, I was just avoiding Thirty Mile Hole. I've lost two shocks over the past ten years by driving through that rut instead of around it.

"Nothing mysterious about the name. I made it up," Gray Wolf added. "The damn hole has never been fixed, and it just happens to be thirty miles from Leo's house.

"Anyhow, as I was saying, if a person meets the first two criteria, then I arrange a visit, usually at my house. Once the person is in deep sleep, I fall asleep beside them and enter their dream. After that, I kind of ad lib it, depending on what plagues them."

"What do you mean, 'you ad lib it'?"

"Well, dreams are kind of a fantasy world based on reality," Gray Wolf explained. "Because it's a fantasy, I can conjure up just about any weapon or tool I need to take care of their problem. I try to keep it simple, you know, knives, guns, arrows. I don't want to traumatize the dreamer by setting off a nuclear bomb."

Togweiler cast an incredulous stare at Daniel. "And this works?"

"One hundred percent; no repeat customers," Gray Wolf said modestly, almost distractedly.

"Now, I'd like you to tell me about your session with Steve Abrams."

Daniel thought for a moment before responding. "Actually, I had several sessions with Abrams. Some in his presence where I solved the nightmare ... and a couple where I recreated the nightmare so I could get back in his head. I'm sure you got the scoop from Deputy Dan over at the Sheriff's Department."

Togweiler smiled. "Actually, the deputy was a little remiss in giving out details, other than he was sure you were involved in the kidnapping. I'd like you to tell me the whole story, from when you first met Mr. Abrams until your last encounter."

Taking a deep breath, Gray Wolf Abrams started with the chance meeting in the bar, the unexpected midnight phone call that set the wheels in motion, then up through yesterday's encounter with Edwin Nagel. Daniel kept objective, involuntarily showing emotion only when describing how he recreated the nightmare. Twenty-five minutes later, just as they cruised through the minuscule town of Caputa, he finished.

Freeman Togweiler was silent for a moment, trying to absorb Gray Wolf's entire story. As unbelievable as the events sounded, he had no doubt the Dream Catcher was telling the truth. Twenty-six years in the Bureau, coupled with thousands of people interviewed, made him a decent judge of character.

"Holy shit!" the agent finally breathed. "Just when I thought I was getting this dream catching scenario in line, you spring a new twist on me ... the re-creation part."

"Yeah," Gray Wolf agreed, nodding his head. "That was new for me, too. Up until this kidnapping, I didn't know I could do that. Grandfather ... Leo ... was kinda surprised by that little turn of events, too. To tell the truth, I think he was more scared than surprised."

"Scared of what—did he say?"

Gray Wolf paused, frowning as he tried to recollect. "No—yes—well, no. Leo just muttered something under his breath as he tromped off into his bedroom. I only heard part of what he said."

"And?" Togweiler prompted, seeing Daniel's hesitation. "I could have sworn he said something about *nawawanica*. It means to turn into nothing; you know, disappear ... evaporate. Kind of like what our old legends say about shape shifters."

Freeman Togweiler stared hard at Gray Wolf, hoping to see a smile or hear a chuckle signifying the Indian was kidding. When Daniel didn't change his expression, the agent felt compelled to respond

"Shape shifting? You mean, like turning into animals and stuff? Come on, Daniel. I might walk around with this big hook hanging out of my mouth believing your Dream Catcher prowess, but shape shifting? Hell, now you're sticking a freaking gaff in my side."

"Can't say as I blame you," Gray Wolf agreed. "It's something I don't even want to think about.

"Besides," Daniel added not too convincingly, "Leo's an old man. He says lots of things he doesn't mean."

Togweiler joined Gray Wolf's silence, comfortable in not exploring any deeper into this Indian's strange way of life.

Five minutes later, Daniel broke the quiet that had permeated the pickup interior. "Uh, Butch, do you want me to drop you off somewhere—you want to come to my house and freshen up—what?"

"We can stop by your place if you feel a real need to clean up, but I'd like us to be at headquarters as quickly as possible. I have a hunch Mr. Abrams' trail is not that old, so the more time we dawdle, the colder it gets."

Gray Wolf shook his head. "If you guys can stand me for a

few of hours, we'll head straight to your office. I only wanted to make a couple of calls; I haven't checked in at work yet."

The remaining drive into downtown Rapid City was a silent one. Each man thought his own thoughts about the kidnapping, what role he played in the bizarre little saga. Only as Daniel turned into the federal parking lot did Togweiler speak.

"Bob Talmedge, the forensics guy you met out in the Badlands, will probably sit in on our debriefing. He's going to ask you a lot of questions ... pointed questions."

"I understand that."

Togweiler nodded. "Just wanted you to know in advance. The Bureau is a rather high profile agency; public opinion of us switches as often as I change socks. We have to be careful about our dealings with events out of the ordinary."

"Yeah," Daniel agreed. "I have to be careful as well. Word gets out I collaborated with the feds and something goes wrong on your case, I can kiss my dream catching career good bye."

"Sounds like you're now sold on staying the Indian nightmare solver. Earlier this morning, you were singing a different tune."

Gray Wolf shrugged. "Things change—like Leo says. I guess I knew what the answer was all along; I just didn't want to admit it."

Parking his pickup in a visitor's slot, Daniel and Freeman Togweiler walked toward the sterile glass and brick federal building. Even without the benefit of the prominent brass lettering on its side, the office structure screamed 'caution—government employees inside' Entering the federally approved seventy-six degree interior, Gray Wolf followed the agent through the maze of white corridors. Their footsteps muted by uniform beige carpet, the men traversed the network of hallways in relative silence.

Freeman Togweiler pushed through a heavy wooden door ladened with opaque glass. Inside, half a dozen agents, most still in suit coats, bustled throughout an ongoing labyrinth of corridors. No one lounged near the water cooler; no idle chatter flowed. This was a place of business as only the government could run it. Two pictures graced the otherwise barren walls of what Gray Wolf half-heartedly guessed was the reception area. The current Director of the Federal Bureau of Investigation, Miles Stedman, hawkishly glared at agent and Indian from his perch on the far wall. Daniel found only slightly more warmth in the second picture of the classic Iwo Jima flag raising ceremony.

"Nice digs."

Togweiler smiled. "It's home. Come in the back with me."

Again, Gray Wolf followed the agent into the hallway puzzle. The interior offices glowed with slightly better light, reflective compliments of hidden windows somewhere deep within the recesses. Just when Daniel figured they had about walked to his home in Rapid Valley, Togweiler stepped into a basically empty office.

"This is my space," the agent said, no gestures, no apologies. "Make yourself comfortable."

Not wanting to sit on the only visible chair—Togweiler's desk chair—Gray Wolf leaned against the wall near the window.

"So, Butch—er—Freeman, how'd you rate the executive suite?"

Togweiler smiled, a friendly warning leer. "Glad you corrected yourself. I'd hate to have to eliminate you before we're done with the questioning. By the way, seniority got me the window seat and, believe it or not, more furniture's due any day. GSA warehouse backorder. You know the routine."

It suddenly occurred to Gray Wolf how ludicrous all this sounded. Guilty conscience slammed into him like a two hundred fifty pound linebacker. Serious now, he asked. "Freeman, is it normal to be kidding around when a little girl's life is at stake? I mean, here we are chitchatting about this and that and Christine Hardesty's still missing. Shit!"

"I'm not a shrink, Daniel, but I can tell you this much," Togweiler said. "What we're doing is a defense mechanism. If I carried the pain of each victim, I'd have been dead, or at least medically retired, fifteen years ago.

"Neither of us has forgotten about the little girl," he continued. "We're just at a point in time where we can't do anything to help her. Kidding around relieves some of the pressure so we don't go bonkers thinking about the bad things people do to each other."

A sharp rap on the doorframe exorcised the maudlin monsters from the room. Forensics expert Bob Talmedge poked his head around the corner.

"I'll have some lab results back by the end of the day."

"You have any preliminary guesses, Bob?"

Talmedge eyed Gray Wolf, uncomfortable with divulging Bureau information in front of non-Bureau personnel.

Togweiler said, "It's okay. Daniel's going to be helping us on this."

The forensics agent's open face displayed genuine pleasure. "Hey, that's great news! I hope we'll get a chance to talk about things ... you know ... "

"I'm sure we'll be talking, Agent Talmedge. With all your studies, you might teach me a few things."

Talmedge blushed with pleasure. "I doubt it, but it'll be a real kick getting to visit with you, Mr. Gray Wolf."

"Call me Daniel, please."

"Are you two done with this mutual admiration stuff?" Togweiler asked. "We've got to get Brudzinski in here to do up a sketch of Mr. Steven Abrams."

"Cool your heels, **Butch**," Talmedge said with obvious relish. "Joe Brudzinski's just down the hall waiting for your call. And, no, we don't have a preliminary yet."

"Would you be so kind—Almost-Agent Talmedge—as to ask Agent Brudzinski to join us? With all that judicial background, I believe you can persuade him to walk the extra mile here. Thanks, and good-bye."

Smug smile still pasted across his face, Bob Talmedge half saluted before sauntering down the corridor. Togweiler wheeled around in his chair until he faced Gray Wolf.

"Bob's the only guy I let get away with the nickname bit. He knows if I put out a contract on him, the Bureau would be up the creek."

Daniel could only smile, caught up in the wondrous normalcy this field office portrayed. *Hell, these guys let their hair down just like everybody else. I haven't seen one guy do an Efram Zimbalist Junior impression yet.*

Gray Wolf registered these thoughts a moment too soon. Three distinct knocks on the doorway frame pulled his attention to the Efram Zimbalist clone outlined against the door opening.

"Agent Togweiler, is this the gentleman I'm to speak with?" Zimbalist asked, brandishing a large sketchpad at port arms.

"Ah, Agent Brudzinski," Freeman purred. "Yes, this is Daniel Gray Wolf."

Daniel extended his hand and received a nod and cursory 'Mr. Gray Wolf' in return.

"I have another composite scheduled in one hour,"

Brudzinski said. "We should begin as quickly as possible to avoid any conflict."

All right! This is the FBI we know and love. "I'm ready if you are, sir."

Gray Wolf followed Brudzinski back into the federally constructed maze, losing track of his location almost immediately. *Helluva testimony to my heritage as a great tracker. I piss old Efram Zimbalist off and he walks away, I'll starve to death in this sheetrock forest.*

Brudzinski's perpetually present sketchpad was not needed. Following Gray Wolf's detailed instructions, the agent developed an uncanny likeness of Steve Abrams on the Bureau composite computer.

"Yep, that's him. That's Abrams. I'm impressed, sir."

Nonplused by the unexpected praise, Brudzinski responded in true bureaucratic form. He praised the computer. "We've got over one thousand distinct hairstyles, eye sets, mouths, glasses, etcetera, in this machine. The combinations are limitless. It's typically a matter of elimination."

Daniel pushed for a human response. "So, what's next? Do you fax this to your field agents?"

"I'm not at liberty to divulge that information," Zimbalist/Brudzinski replied. "Now, if you're sure this is a reasonable likeness, I'll direct you back to Agent Togweiler."

Mild claustrophobia tickled Gray Wolf. "Any chance you can lead me back? I know you're on a tight schedule, but I'd hate to wander these halls until the first snow."

Brudzinski either chose to ignore, or didn't recognize, the humor. He checked his watch, mentally calculating how many seconds his timetable would be altered by leading this feckless Indian back to the smart ass Togweiler.

"Follow me," Agent Joseph Brudzinski sighed. Having to

mingle with civilians was bad enough; baby-sitting them and wiping their noses was not part of the job description.

"Thank you," Gray Wolf called after the retreating sketch artist, having been safely deposited back in Togweiler's presence. Turning his attention to the field agent, he asked, "What's next?"

"I guess we wait for the next ransom note. Abrams' picture is being faxed to all the field offices, along with a description of his car.

"That is ... unless you intend to get involved further," Togweiler added, more or less as a planned afterthought.

"Yeah," Gray Wolf nodded soberly. "I was afraid you were going to mention that. You have any ideas?"

Butch shook his head. "You're the Dream Catcher. You know, I wouldn't admit this in public, but this Abrams guy has me—us—stumped. Could be his mental instability, or genius; who knows. That's one reason why I decided to kind of pal around with you this morning after we discerned you weren't the kidnapper."

Daniel didn't figure the words had been said to hurt him. He knew Togweiler was a serious federal cop, conducting a serious federal investigation. Old Butch was using any available resource. He just happened to find a budding kinship with a former suspect.

"Okay, I know what I have to do," Gray Wolf said reluctantly. "But, I need to do it my way, in a controlled environment. This dreaming thing with Abrams has presented me with some real health hazards, not to mention scaring the bejeezus out of me."

"We'll accommodate any way we can, Daniel. I need to be present—at the very least—have Talmedge there as a Bureau representative."

Gray Wolf thought for a moment. "I guess the size of the

crowd isn't important. Hell, I might even feel safer surrounded by the FBI. *Like, they're going to be able to subpoena the fucking dogs once I put their heads back on.*

"Can I make a couple of calls now? I need to let work know where I am. Then I want to call my newest best friend to hold my hand while I bring back the dogs." *Yeah, dazzle them with humor. Pretty bold talk for a brave shaking in his moccasins, kola. Macho shit so don't let 'em see you pee in your pants.*

Gray Wolf called Dakota Steel, letting his mildly concerned boss know everything was all right. He couldn't think of a plausible lie so he told the truth which, after hanging up, sounded like a pretty farfetched lie anyway. *Oh well, I've got vacation time coming; can't take that from me.*

His second phone call, to Edwin Nagel's office, made connection. Two rings, followed by a professionally bored receptionist's voice. "Doctor Nagel's office."

Don't be there, Edwin. "Is Doctor Nagel in?" *C'mon, be out on the golf course ... damn, it's only Monday.*

Miss Bored asked, "Whom may I say is calling?"

"This is Daniel Gray Wolf. Listen, if the doctor's busy -"

A muted ring interrupted Gray Wolf as he was connected with the inner sanctum. Edwin's manicured voice answered. "Doctor Nagel."

"What has eight legs, no heads, and scares the piss out of Indians and kidnappers?"

"Who the ... " Nagel sputtered before recognizing the voice. "Gray Wolf? Where the hell are you and what the hell does that mean?"

"Oh, I'm at the Federal Building chatting with an Agent Togweiler," Daniel responded with a lot more gaiety than he felt. More subdued, he added, "What it means is I need to get back into the kidnapper's dream and I'd appreciate your help again."

CHAPTER 20

Y ou know, I should insist on you not going through with this," Edwin Nagel said. "Or, I could refuse to aid in this lunatic plan."

Introductions had been made. Freeman Togweiler and Bob Talmedge now listened intently as they sat against the back wall of Nagel's office.

"I almost wish you would," Daniel said. "I'm not exactly looking forward to going back into that world. But, that's why I'm here. If you can think of a better way to drum out Abrams, I'd really appreciate hearing it."

Nagel couldn't, but felt compelled to offer a professional resistance. "Daniel, it was only yesterday you had such a horrible episode. You're not ready. Hell, I can still see the physical signs of your last encounter. What happens if you experience another hysterical conversion reaction?"

"Excuse me," Togweiler said from his vantage point. "What's this hysterical conversion reaction you're speaking of?"

"Physical manifestations resulting from a subconscious, or dream, activity," Nagel answered.

"I got shredded pretty bad by the dream dogs. Scratches, ripped clothes, that kind of stuff," Gray Wolf added with feigned nonchalance.

"How dangerous is this manifestation, Doctor?" Togweiler persisted.

"Please realize study on the subject is incomplete because of the rarity of its occurrence. Significantly more data is needed to ... "

"Ballpark guess, Doctor." Togweiler didn't want to hear the full-blown case history.

Nagel looked at Gray Wolf, gauging his reply based on what he saw in the Indian's eyes. Getting no hint from Daniel's down turned gaze, he said, "In rare instances, it could prove fatal. These are rare instances, mind you. Typically, the victim wakes out of his trance before permanent harm is rendered. Permanent physical harm, that is.

"Dammit, Gray Wolf," the psychiatrist added quickly, "this is why I want you to hold off. A child's life is already in danger. I'd hate to unnecessarily expose another person to risk."

"See, Edwin," Daniel said resolutely. "That's just the reason why I have to go back in. Odds are in my favor I'll only be scared shitless again. Maybe get scratched a little. I'd venture to say Christine's odds are worse than mine right now."

Bob Talmedge, silent until now, offered a startling suggestion. "Daniel, you know I've studied a little about this phenomenon. Legend speaks of the old Dream Catchers having the ability to shape shift. Heck, it's farfetched. But, I mean, every creature is afraid of something. What would happen if you entered the dream as a bigger, meaner animal than these two hell hounds?"

"Shit, Talmedge!" Freeman Togweiler said through gritted teeth. "Don't go muddying the waters here. Gray Wolf's got enough on his mind about resurrecting two dead dogs. He doesn't need any other crap to worry abou -"

"Wait a minute!" Daniel's eyes lit up. "What did you just say?"

Somewhat taken back, Togweiler repeated, "I said something about -"

"No! No, not you. Agent Talmedge—Bob—what did you say? Something to do with being bigger and badder. Like shape shifting."

Gray Wolf jumped up from his seat and strode toward the startled agents. "This may not be as tough as I thought. I killed the dogs last time around." Unconsciously rubbing his birthmark as he speculated, the Dream Catcher continued. "That means I either have to re-animate them ... or emulate them ... become one of them. Maybe, just maybe, this will work.

Turning toward Edwin Nagel, Gray Wolf said, "When I visited your dream, you were prepared. You set up mirages of yourself, roadblocks, obstacles, stuff I wasn't suppose to get through. How'd you do that?"

Nagel leaned back in his chair, an exasperated look on his face. "Daniel, I've had years of training in the control of dreams. I don't think a crash course is going to–"

"Edwin, I've had just as many years controlling dreams as you, only it's been inside someone else's head. I always entered as Daniel Gray Wolf. It's always been spur of the moment ... making up defenses to suit the problem as I see it.

"Now, how do I set up my own dream?" Daniel added, sitting back down beside the psychiatrist.

CHAPTER 21

Steve Abrams low crawled through the last few yards of pitch-black tunnel, his path illuminated only by a two-cell flashlight threatening to go on strike at any moment.

"Better. Yes, this is a much better place than the Badlands," he said, feeling the protective closeness of limestone scraping his back as he tried to straighten up.

Abrams had found Brooks Cave by accident. After hurriedly exhuming the live-but-terrified Christine Hardesty, he had instinctively driven toward the Black Hills. The tree-clotted mountain range offered countless places to hide his living paycheck. Lightly populated, the northeast edge of the hills housed no tourist traps, held no heavy traffic paths. ·

His original panicky intention was to gag the young girl and tie her to a tree, somewhere half way up a mountainside. But the gods of abduction had showed him an alternative, a much safer haven. Thirty feet up the chosen bluff, Abrams spotted a small hole. Nearly concealed by scrub brush and low-lying pine, the two-foot square cavity had proved invisible from ground level.

Pushing Christine Hardesty ahead of him, Abrams slipped into the confining entrance. One hundred restricted yards inside the mountain, the tunnel widened. Steve crawled up beside the shivering girl, extremely conscious of the erection he now owned thanks to the constant rubbing against the rock floor. Again, thoughts of forcing himself on the girl had passed through his mind.

"Not yet—not yet," he breathed into Christine's hair. "Patience now. We'll dance the nasty later."

Abrams splayed the dim flashlight beam around the cave's interior. A craggy, semi-circular room greeted him through the faltering pallid glow. Saw-toothed peaks of limestone grinned from across the room. Shuffling forward on the uneven surface, Steve kicked up pebbles as his toe stubbed into an obstruction.

"Shit!" he yelled, bending to rub his injured foot. Once again, karma smiled on the wicked. Looking down into the murky darkness where his shoe should be, Abrams saw nothing but black, heard nothing but the distant ricochet of stones bouncing off unseen walls far below him.

"Wow, what a fucking hole!" Excited by the near fatal step, a thrill of danger tingled through his body, centering in his already hard groin area. "Hey, this is a great hideout, kid. Wonder how many bodies are at the bottom of this pit?"

Carefully stepping backward, Steve wheeled toward the young girl. "I said, I wonder how many bodies are at the bottom of this pit. Maybe we should find out. Do you wanna join the skeletons down there?"

Christine sobbed, "Please, mister. I want my mom and dad. Please let me go home. Daddy will do whatever you say. Please!"

Abrams leaned down, shining the dull light into the child's eyes. "Aw, there there. Aren't we having fun yet?"

Christine buried her face in her hands. Pitiful snuffles escaped between her clasped palms.

"Stop your fucking crying right now," Abrams whispered, his voice menacing in its softness. "Stop whining or I'll toss you down the fucking hole where the skeletons will get you.

"Now put your hands behind your back. C'mon, I don't have all goddamned day. Do as I say and the bony monsters won't get you. Fuck with me and you become skull bait, you understand what I say? Hands behind the back. Now!"

Abrams looped nylon cord around the child's compliant wrists, cinching the knot unmercifully tight. Pulling her legs up, he bonded wrists behind ankles. Grunting with the exertion, Steve shoved Christine Hardesty into a sitting position.

"I'm going back outside now, so you're going to be in the dark. Move and you'll fall in the hole. And we know what's down there, don't we? Don't even think about trying to sneak through the tunnel because I'll be right outside. I see your shitty little head poke out and I'll personally chuck you to the skeletons. Got it?"

Without looking back at his prize, Abrams hunkered down and entered the narrow outlet.

CHAPTER 22

"You have to figure Abrams won't show back up at his apartment after he's stashed the girl," Freeman Togweiler said. "Fact is, he'll probably hole up somewhere in a motel. How close do you have to be to him for the dream to be effective?"

"I don't know," Gray Wolf responded. "When I set the dogs loose the first time, I was seven, maybe eight, miles away.

"Oh, shit!"

"What? What's the matter now?" Nagel asked with some concern.

"This isn't going to work."

"Why won't it work, Daniel?" Togweiler asked.

Gray Wolf sighed, a heavy exhalation of defeat. "Even if I could turn myself into ... into something other than Daniel Gray Wolf, I don't have a dream to hook up with. I mean, when I let Abrams' nightmare dogs loose, they were his to start with so they found him again. If I go in and conjure myself into some kind of Frankenstein dog, how do I hook up with Abrams? How do I know he's sleeping?

"No, there's only one way around it," Gray Wolf said. "I've got to set Stevie's own freaking dogs on him again."

Edwin Nagel slumped in his chair. "So, we're right back where we started. Should I warn you once more about the danger you're placing yourself in, or do you remember having this conversation a few minutes ago?"

"Screw you, Edwin," Daniel said conversationally. "You're not making this any easier. I need your help, not a prognosis."

Nagel pursed his fingers, placing them against his lips as this thoughts deepened. "How did you dispose of these nightmare dogs?"

Gray Wolf closed his eyes and vividly recalled the means of demise. "I chopped one's head off; the other got a machete stuck in its chest. Is that going to pose a problem?"

"How the hell should I know." Edwin Nagel shrugged his shoulders. "I've never pieced a metaphysical dream creature back together again. I only asked because if you had obliterated the beasts, say with a bomb, reassembly may be impossible."

"No, they're basically intact." Gray Wolf leaned closer to the psychiatrist. "Edwin, you're going to have to let me in on some of your dream tricks. Between us we should be able to figure this thing out. Christ, we have to!"

Nagel studied the Dream Catcher's face for a long time before looking toward the agents. "Gentlemen, would you excuse Mr. Gray Wolf and me? Doctor patient privilege here. Nothing personal, but I've worked with the Bureau before. What I have to say is strictly between Daniel and me.

"Margaret will pour you some coffee while you wait in the lobby," Nagel added, dismissing the two agents.

Turning back to Gray Wolf, Edwin said, "Now, Daniel, are you positive you want this journey to begin? I can't swear what I tell you will work. I won't guarantee your safety. It is truly your decision, my new friend."

"Just stick around to pull me out if you see things aren't going my way," Daniel said, meeting Nagel's eyes.

Nagel sighed. "As I said … no guarantees."

CHAPTER 23

"Thank you for letting us back in, Doctor," Freeman Togweiler whispered. Carefully, he and Bob Talmedge sat in their original seats, both staring at Gray Wolf's supine form.

"Daniel's asleep now," Nagel said in a low voice. "He requested you be allowed to watch the proceedings. I was reluctant at first, but one thing changed my mind."

"What was that?" Talmedge asked.

The psychiatrist stared at both agents as if judging what their reaction would be to what he was about to say. "I want witnesses in the event something happens to Daniel."

"But, this is only a dream he'll be going through," Togweiler protested. "What the hell could happen to him?"

"Gentlemen, please. Just keep your eyes on him. Don't ask any questions, only be ready to help me wake him if necessary. Please!"

Nagel's words pounded into the dimensionally trained agents. They shared a look, each seeing puzzlement and concern on the other's face. What could go wrong? How could a man be physically challenged by a dream?

"He's started," Nagel said.

***

The street scene was as he remembered it; damp, with bad lighting courtesy of a distant street lamp. The silent, blackened alley beckoned from the left. His alley. The dogs' alley.

"Just follow the doctor's orders, *kola*," Gray Wolf muttered to himself as he produced a flashlight.

He cautiously directed the beam of light around the darkened corner. Reflected in the illumination was the dumpster, an unbecoming hulk of black-green steel. At its base lay two indefinable lumps. He knew closer inspection would turn the lumps into dog beasts.

Heart stuttering, Daniel crept toward the still forms. *Easy now. Stevie's dogs may be dead, but this is **my** dream. Anything can happen in a dream.*

Veils of mist threaded toward him, then nonchalantly drifted aside, only to form again behind him. Swirling, touching, cold tendrils of fantasy fog weaved a vaporous connection between the Dream Catcher and the yet-silent creatures. *Was the fog here before? Is this something new I added to spice up the dream a little?*

Three incredibly brief strides brought him in contact with the dumpster. Chilled metal slid against Gray Wolf's side as he edged toward the front of the bin.

"Don't wake up. Please don't wake up!" Daniel whispered a silent plea to the misshaped piles of fur.

All right, kola. Time to protect yourself here. Do like the good doctor said and conjure up some armor.

As quick as his thoughts, Gray Wolf's arms became clad in dog training pads. Thick rolls of cotton-stuffed canvas circled his arms, chest and groin area. *All right! Uptown stuff. Okay, which one first?*

Comforted by the protective coat, the Dream Catcher chanced a few seconds to mull out his options. *I snug that bastard's head against his body over there and I'll have a whole dog. Or, do I pull the knife from this one's chest first? Which way gives me the most time?* Acting on instinct, Gray Wolf reached down and tugged at the machete buried in the closest beast's chest. At first, the blade held firm, embedded deep in a solid fusion of thorax muscle and ribs. Planting a foot on the oversized mastiff, he pulled harder. An inch of blood-covered blade slid free. Dull red sparked into the beast's eyes; a weak growl emanated from its yawing mouth. *Oh, shit! That was quick!* He yanked the handle and was rewarded with a grating, wet, sucking sound as the machete freed itself.

The beast stirred, a louder and more menacing growl accompanying its erratic movement.

Daniel hurriedly stepped over the writhing form, then reached for the severed head of the other creature. Grabbing at the short floppy ears, he lifted the second monster dog's impossibly heavy head and leaned forward to set the horrible skull in place against the bristled torso.

Two hundred and fifty pounds of reborn fury drove into Gray Wolf's back. Pinned beneath the beast's massive body, he heard the sounds of canvas, then flesh, being torn apart. Gouts of red-hot pain flashed into his eyes. *Noo! Oh God, my legs! Wake up wake up wake up –*

"Grab him. Quick goddammit, get him!" A stream of frenzied words, seeming to pour from the attacking Mastiff, pounded into the Dream Catcher's pain-dimmed mind. Numbly, he clasped the other creature's head to his chest.

No … not the dog talking! A voice was trying to draw him from the nightmare. Nagel's voice. Gray Wolf reached for the sound, grasped at the words. Tried to drag himself back to reality. Tried to escape.

Fresh waves of pain hammered Daniel as the creature renewed its violation of his body. Slavering jaws pulled him back. Too powerful, too big. So much pain.

Seconds before blackness swallowed him, before he let his

spirit slip from its ravaged host, *Ihanbla Gmunka* pushed the severed head against its waiting body. *This is for you, Stevie. Eat shit and die* .

CHAPTER 24

"You are a brave man, my son."

"Leo?"

No other words emanated from the white mist.

"Leo? *Tunkasila*, is that you?"

Gray Wolf pushed himself upright, wincing in anticipation of the pain he knew would assault him. Yet, there was no pain. Not in his legs, not even the familiar headache that always formed.

"*Tunkasila*, where are you?" Daniel whirled in the liquid cloud, searching for the owner of those comforting words.

"Feel the happiness, *Ihanbla Gmunka*. You are the chosen." The voice was directly behind him.

"Leo? C'mon, this isn't funny. I just had one mean fight in the dream world. Even thought I lost for a minute. Leo? Red Hawk, goddammit, quit messing with me. I'm tired, I think I'm hurt and -"

"Leo is not here, my son."

Gray Wolf pivoted in the direction of the voice. "Then, who is this? Where is this?"

"I am your guide."

"Woniya?" Daniel squinted into the brilliant haze. "Where are you? Why can't I see you?"

"It is not yet time to see me. Your grandfather has asked me to watch over you. I am to protect you."

"Am I dead? Is this what the Other Plain looks like?"

"I have done as your grandfather asked. The Other Plain waits for you but only when it is your time. There is much work to be done before you can join your fathers. *Ihanbla Gmunka*, your path is chosen. You must journey this path always with care. Look for the signs. There will always be signs."

"But ... "

"You must now go, Dream Catcher. Your work is not finished."

"Wait! Woniya, my spirit guide. Tell me what is expected of me."

"Daniel!"

"Woniya! What am I to -"

"Gray Wolf, wake up, for chrissakes!"

Daniel opened his eyes. Three concerned, and very frightened, faces stared into his. Three mouths moved in perfect unison.

"He's coming around. I think he's ... "

" ... must check his vitals. This is so unbeliev ... "

" ... how the fuck do we stop the bleeding?"

Cottony clouds of well being skittered away as a gale of pain struck Gray Wolf full force.

"Oh shit! I hurt ... I really hurt!"

CHAPTER 25

I don't believe there's any muscle damage, Daniel. At least, not permanent damage." Edwin Nagel's prognosis was meant to comfort.

Daniel sipped at the heavily laced coffee, then leaned back on the couch. As much as the psychiatrist tried to soothe him, each word about his physical condition drove another pain spike into his damaged legs.

" The lacerations are deep enough to require stitches, but I -"

"Edwin, with all due respect, please shut the fuck up." Muted conversations ceased as Daniel tiredly issued his order.

Usually stolid Agents Togweiler and Talmedge shared a look of concern. And a tinge of fear. Talmedge broke the silence first.

"Christ, Daniel, where the hell were you? First, these marks start showing up on your legs and you're flopping around on the couch like a ... like a ... I don't know. The next thing we know, you just kind of curl up almost like you're dead."

Togweiler added analytically, "Doctor Nagel couldn't find a pulse. Figured you were in some sort of arrest."

Unperturbed by the Dream Catcher's earlier outburst, Nagel said, "Daniel, we need to talk this out. You've just experienced a horrible trauma; possibly more dramatic than even a similar real life encounter. And, Agent Togweiler's correct. For a moment, I believed you were dead."

"I was, kinda sorta," Gray Wolf answered, looking at the pale doctor. "Look, I'm sorry for what I said. See, just for a minute I didn't need to be reminded about what happened to my legs. I feel a little better now. Legs hurt like hell, but I'm back in control."

Bob Talmedge persisted. "Maybe you can tell us what happened now. You bear some pretty vivid evidence that you encountered the dogs again. But I still want to know where the heck you went afterward."

Gray Wolf looked at the agent, gauging what to say. The truth sounded a little outlandish at the moment.

"Oh, I paid a visit to Woniya. You know, my spirit guide? Never saw him, but we chatted for a while. I think he's the one that pulled me out of the dream."

"We tried like a sonofagun," Togweiler said almost apologetically. "But, you wouldn't release."

"Doctor Nagel, Freeman, me ... we were all shaking you and slapping your face trying to bring you out," Bob Talmedge explained.

Gray Wolf smiled at his inquisitors. "Yeah, I heard you in there. Looks like my guide beat you to the punch."

The men sat in their tight little concerned grouping, three of them silently coaxing the fourth to continue his story. Daniel took another sip of his brandied coffee. He stared down at the bloodied gauze circling his legs.

Heaving a sigh, Gray Wolf added. "I followed your directions, Edwin. Followed them up to the point when that first mean sonofabitch started eating me. No doubt in my mind he's intact. The second bastard? Well, I think I finished the job, although I was kinda busy trying to survive as I reattached his head. Might have put it on a little crooked. Shit, that'll just make him all the uglier when Abrams meets him again tonight."

Bob Talmedge was enthralled by the Dream Catcher's story. All his research, all the studying on Lakota culture, couldn't top the spiritual history lesson he was receiving here in Doctor Nagel's office. "I've got to know. When you ... you know ... kind of conked out on us. Did you go to the Other Plain? What's it like over there?"

Gray Wolf smiled at the inquisitive agent, knowing Talmedge's questions weren't just for morbid curiosity's sake. "I've got good news and bad news, Bob. The good news is I think I was just on the edge of entering the Other Plain. A heavy, white mist surrounded me. I spoke with Woniya but he wouldn't let me see him. Man, it was really peaceful there what with no cares, no worries, and no pain. But, I couldn't go any further. Woniya told me it wasn't my time. Told me I had to leave."

Togweiler asked the obvious. "So, what's the bad news?"

"There are no white men in heaven," Gray Wolf intoned. "Only red men."

Five extra long and dead silent seconds ticked by on the Sony wall clock, before Daniel broke the silence.

"Just shitting you. It seems you guys apparently haven't been listening very good," Daniel replied, eyeing the three men. "It was bad news for me. Woniya told me I **had** to leave. I **had** to leave that peaceful place and come back into this shithole called reality because my job isn't done."

"The important thing is you succeeded," Nagel summarized. "The dogs are intact, at least one of them is. If Abrams is as fearful as you say, he could well contact you."

Freeman Togweiler asked the question the others were afraid to voice. "Abrams knows we're on to him. He's moved the girl and will undoubtedly be on the alert. What happens next if he doesn't call Daniel?"

Nagel thought only for a moment before responding. "This man appears to be deeply psychotic, yet he still can separate reality from fantasy. Strange as it may sound to you—hell, it sounds strange to me—these dream dogs are a very real physical threat to Steve Abrams. I strongly believe he won't be able to face them without Daniel's help."

"Look what those dogs did to Daniel here," Talmedge said, nodding his head toward the Dream Catcher's bandaged legs. "When Abrams hits the sack tonight, what if he can't wake up in time? What happens if the dogs win?"

Gray Wolf answered for the doctor. "Then we have a dead kidnapper and a dead little girl. But that's not going to happen. I have to believe Abrams will wake himself. He may get chewed up—and I hope the little turd does—but he **will** wake up."

"I think we need to get you home," Togweiler said to Gray Wolf, "just in case our friend decides to take a nap. Our guys will finish tapping into your phone line and -"

"Finish tapping? Someone's messing with my phone?"

Unflustered, Togweiler continued. "You were a suspect until late this morning, remember? Standard procedure, you know. Anyhow, once my boys are finished, we'll be able to trace Abrams' call. It'll give us an idea which way he headed after leaving the Badlands."

Gray Wolf stared hard at the federal agent. "I'll be pissed at you later, Butch. But, right now I agree with you. Can one of your suits give me a ride home? I don't think I'm in much shape to be driving right now."

"*Touché*, asshole," Butch Togweiler replied.

Edwin Nagel wasn't ready to release his new patient yet. "First, we have to take care of those lacerations. They need to be irrigated and sutured. You'll need a tetanus shot at the very least and I'm very seriously leaning toward starting you on a hydrophobia vaccination series."

"Uh uh. No way with the shots in the stomach! I'll agree to the other stuff, but you can just forget about the rabies treatment. I'll take my chances, okay? Problem is, where do we find a doctor on Sunday, especially one that makes house calls?"

Nagel pursed his already thin lips. "You forget I'm also a medical doctor. I'd prefer to treat your wounds here or in a clinic, but I understand the immediacy of the situation." The psychiatrist stood up then walked to the far wall. Unlocking a glassed cabinet, he rummaged through the bottled contents as he muttered, "Who the hell would've thought I'd be making house calls ... on Sunday, no less!"

***

Gray Wolf leaned back into the familiar curves of his sofa. Edwin Nagel had performed an admirable piece of impromptu surgery, stitching the worst of Daniel's gashes. His legs still hurt, but the pain was more bearable because he was on home turf with three stiff brandies under his belt.

Togweiler and Talmedge kept busy with their own brand of surgery. In a matter of forty minutes, state-of-the-art listening devices had been connected to Daniel's phone lines. Any incoming call would now be traced in just a few seconds.

Daniel grew restless watching the constant bustle of FBI throughout his house. Though the feds were fastidious in their work, the Dream Catcher frequently glanced around, searching for anything out of place. It had to be the slight feeling of invasion, not being in total control of his own territory.

"You guys about done?" Daniel groused for the third time. "Hell, I could've had this stuff slapped together half an hour ago."

"We appreciate your patience, Mr. Gray Wolf," answered a stereotype federal technician. "Just a couple of more minutes and we're out of your hair."

"Some of my stuff is going to get busted the way you're whipping around. Hey, watch out for that doily; that was my gramma's."

Togweiler magically appeared, towering over the reclining Gray Wolf. "If I was more familiar with you, I'd chew your ass for being a cantankerous fart. But, in deference to your war wounds, I'll just conversationally say 'lay off', okay? These boys know what they're doing and they sure as hell won't hurt Gramma's doilies. Besides, anything gets broken, the Bureau will reimburse you for it."

"Kinda hard to replace a family heirloom," Gray Wolf grumbled under his breath.

"Kinda hard to bust a doily by running a rubber-coated wire over the top of it," Togweiler countered.

"This crap going to work? Hell, Freeman, you got three tons of wire strung inside my house. We could shoot all of Rapid's phone business through here."

Togweiler sighed, a very human sound for a normally stalwart federal man. "You're beginning to tax me, boy. If you'd ever get the jaundice out of your eyes you'd see there are exactly seven cables. Compared to that spider web of wire you have running behind your TV, connecting VCR to stereo to your set, this rig out here is small potatoes.

"Now just let the guys take care of things, okay?" The agent walked away before Gray Wolf could retort, busy in his last minute preparations.

"Okay, Central, give it a try." Stereotyped Agent Technician Number One spoke into the mouthpiece of his high tech headset.

The jingling of the telephone interrupted Daniel's funk. Automatically he reached for the handset.

"Don't answer that!" Number One commanded, then finished in a milder tone. "That's headquarters calling in a scrambled number for a test."

Two more rings and the technician spoke into his mouthpiece again for only a few seconds "Got it, Central. 2131 West Chicago Street. Okay, we're set."

"I thought you guys were just downtown. What do you have over on West Chicago, a safe house?" Gray Wolf's curiosity overcame his grumpiness.

Togweiler answered for the technician. "Nothing over on West Chicago. State-of-the-art equipment here and downtown. This interceptor picks up the incoming call and traces it to its origin in a matter of seconds."

"Ma Bell offers me the same thing and hides the wires. Caller ID, I believe is the name?"

"You're absolutely right, Mr. Electrical Engineer, but Ma Bell would charge you about a four hundred thousand dollars to give you what we set up here at government expense. All the phone company can give you is a readout of the phone number, maybe the party's name unless they have it blocked. This little baby analyzes where the call originated, performs a voice analysis, and spits out the data in a little over fifteen seconds."

"Headquarters emulates a call from a randomly picked number," Number One added. "South Dakota's easy because it's all one area code. Somebody calls from a different area code, we slow down to about twenty-five seconds' interpretation time."

"We figure Abrams is still within the state," Togweiler continued. "Let the phone ring three times, max, and we've got the caller's location pegged. If you answer too much quicker than that, you might make him suspicious anyway. Then you converse with him nice and easy so we can analyze his voice—make sure it's the kidnapper. Again, nice and easy so we don't spook him by you appearing over eager."

Lulled by the convincing explanations, Daniel looked about the room again. Instead of the chaos he imagined earlier, he now saw cohesive teamwork. Three agents in his house, combined with however many working the detail from the Federal Building, gave him a scope of the effort being expended to find Christine Hardesty.

"So, now we wait?"

"We wait, and hope Abrams gets scared enough to call you." Togweiler replied.

Edwin Nagel had remained backstage as the bureau specialists laid their wire. Now that their job was done, he stepped forward. The onus was back on Gray Wolf, a demand for the Dream Catcher to perform once again at what he did best. Nagel wanted assurance his new ally was up to the task.

"When Abrams calls, don't act surprised. Don't play dumb either. Remember, he knows you know.

"He'll be upset, agitated, and above all, suspicious," Nagel continued. "In his particular psychotic state, Abrams will be reaching for assurance, yet he probably won't want you near him. The Hardesty girl is undoubtedly not with him. She's hidden somewhere equally devious as the first site."

Gray Wolf stared at his injured leg, a dull but constant reminder of Abrams' innermost terrors. "How do I respond to the guy? He needs me but he won't want to see me. He's scared shitless, yet he's going to doubt everything I say. Just what do I say?" Nagel paced away from the Dream Catcher. He'd developed several theories over the past few hours, analyzed them, then trashed each approach as he found voids. A second-hand diagnosis based on this Indian guy's mystical ability to sneak into other people's dreams. Besides, Nagel had never had direct contact with the afflicted person. How do you handle a mentally ill person long distance? A little girl's life was at stake. It was time to decide.

"You need to make Abrams aware you are his savior ... or his executioner. He needs to be told you control what happens to him. You have to tell him the truth."

Freeman Togweiler had been listening to the interchange, trying to conjure up a comparable experience from his long list of supervising abduction cases. "Dr. Nagel, I have serious doubts about Abrams' ability to understand, let alone believe, what Daniel' going to say. It's been my experience that -"

"Agent Togweiler," Nagel suspended the bureau rep with an icy voice. "Let's just say I have much more experience in dealing with mental instability than you. Therefore, let's assume, if the Bureau is willing to listen, that I just may know what the hell I'm talking about."

Quieted, but unperturbed, Freeman Togweiler nodded slowly.

Turning back to Gray Wolf, Nagel continued, "Remember one thing, Daniel. Steven Abrams is a criminal, but I believe he is criminally insane. This means he is not necessarily in full control of his faculties. He must be handled quite delicately. You can't bully him, but you have to let him know you're in control of the situation. Too strong, and you anger him or make him more afraid. I trust your many years of dealing with people will allow you the proper mixture."

Gray Wolf answered the question on everyone's mind. "I've got to do it right, or Christine's dead."

CHAPTER 26

Sleep. Steve Abrams needed sleep more than he needed the million dollars that would soon be his. He'd had only snatches of slumber since being forced to move the Hardesty brat from a perfectly good hiding place.

"Got too cute, Gray Wolf. All this bullshit about only being able to stay in my nightmare. Injun speak with forked tongue. How much of the other stuff was lies, huh motherfucker?"

Abrams knew for a fact the Dream Catcher screwed up big time. Despite his deteriorating mental condition, he knew Gray Wolf had killed the dogs this last time. Watched him kill the fucking dogs. They wouldn't be back.

"And now, you're just a bad dream, asshole red man."

Abrams stretched, then assumed his favorite reclining position. Hands folded across his chest, the kidnapper started his slide into oblivion.

"Hope I dream about that broad with the flabby tits again. Man, what I could do to her with my … "

Slumber found the contented man, gently folded him in her nether arms and lifted him to the place of dreams.

Abrams glided from light into a dark void. So dark, he couldn't see his hands or feet. *Yeah, this is where the chick comes in!*

Anticipating a light caress from the flitting, Romanesque lady of his desires, Steve reached out into the blackness.

His hands touched something, but it wasn't the clay-like consistency of his dream girl. It was bristly soft, damp, and the light contact rewarded him with a deep-throated growl.

Oh shit! Shitshitshit.

Knife-like teeth grabbed his fingers, closed on them with horrible strength. And then Steve saw.

You're dead. You're fucking dead! Yet, attached to his arm was one of the devil dogs, red eyes glinting with a horrid expectation. *Nooooooooo!*

Abrams frantically tore his hand from the beast's mouth. Shredded skin pulled down the length of his fingers; hung in tatters from the grinning jowls of the Mastiff creature. Wheeling clumsily, he ran back toward the darkness, a painstaking, slow motion canter compared to the sprint he wished for.

Steve only saw a blur of the other bristled hound. He saw the son of a bitch leave the ground in a massive leap. Dreamlike ineptness kept him from dodging the attack. *Not fair!* Any hope of escape sputtered as the second creature broadsided him.

Oh shit help! Ow, my back! Rough, sharp-clawed forefeet scraped a frenzied pattern on Abrams' back. Razored teeth slashed at his sides, sought his belly and its vulnerable contents. Abrams curled into a ball, subconsciously covering his vitals from the enraged beast. The new position brought him face-to-face with his feral nightmare beast.

God, its head! Head's all crooked. Wake up! Please God wake me up wake me up wake me up. But, God was apparently busy or, at the very least, choosing not to listen to Steve Abrams for the moment. Alone, Abrams fought the Mastiff-beast with a crooked head. Even under the enormous handicap of having its head attached at a forty-five degree angle, the creature was winning. The nightmare hound adapted well, canting its body to the left so its mouth could tear at the kidnapper's bloodied side.

Hot coals burned a path into Abrams' stomach. Weakened, exhausted, dying, Steve detachedly watched as dog number one joined its misshaped partner. He watched the curs gut him, then tug his intestines from the slit. Quick-time thoughts seared his mind as the hounds languorously pulled on his guts.

I'm sorry, Bowser. Sorry I did to you what these things are doing to me. Mom ... Mom, I love you. Wish you could get me outta this. I'd be a good boy, honest!

God must have decided the kidnapper was temporarily sincere in his thoughts because a quirky kind of dream thing happened. Instead of continuing their teamwork, the beasts started to fight over a particularly tender morsel of Steve. Number One gnashed viciously at Misshaped's snout. Misshaped retaliated, snapping crookedly back at Number One.

Entrails forgotten, the dogs now tore at each other. Even in dreams, turf was an issue for the creatures.

Abrams may have been dying, but he wasn't yet dead. Instinct for survival flared and Steven began dragging himself away from the fighting Mastiffs. Dragged himself deeper into the black until he reached the darkness' edge. Pain stabbing at his torn body, he rolled into the welcoming light and woke.

"Goddamned dogs," Abrams whimpered. "Goddamned dream dogs and your whoremaster Indian."

Steve reached up to wipe the sleep from his eyes. The movement glazed him in a sheet of pain. Opening his eyes, he looked at the torn and bleeding hand suspended six inches from his face. *Noooo, no no no. It really happened! Oh God, my belly!* Detaching his gaze from the ruined hand, Abrams forced himself to look lower. Morbid curiosity told him he needed to look at his body.

He had gone to sleep wearing a soiled white T-shirt. Awake now, Abrams saw he was wrapped in a gaudy red and white ensemble, tie-dyed patterns of blood swirling among the food and sweat stains on the belly of his T-shirt.

"No! No, not my guts." The kidnapper frantically yanked the clotting material away from his skin. Jagged ugly tears striped his belly. Three, sometimes four, parallel gouges criss-crossed his abdomen and side like a tic-tac-toe board designed by Charles Manson. But, no intestines poked through the ridges. No guts trailed down off onto the bloodstained bed. Terror gave way to relief. Almost as quickly, the relief turned to rage.

"Gray Wolf, you bastard. I need you. I need you one last fucking time then I'm going to kill you ... real hard and slow."

Abrams knew the score, knew Gray Wolf held him by the short hairs. Pain intensified his recognition of the situation. *I get you to kill the dogs one more time, then I do you before you can set the bastards free again. No more Gray Wolf. No more dogs. Simple as that.*

CHAPTER 27

Despite the bustle of activity, Daniel Gray Wolf dozed. A fitful couple of hours sleep in Leo Red Hawk's rickety lounge chair, the handcuffed drive into the Badlands, a guided tour of the FBI office maze, and the near fatal visit into the dog dream hadn't left him overly refreshed. The light buzzing of agent talk lulled the Dream Catcher. An overbearing sense of safety and relief, compliments of the presence of several armed men, pushed Daniel toward the land of nod.

The abrupt ringing of the telephone surprised him. Reflexes, honed by years of practice in answering midnight calls, moved his arm toward the offending instrument. Number One Agent's reflexes were faster. The agent laid a firm hand on Daniel's, stopping him from picking up the receiver.

"Remember. We wait three rings."

Nonchalantly as possible, Gray Wolf waited until the third ring had subsided. "Hello?"

"They're back, you prick! The sonsabitches almost killed me this time."

"I know, Steve. I brought them back."

This short interchange of frantic and casual words allowed the first locator grid to be established. Number One motioned for Daniel to continue.

"I got your note, Steve. You must have spent a lot of time pasting that little poem together."

"Fuck the poem, asshole!" Abrams screamed, then abruptly changed to a dangerously calm voice. "But, I suppose I shouldn't use that kind of language over the phone. You probably got the feds there trying to trace me. I'm cutting this conversation off in one minute."

More calmly than he felt, Daniel answered, "Why would I need the FBI, Steve? I control the dogs, remember?"

Locator grid two locked in place. Number One held his thumb and forefinger half an inch apart. They were close.

"But I control the brat, Daniel. Don't you forget that."

"I'll make you a trade, Steve. You give me the girl and I promise the dogs are gone forever."

"The bitch is my meal ticket, Gray Wolf. I'll make you a deal. Call off the dogs and I promise you she'll live—after I get my money."

Number One circled his thumb and forefinger. They knew where Abrams was.

"See Steve, I don't think I can do that. I don't know whether Christine is alive or not. Why don't you let me talk to her for a minute."

Abrams barked a nasty laugh. "Kinda hard for her to come to the phone right now. She's, um, busy, you know? No, Gray Wolf. We do it my way or the girl dies."

Edwin Nagel had been listening in on a headphone set. He must have heard something in Abrams' voice, something that scared him. Silently, he mouthed the words, "go go!"

Heaving a sigh, Daniel said, "All right, Steve, we'll do it your way. Where do you want to meet?"

"Minute's up, asshole. I'll call back." The phone line abruptly went dead.

"Hillside Motel, I-90 at the Elk Creek Exit," Number Once announced. "Do we send a unit?"

Freeman Togweiler, silent up to this point, said, "Send a team but don't have them close in. If Abrams leaves, normal surveillance routine. Let's see if this dude calls back."

Gray Wolf turned toward Nagel. "Something's bothering you about the way Abrams spoke. What is it?"

"The man's slipping. He's terrified one minute and coldly calculating the next. He called you because the dogs are back, but most of his message was dictative. I'm worried about a man who can shove a life-threatening situation to the back of his mind to cast threats."

"Do you think he'll call again?"

"Oh yes, he'll call. Right now, Steve Abrams is realizing he didn't accomplish what he wanted. He still isn't rid of the dogs."

"How should I handle him the next time?"

"Comply. Don't grovel or he'll feel he's gained the upper hand. Remind him who controls the dreams, but grudgingly acquiesce."

The jangling of the telephone interrupted further conversation. Gray Wolf received a nod from the monitoring agent. He picked up the receiver.

"Yes, Steve."

"I'll keep it short, Daniel. Call off the goddamned dogs and the girl will be safe."

"Okay, I already said I would. Where do we meet?"

Abrams chuckled. "See, Mr. Dream Catcher, I've been thinking about that. You don't seem to need to be around me to set the d-dogs loose. I got a suspicion we don't have to sleep together for you to make them go away either."

"Steve, I've explained this to you before."

"Cut the bullshit, Gray Wolf. You dream the dogs away now, or I swear to Christ the Hardesty kid will be dead before tonight."

"Wait! Steve!" A loud click told Daniel no one was listening. Receiver still in hand, he turned to Nagel, a stricken look on his face.

"Shit, Edwin, he's right. What do we do now?"

Nagel shared Gray Wolf's expression. "I truly didn't expect this reaction. Abrams' new-found acute rationality concerns me."

"Which means what, Doctor?" Togweiler asked.

"Which means, I don't know what he's capable of. Intermittent bouts of reality and psychosis mean he's unpredictable."

"What if I met with him face-to-face?" Daniel said suddenly. "I show up at his motel room. What does that do to him?"

Edwin Nagel studied the man in front of him, using the time to gather his thoughts. What Gray Wolf proposed bordered on ludicrous, except ... except for the one slight chance the Dream Catcher could regain Abrams' confidence. Odds were that the kidnapper would resist, flee, or even worse, clam up.

"That's a risk I don't want to take, Daniel. We're dealing with an increasingly unstable character. In your current condition, this man could even overpower you. Your one hope would be to make Abrams believe you're his only salvation."

Daniel smiled, a grim sort of tightening of his lips. "See, Edwin, I am his only salvation. I'm the key. If those canine bastards did to him anything near what they did to me ... shit, he'll be dead tonight before he had a chance to kill Christine. Either way, the girl's going to die if I don't pow wow with this asshole."

"We all heard Abrams," Togweiler interjected. "The man's close to the edge and we don't have time to rip up several million acres of territory looking for the girl. We've got to decide now."

"I think we need to check with Congressman Hardesty," Nagel said, vacillating away from the ultimate responsibility.

"Hardesty's not running this campaign, Doctor," Togweiler said heatedly. "What I want from you is medical clearance that Daniel is up to meeting with this guy. My responsibility; my case, got it? Now, can Daniel do it?"

The look on Gray Wolf's face gave Nagel the answer. Resigned, he directed his answer to Daniel. "You're a bit lame, yet you appear to be in control of your mental faculties. But, I will not condone another John Wayne bout with those dogs. I can almost guarantee you'll lose." Nagel paused before adding, "And if you lose, you'll be dead."

Daniel Gray Wolf turned to the agent in charge. "Freeman, will you help me to my truck?"

Togweiler nodded, then turned back to his crew momentarily, issuing crisp orders for the gathering of a search party. Just in case.

CHAPTER 28

H ello, Steve. Can I come in?"

Abrams stared, open-mouthed, at the bedraggled Indian standing at his motel room entrance. "Gray Wolf! What the fuck are you doing here? How the hell did you find me?"

With studied nonchalance, Daniel limped past the shocked man. He spoke over his shoulder to Abrams. "I'm the Dream Catcher, remember?

Steve Abrams regained some of his dwindling senses. "I should kill you right here after what you've done to me. Kill you, then whack the bitch girl."

Daniel nodded slowly, then turned and inspected the kidnapper. "Yeah, maybe you could do that, but then, look at you. What's that bandage around your waist for? Cut yourself shaving?"

"Your fucking dogs did that."

"No, Steve. Remember, they're your dogs. Also remember, you kill me and you got two choices left. Stay awake or die!"

Reality flashed in the kidnapper's eyes. Daniel noticed. "I've come here in good faith, Steve. You can see the dogs haven't been too friendly toward me either. All bullshit aside now. See, when I dream the dogs up by myself, they become my nightmare. They come after me and I don't like that at all."

"So, why don't you get rid of them for good?"

"Because you've still got the girl, Steve," Daniel answered softly.

"I already told you, get rid of the dogs, get me my money, and the girl goes free. I promise! I swear to God."

Gray Wolf braced Abrams with a flint-eyed stare. "You believe in God, Steven? You think God's happy with what you're doing to this little girl?"

Abrams offered a crooked grin, bordering on childlike. "God knows I'm a little bit unstable, okay? He also knows what happened to me as a kid, so I'm sure he takes that into account. 'Sides, when anything bad starts happening to me, I beg for his forgiveness. God always forgives you if you're sincerely sorry about your sins."

The statement struck Daniel with its absurd naiveté. *He knows he' crazy. The little shit thinks he can get away with anything just by saying I'm sorry.*

"You're forgetting one thing, Steve."

"Yeah?"

"I don't forgive you. And I'm your god right now because I control the dogs. As far as you're concerned, I know all and see all. I knew you were the kidnapper from the minute you took the little girl. I arranged to set the dogs loose so I could get back in your dreams and find where you hid Christine. That was me, Steve, me! Not God up there, you got it?"

Abrams wiped away the tiny drops of moisture from his forehead. His voice was quavering as he spoke. "Yeah, but if I die, the girl dies."

Daniel shook his head slowly. "I don't think so. You're a dreamer. Asleep or awake, you're a dreamer searching for your perfect little world."

"You're wrong about that, Gray Wolf. I -"

"No," Daniel interrupted. "I'm right. It's just a matter of

time. When you fall asleep, and you will fall asleep, I'll be watching. The dogs are going to tear you up this next time. But, you won't die right away. You'll die slow and as you sink towards hell, I'll be in your dreams finding where you put Christine. You're easy, Abrams. See, you can't stop dreaming."

Real panic ripped into Abrams' heart. The goddamned Indian had him pegged. He knew Gray Wolf's power; had seen it firsthand. Worse, Gray Wolf knew him—knew his deepest secrets. His fears. He tried one last time. "You're hurt pretty bad. Probably couldn't stop me if I decided to kill you. So, if you're going to let me die, I might as well take you with me. That way everybody loses. You're dead, I'm dead, and the girl's dead."

Daniel nodded slightly. "I guarantee you one thing. Kill me and I'll be waiting on the other side for you. We might not meet again until tonight, or tomorrow, whenever you finally fall asleep. But when we do meet again, I'll drag your sorry ass straight to hell. And you know what hell will be for you? One big fucking dog kennel full of your dream friends. You'll get to play with them forever then."

Abrams' imagination was too strong. Moaning, he sagged to the floor, a tired little balloon sputtering out the last bit of air.

Softly, with much more sympathy than he felt, Daniel said, "Let's go find the girl, Steve. Take me to her and you'll never see the dogs again."

Abrams looked up, his pleading, myopic eyes locking with Gray Wolf's hardened brown stare. "Swear to God! Swear to God I'll never see those bastards again."

"As soon as the girl's safe, I swear the dogs will never bother you again."

Steve Abrams grabbed Daniel's arms, squeezed them with

terror-induced strength. "I really want to believe. I really need to believe you," he sobbed.

Grunting at the pain Abrams' fingers were causing, Daniel pulled the man up off the floor. "If there was ever a time to trust me, it's now, Steve. I don't like who you are, but I don't want to see you hurt either. Now take me to the girl, please."

Using his forearm as a handkerchief, Abrams wiped the snot dribbling from his nose. Magnified eyes behind thick glasses stared out at Gray Wolf with childlike trust. "You won't let the FBI hurt me either?"

"No one's going to hurt you, Steve. We just want the girl back safe."

Abrams hung his head, a tired, defeated man-child. "I put her in a cave, up in the hills."

"Let's go get her, Steve." Daniel opened the door, standing aside so Steve Abrams could walk through.

Outside, Gray Wolf drew in a deep breath of clean summer air. Four doors away, a motel maid pushed her cleaning cart toward the two. Daniel called to the lady, "Steve's taking me to Christine."

Immediately, the maid pulled a handset from her cart. She spoke brief, hushed instructions into the tiny transmitter.

Abrams gawked at the woman's transformation from housekeeper to government official. "She's a fed?"

Daniel nodded and added a carefully nondescript smile. "So's the desk clerk and the gift shop manager. You did right, Steve. This will look good for you."

"But, how -?"

"Doesn't matter right now. We'll talk later when we take care of the dogs. Right now, we need to find the girl, don't we?"

Steve nodded, then fell into step with Gray Wolf as they

walked into the rapidly filling parking lot. The suddenly intelligent looking maid/agent walked closely behind the men.

Freeman Togweiler reached the pair first, followed closely by Edwin Nagel. Casting a quick glance at the doctor for assent, Togweiler said, "Steven Abrams, you're under arrest for the kidnapping of Christine Hardesty." The agent finished his Miranda spiel in a surprising, conversational tone. No hint of anger, malice; nothing offensive. "Do you understand these rights?"

"Yes," Abrams answered in a small voice.

"I understand you've volunteered to lead us to Christine, Mr. Abrams." Togweiler spoke in the same moderate voice as he gently clasped handcuffs around Abrams' wrists. "We'll drive in my car."

"Daniel's got to come with me!" Abrams blurted.

"Daniel will be in one of the other vehicles, Mr. Abrams. You'll be riding with two federal agents and me."

"Gray Wolf's got to come with me," Abrams insisted, a dangerous, wild tone entering his voice. "We ride together or I don't lead you to the bitch ... the girl."

Togweiler didn't wait for Daniel's answer. "All right, Mr. Abrams. Daniel will ride with us."

Abrams turned to Daniel, a frenzied look creeping into his eyes. "You've got to stick near me, Gray Wolf. We got a deal and you have to stay with me, okay?"

"We got a deal. I'm with you all the way, Steve."

Freeman Togweiler led the kidnapper to the light blue sedan. Opening the rear door, he assisted Abrams into the back seat. Special Agent William Anderson opened the other door and slid in beside Abrams.

"No. No, no, no. Gray Wolf sits back here." Noticeably agitated, Steve Abrams issued orders with childlike insistence.

Nagel spoke to Togweiler in a hushed voice. "He's becoming increasingly unstable. If there's no real danger, you should comply."

Togweiler looked around the parking lot as if counting his reinforcements. Nodding tersely, he ordered, "Bill, ride up front with me. I want one car up ahead, and the three search teams behind us.

"You can ride in back with Mr. Abrams, Daniel," he added. It wasn't a request.

***

"Turn left here."

A barely visible gravel trail materialized, hardly noticeable in the thick undergrowth along the asphalted main road. The federal caravan pulled onto the access, driving slowly to avoid the numerous ruts. Five hundred yards into the journey, they were confronted by a fork in the road. The lead car stopped, waiting for instructions from Togweiler's vehicle.

"Which way, Mr. Abrams?"

"Um, left again—no, wait—right. We go right."

Togweiler gazed over his shoulder. "You're sure?"

"I said right, didn't I? The cave's just up over this hill."

Togweiler nodded in agreement, yet his radioed orders differed. "Schmidt, take the lead car left. I want two search teams to follow me; the third goes to the left with Schmidt. Got it?"

Pulling around the front sedan, Togweiler made his way up the slight incline. He didn't bother checking in his rear view mirror. His instructions would be followed.

Two hundred feet down the slope, Abrams said, "Okay, stop here. The cave's up on that hillside."

Togweiler radioed again, "We're at the site. Cars one and

five, you're probably no more than three, four hundred yards south of us. Leave the driver but start the teams north over the hill toward us."

"I told you this is where the girl is. Why're you wasting your guys' time?"

"Standard procedure, Mr. Abrams, just in case you may have forgotten which road you took."

"She's right up there, in the cave. I didn't forget."

Togweiler ignored the childish response. "Shall we go get Christine now?"

Agent Anderson opened Abrams' door. Using just the proper amount of effort, he helped the manacled kidnapper from the auto.

On the opposite side, Daniel pushed opened the door, grunting in his effort to slide from the vehicle. Pain danced through his torn calves. *Man, once this is over, I'm sleeping for a week. By myself ... no bad dreams, no people with bad dreams ... no nothing.* But, right now, there was work to do. Christine was somewhere inside the hill facing him, somewhere only Steve knew for sure.

"You're looking a little ragged, Daniel." Freeman Togweiler studied the tired, pale man before him.

"I agree," Edwin Nagel said, trotting up from the vehicle behind Togweiler's lead sedan. "I insist you get back in the car and stretch out in the back seat. You need to elevate those legs to prevent further bleeding."

"Daniel's gotta come with me. He's gotta come with me. I need him with me and I'm the only one who knows where the girl is." Steven Abrams yelled as he wrestled against Agent Anderson's grasp.

"You're in no condition to go walking through caves, Daniel," Nagel insisted. "Let the FBI take it from here."

Abrams practically dragged his captor around the car. "Gray Wolf, I need you in there. What about the dogs?"

"Steve, why don't you let these able-bodied guys find Christine with you? Doctor Nagel's right; I'm not up to hiking right now. Besides, the dogs can't bother you when you're awake."

"It's dark in there ... and real strange looking ... anything can happen. The damn dogs **could** get me."

Daniel looked at the spectacled man in front of him. Abrams had aged appreciably since their first visit, a victim of his terror and greed. The Dream Catcher whispered, "I can't, Steve. I just don't think I can make it."

Steve Abrams stiffened, a glint of madness creeping back into his eyes. "You don't go, then I don't go. Let these guys try and find her. Heck, I've set up booby traps all around inside."

"Mr. Abrams, you've cooperated up to this point," Togweiler said. "We're only asking you to finish this effort. Lead us to the girl."

"And I'm only asking Daniel to go with me," Abrams insisted. "You can send in as many guys with us as you want, but I need Gray Wolf to protect me."

Shit! What's a couple more minutes, kola? "Will these bandages hold up for awhile longer, Edwin?"

"Daniel, I really must insist this time."

Gray Wolf waved a heavy arm at the doctor. "I know, I know. But, hell, I'm a fast healer. All that mystical Indian medicine stuff, you know?" A tired smile found its way to his pale lips.

"We've got a little girl to find," Togweiler reminded the group. "I think we need to get started. Now!"

"All right, Steve. I'll go. Now, where's the cave?"

Abrams cackled, a delighted childish sound. "Boy, are you in for a treat."

***

"Shit, Steve, this is just a hole in the ground."

"It's okay, Daniel, it gets bigger inside." Abrams grinned his kid grin once more. His spirits had lifted considerably since Daniel had acquiesced and since the agents had manacled his hands in front.

"Let's go, Mr. Abrams," Togweiler said as he finished knotting the tether to the kidnapper's rear belt loop. "You lead and I'll be right behind you.

"Bill, you fall in behind me, then Daniel," he added. "Keep your flashlight handy in case mine dies."

The foursome of unlikely spelunkers, a kidnapper, two federal suits, and a wounded Indian, crawled through the tiny entrance single file. Once inside, Togweiler's flashlight cast a barely adequate beam in front of Abrams' profile. Painstakingly, the group inched along the rocky surface. Mutters from the cramped agents interspersed with grunts of pain as Daniel knocked his injured legs against the confining sides.

One hundred yards into the needle hole journey, Togweiler expressed his doubts. "Are you sure this is the correct cave?" His subdued voice resonated through the narrow shaft.

"Only a little further," Abrams panted.

Daniel Gray Wolf hung on only through sheer determination. The banging against sharp granite walls had taken their toll. He knew his legs were bleeding again, felt the warm trickle of blood cool as it slid down his calves. Only the faint glow of Togweiler's flashlight and the occasional bump against Anderson's feet kept him moving forward. *Gotta keep up. Shit, where would I turn around anyway?* Gray Wolf barely caught the muffled "we're here" amidst the grunts of exertion and the eerie ringing that had recently taken up residence in his ears. Then the tunnel snapped dark.

With no flashlight beam to guide him, Daniel stumbled forward, panicking in the total darkness. Hands firmly grabbed his shoulders as he emerged from the burrow.

"Whoa there, pardner." Bill Anderson's blessed voice greeted him. "Just stop where you are. There's a hole 'bout as deep as Grand Canyon just ahead of you. Move a little over to the right. Can you stand?"

"What about the girl? Is Christine okay?"

"Freeman's tending to her right now. She appears all right. Just relax now, Daniel. You did good."

Daniel squinted against the darkness, his eyes slowly adjusting to the miniscule light emanating from Togweiler's flashlight. Following Anderson's directions, he pushed himself semi-erect and shuffled to the right onto a ledge four feet wide.

"I told you she was okay. I told you she wasn't hurt." A plaintive tone pulled Gray Wolf's attention to the kidnapper.

Steve Abrams stood on a tiny outcropping of limestone, a scant three feet separating him from the huddled group.

"I told you she was okay," Abrams repeated. "I wasn't going to hurt her or anything. I just wanted the money, you know? Daniel, you're going to make things better now, aren't you?"

Abrams' flurry of questions drew no answers. Togweiler preoccupied himself talking softly to the young girl clinging to him. Anderson watched the kidnapper, alert for any sudden moves. Daniel hung his head and sucked in cool cavern air.

"Daniel? C'mon, I held up my end of things. You're going to make it right with the dogs now, aren't you?"

Gray Wolf slowly raised his head, then focused on the

man in front of him. *I could just back off. Let this little shit suffer for what he did.*

A slight movement to his left caught Daniel's attention. He turned his head just in time to spot a brown and black creature pull itself through the tunnel entrance. Righting itself, the dog loped toward the group of men. Toward Steve Abrams.

The kidnapper's eyes bulged behind their glasses. "No! No, it can't be the dogs. I'm awake! Daniel? Help me, Daniel!"

Abrams stepped backward, a natural, self-preservative instinct.

"Steve, wait! It's not what you -" Gray Wolf's cry was cut short as he watched Abrams lose his footing.

Twirling clumsily, Abrams fought to regain balance, but the backward momentum was too great. He teetered, handcuffed arms windmilling furiously. A moment later he disappeared over the ledge, a loose-jointed rag doll silently fluttering in the still cavern air.

A soft, wet sound signified Abrams had found the cavern floor two hundred feet below the rim. Only then did the group react to the incredulous spectacle.

"Jesus, we need to get an ambulance," Bill Anderson breathed.

"Too late," Freeman Togweiler's terse answer echoed throughout the still chamber. He clutched the young girl to his chest, hoping she had not witnessed the last few seconds.

Daniel tore his gaze from the empty ledge. The complacent animal sniffing at the young girl came into view. "Good God, where'd the dog come from?"

"Canine search team," Togweiler replied. "It probably followed Christine's scent into here."   Kneeling down, the agent spoke in soft tones to the young girl. "We're taking you home now, sweetie. It's all over."

CHAPTER 29

Daniel almost didn't answer the knock at his door. *Just more freakin' reporters anyway.*

For the past two days he had wanted nothing more than to sleep and heal. Deep bouts of dreamless slumber had worked wonders on both his mind and body. His legs, though still sore, showed signs of recovering nicely. His mind, equally scarred by the past week's events, mended even faster. Daniel sensed a return to normalcy. *Yeah, if that's what you can call my life.*

Yet the knocking persisted, a gentle, steady rapping on his storm door. *Go away! I don't want to play anymore.* Gray Wolf backed further into his mental cave.

"Who's there?" A hermit's question, asked with a tinge of mistrust.

"Daniel? It's Linda. Linda Paxton."

Gray Wolf instantly transformed into a civilized human. Nervously smoothing his hair with one hand, he reached for the doorknob.

"Geez, Linda, what are you doing out here ... at this time of night?"

"It—it's only nine. I didn't think you'd be in bed."

"My gosh, come in! Only nine? God, I thought it was two, maybe three in the morning."

Gray Wolf's former high school sweetheart sidled in past his still-protective stance at the doorway. That perfect, light smile touched her lips.

"Biological clock's all messed up?"

Daniel smoothed his hair back even further. "I'm sorry. I guess I've kinda been out of it for a couple of days."

"I'll understand if you want to be alone. What you did has been on national television non-stop. The papers say you're a hero. You're probably sick of people pounding on your door for an interview."

"Well, you know the media. Always blowing things out of proportion. The feds did all the work. I was just along for the ride."

Linda's smile brightened even further. "That's not what Special Agent Togweiler says."

"Think about it, Linda. He's a federal agent. He's trained to lie." God, she smelled good, standing there just a few inches away.

Daniel mentally splashed water on the smoldering fires of long ago memories. "Anyhow, to what do I owe this honor?"

Linda squirmed slightly, showing a touch of discomfort. Or was it embarrassment? "I just wanted to talk. Thought maybe you might want to talk. But, it can wait for a better time."

"No—no, come on in. I could stand some real company."

Linda ducked slightly under Daniel's arm and stepped into the foyer. She quickly gazed around the living room. "Daniel, this is ... this is ... "

"God, I'm sorry, Linda. I haven't had time to clean or anything." Gray Wolf limped past her and began fluffing at the already fluffed pillows.

"I was trying to say that this is really a lovely room." Linda turned and faced Daniel, the solemn look on her face cracking into a lovely grin. "You were such a slob in high school. I can see you've changed."

Embarrassed, Daniel replied, "Well, you know … red man who keep dirty teepee, no gettum squaw."

"Well, you keep an immaculate teepee, and still you no gottum squaw," Linda quipped. A stricken look crossed her face as she quickly added, "I'm sorry. I was just kidding. You—you told me you'd never married. I'm sorry, that was insensitive of me."

Gray Wolf laughed for the first time in several days. "God, look at us. Here we are like a couple of high school kids trying to 'out nice' each other. I'll make you a deal. I'll be normal Daniel if you be normal Linda. Want a beer?"

"Thanks, that would be nice."

Daniel shuffled toward the kitchen. Knowing Linda was watching, he made a concerted effort not to limp. "Sit down and relax. I'll just be a sec."

Rummaging through the refrigerator, he spotted the last two bottles. *Gray Wolf, you idiot, why the hell don't you have some wine around the house? Real smooth, offering the lady a bottle of beer.* "Listen, if you'd rather have some wine, I'd be happy to go get some."

"Beer's fine."

God, what a voice! She even makes the word beer sound sexy. He pulled a clean glass from the cupboard then expertly poured the golden liquid into it. Armed with Linda's glass and his bottle, Daniel ambled into the living room.

"You're limping."

"Yeah, I barked my shin crawling around in some caves."

Linda smiled. "Still keeping things close the vest, aren't you, Daniel?"

"I don't know what you mean."

"I guess what I mean is you find it easier to lie to people than to burden them with the truth."

Daniel squirmed, uncomfortable that Linda could still read him so well after a twenty-year absence. He felt her deep brown eyes, sensed them pulling at his face to make him look up. *Don't look up, kola. She'll have you for sure.*

"Really, Linda, it's no big deal. I've just got some scratches. If it's okay with you, I'd just as soon not talk about it."

"I know. You never did want to talk about it." Her voice was still soft, no hint of reproach in it. "You would never really open up to me. Ever."

Drawn by her words, Gray Wolf lifted his gaze. His eyes made tentative contact with hers. "What is it you really want to know—why I left you? Is that it?" he asked quietly.

Linda smiled again, a gesture of pure understanding. "No. I already know why. But, you're making progress. At least you're sharing with me now."

"You know why I left, why I felt we couldn't get married?" Daniel's surprise was evident.

"I knew your family, remember? I saw what being *Ihanbla Gmunka* did to your dad. I saw what it was doing to you."

Dumbfounded, Daniel stared at his former sweetheart. His only sweetheart. "But, why did you bother staying with me? Geez, Linda, we were just kids. You could've had any boy you wanted. And now you're telling me you knew what this ... this thing was doing to me. Why did you stay?"

"Because I loved you. Daniel, even then, as a funky little high school girl, I saw the goodness in you. I saw your need to help others."

Gray Wolf's voice husked as he said, "And you still wanted to be with me. Despite what you knew, what you saw. You wanted to stay with me?"

"I loved you." The answer was simple, emotional.

Whoa, this is too much. Get out of it now, kola! "Well, at least you found happiness. It sounds like you married a good man."

"Yes, I did. I needed a father for my child."

The words caught him off guard. Maybe it was just the way she said it; maybe it came out a little wrong. "David's a fine boy. You and your husband must have been thrilled to bring a kid like him into the world."

Linda's warm brown eyes smiled at Daniel as she said, "David wasn't Allen's child."

"But then, who? I mean ... no, wait, it's none of my business."

"Allen was white, third generation English. David's full-blooded Oglala. And, don't be shy, Daniel. It's really more of your business than you know."

Daniel leaned back and nervously swigged at his beer. *What's she saying to you, kola? Is she going to make you ask? Do this right.*

"I guess this means you're going to tell me who David's father is." *Real nice hedge, dummy.*

"I've been with two men in my life, Daniel," Linda answered softly, though her eyes weren't smiling anymore.

"I see. I see." *Jesus, Gray Wolf, she's just told you the kid is yours and all you can do is make sounds like Edwin Nagel.* "Does David know this?"

"David knows Allen wasn't his real father. But, no, he's not aware, although I'm sure he suspects."

A wide range of emotions buffeted Daniel. Surprise had initially struck him squarely in the face, but now only pushed at him like a faint breeze. Guilt sidled up against him and leaned on his resolve. But, a tingling of pleasure purred down his spine, then nestled in his stomach. "What is it you want from me, Linda?" The question held no offense.

Linda Paxton stared at Daniel for several uncomfortable seconds, trying to discern his reaction. "Want? Nothing, other than to let you know. Now that Allen's dead, you have a right to know."

A brief urge to run overcame Gray Wolf. *Settle down! Where the hell you going on two gimpy legs anyway? What do you say to the woman now? Tell her the truth about how you feel? Tell her you still love her after ditching her twenty years ago? She doesn't want to hear that.* For the first time in years, Daniel didn't have an answer. Instead, he studiously peeled at the beer bottle label.

Linda sensed his confusion, his inability to articulate. She smiled at her first lover. "I guess it's up to me to break the ice. I still love you, Daniel. That never stopped. I loved Allen too, but it wasn't the same as what I felt for you ... what we felt for each other."

Daniel poured all his attention into the nearly naked beer bottle. The flimsy, yet intact, label clung to the smooth glass surface by a single smudge of glue. His nervous fingers dug at the final barrier until the limp paper fell loose.

Linda Paxton rose then smoothed her skirt front. "Well, it's getting late. I'd better be heading home. I just wanted ... I thought I should ... "

Daniel caressed the glass bottle, studied its contours. "I love you too, Linda," he said quietly. *There! You got it out, butthead.*

He caught a peripheral flurry of motion before being smothered in Linda's embrace. Pressing his face against her shoulder, the Dream Catcher asked in a muffled voice, "So, what do we tell David ... later?"

CHAPTER 30

Daniel Gray Wolf looked in the bathroom mirror and smiled at what he saw. *Hey, kola, not bad for a guy who didn't get much sleep last night.* Even puffy eyes looked good when they held the light of love in them.

By unspoken agreement, Linda had spent the night. Amid much hand holding and several bouts of joint tear shedding, the lovers talked through twenty years of anguish. Finally, after all the sadness was drained, they shared Daniel's bed and revisited their one previous night of pleasure.

Whistling a brand new, nameless love tune, Daniel sauntered into his bedroom—their bedroom. Kneeling down on miraculously pain-free legs, he smoothed the mane of hair from Linda's face.

"Good morning, sweetheart. Time to get up if we're going to visit Leo."

A muffled sigh, then a smile greeted Daniel. "What time is it? Didn't we just go to bed?" Linda's unabashed, naked stretch almost canceled the morning's schedule.

Gray Wolf willed himself to concentrate on Linda's face. "You've been sleeping for about—oh—an hour and twenty minutes. C'mon, baby, I think it's important we tell Leo about us."

"Hold your horses, you wild stallion you." Linda slipped from between the sheets in a languid, graceful move. "I was only teasing. You know I want to see Leo just as badly as you."

Daniel watched as his lover padded toward the bathroom. *Hold on, kola! Put your damn eyes back in your head before it's too late.* Shaking himself free of the burgeoning erotic daydream, he rustled into the closet. Nervous fingers picked at the first available shirt, then grabbed a pair of clean Levis.

Half an hour later, Daniel pointed the reliable Ford pickup south on Highway 44 and set the cruise control. Linda snuggled against his right side, gently caressing his arm with her hand. *Okay, boss, you got an hour and a half to think up something to tell Leo. You're a smart guy. You'll come up with something.*

"So, what do we tell Leo?"

"How about the truth, Daniel? I think it's going to be rather obvious to him anyway."

"Okay. Yeah, that's good. So, what do we tell David?"

"Daniel!"

***

Badger sprawled into view as Daniel steered through the final corner. Tiny houses, trailers, and two stores lay snugged into the valley below him, basking in the mid-morning sun.

"We've got to stop at the Emporium. I didn't get a chance to stock up for Leo this weekend."

Linda answered with a gentle squeeze to his arm.

Pulling into the dusty gravel parking lot, Daniel braked to a halt then hopped out. A slight twinge plucked at his calves, warning him all was not yet perfect with his legs. Linda sidled out the driver's side while he held the door for her. *Gilbert and William will appreciate the gentlemanly gesture; probably rag you about it, too.*

But Gilbert War Pony and William Yellow Feather weren't stationed at their usual posts. Empty, mismatched rockers stood guard on the Badger Liquor and Grocery Emporium porch.

"The guys must be inside," Daniel said as much to himself as to Linda. "It's pretty warm out here already."

Sauntering up the three steps, his girl on his arm, Daniel pulled open the screen door. Inside the cluttered store, Gilbert and William leaned against the counter. Ralph Trudeau looked up from behind the cash register then smiled as he recognized the couple.

"'Morning, Mr. Yellow Feather. 'Morning, Mr. War Pony."

"'Mornin', Daniel," the pair responded, one voice a ragged echo of the other.

"'Mornin', Linda," William Yellow Feather added warmly. "Good to see you again."

"Gentlemen," Linda acknowledged.

Uncomfortable silence surrounded the group. *Something's wrong here. Where's the usual greeting? Is it because Linda and I are together?*

Gray Wolf brushed aside the feeling of unease. "Hey, Mr. Trudeau. Sorry, I didn't get here this weekend. Guess I'd better pick up an extra special surprise for Leo, otherwise the old fart will -"

"Uh ... Daniel ... Leo died early this morning." Ralph Trudeau's words, softly spoken, cut through the still air like a war lance.

"Passed away in his sleep, Daniel," Gilbert added.

"Real peaceful-like. He just didn't wake up," William snuffled, immediately tweaking his nose with gnarled fingers. A nervous reaction; one intended to cover the sob dwelling just below the surface.

Daniel didn't feel the reassuring pressure of Linda's fingers against his arm. "Where is he? Is Leo still here?"

"Leo's still down at his house," Trudeau said. "Mary

Twilight found him about an hour ago. We tried to call you, Daniel, but you must have been on your way here. I'm real sorry."

Gray Wolf ran shaking fingers through his hair. "I'd better get down there. Linda, you might want to stay here for awhile."

"Leo was my friend, too, Daniel. I'd like to be with you."

Daniel nodded, then looked up at the three Badger citizens. "He died peacefully, you say?"

Only Gilbert War Pony was able to respond. "Yep, he looks happy. Should be, I guess; he's with all his family and friends right about now."

Daniel turned to leave, lightly grasping Linda's hand in the process. He paused at the screen door, then turned back to the somber group at the counter. "Feels kinda strange, walking out of here without any treats for *Tunkasila*. And, I guess I forgot my manners. Would you gents care for a beer before Linda and I go?"

"Appreciate the thought, *kola washta*," William responded. "I think me and Gilbert will pass today. We'll probably toast old Leo tonight after Ceremony."

Gray Wolf nodded, then held the door open for Linda. Outside, he drew in deep breaths of hot air.

"Are you all right, Daniel?" Concern tinged Linda's voice.

"Yeah, everything's fine. Sort of. I'm feeling a little bit sorry for myself is all. Leo's at peace, but damn, I miss the old coot."

Linda hugged Gray Wolf's arm. "I know what he meant to you. And I know what you meant to him."

"Well," Daniel sighed. "We'd better get down there. I don't want *Tunkasila's* spirit ticked off at me for being late."

Forty-five long seconds later, Daniel carefully pulled into

Leo Red Hawk's dusty front yard. Only upon braking to a halt did he realize there were several other cars and trucks already parked around the house. He recognized most of the vehicles, neighbors and friends of Leo's here to pay their respects.

The curtains gracing the shack's only front window parted and a weathered face peered out. Daniel started, briefly imagining the face was that of his old friend. *C'mon, Gray Wolf. Back to reality. It's just one of the neighbors checking to see who showed up.*

"What do we say to these folks, Linda? Hell, what do you think they're going to say to us?" Gray Wolf was experiencing a mild case of guilt. "I should have been here for Leo."

Linda halted half way between the truck and Red Hawk's front door. Her hands, linked through Daniel's arm, pulled him to a stop. "Leo was almost a hundred years old, my love. These people are here to assure his safe journey to the Other Plain. If they are concerned about anything, it will be for your reaction to Leo's death."

The door to Leo's home opened, saving Daniel from any further retrospect. An elderly Lakota woman bustled down the path toward them. Placing herself squarely in front of Daniel, she threw her arms around the startled man.

"He's finally gone home," Mary Twilight whispered into Daniel's chest.

Gray Wolf tightened his arms around the stout little woman and kissed the top of her head. "I miss him, Grandma Mary. Linda and I came here to give *Tunkasila* some good news, but now ... "

Mary Twilight leaned back from Daniel's embrace. She gazed first at Linda, then at him, with tear-brightened eyes. "Maybe Leo already knows. Maybe that's why he let his spirit go."

"I don't know, Mary," Daniel replied as he escorted the two women into the house. "I'd like to believe that."

"Well, believe it then, Daniel Gray Wolf," Mary admonished softly. "All the old man talked about was his Daniel and the little girl who wore a red and white coat too big for her, finally getting together again. He waited a long time. But, enough of this. Now you must visit Leo."

Inside, the house was surprisingly cool despite the number of people present. Daniel moved through the tight-packed group, accepting brief handshakes and murmurs of condolence. Pressing through the final gathering, he stood at the doorway leading into Leo's tiny bedroom.

Leo lay at peace on his ancient bed. Someone, probably Mary, had dressed him in a fresh white buckskin beautifully adorned with multi-colored beads. Traditional medicine wheels in red, white, black, and yellow guarded the old man's headboard. A light scent of burning sweet grass lingered in the air. Leo Red Hawk was prepared for his Ceremony of Passage.

Tears slid from Daniel's eyes as he knelt beside the bed. He grasped the gnarled hand of his friend, mentor, and spiritual guardian for the last time. "Good bye, *Tunkasila. Tohanl wi mahel iyaye kin hehanl yaupi kte.* When the sun goes down, then you will be home."

Rising, Daniel turned and saw Linda standing in the doorway. He stepped toward her, then gathered her in his arms. Their tears joined as he touched her cool cheek with his.

"I hope you don't mind. I went back out to the truck to get this." Linda drew a small red willow hoop from her pocket and placed it in his hand. "I thought you might like to give it to Leo for his journey."

Daniel studied the dream catcher symbol, traced the lacy sinew spider web in its center. "Leo gave me this when I … when I came of age."

With Linda at his side, Daniel hung the dream catcher on the headboard directly above Leo's head. "For your journey, *Tunkasila*. And to remember me."

Morning passed slowly; a haze of subdued activity, muted conversations, and frequent bouts of tears. At noon, Leo Red Hawk left his house for the last time accompanied by Shannon County Coroner, Robert Pony Soldier A throng of mourners guided the hearse to the Ceremony House where Leo would be sent on his way to the Other Plain later that evening.

"I can't go with Leo just yet," Daniel explained to the few people remaining at the house. "There are things I need to take care of around here." He and Linda lingered, touched the sparse collection of things Leo had surrounded himself with, and remembered the living Red Hawk. There would be plenty of time to say good-bye, tonight at Ceremony.

When they were finally alone, Daniel sat down in Leo's ancient lounge chair and stared out the solitary living room window. "I want to remember him like he was, Linda. I want to remember the ornery old coot who guzzled beer and chain-smoked cigarettes. If I go there now, well, whenever I think of Leo, it will be of him laying on his bed decked out in a burial robe."

"He'll always be alive in your heart, Daniel. Grandfather lived a full life and spent most of it helping others. Helping you. That won't stop just because he's not here to speak with you anymore."

Idly, more out of need to do something with his hands, Daniel turned on the old Sears television. Static noise filled the room as the TV valiantly fought to locate a readable signal. Blurred images emanated from the screen, then sharpened into an early afternoon soap opera. Daniel turned the channel knob until a game show appeared.

"Strange," he murmured, flipping through the remaining channels. Four programs struggled to appear. Three soaps and the game show, all of them modern day vintage.

"What's strange?"

"Leo used to be able to pick up some really old programs; The Lone Ranger, Rin Tin Tin, Lassie; that kind of stuff. Now it's just normal television, and pretty cruddy reception to boot."

"You usually visited him on weekends. Maybe there's a nostalgia channel that plays those shows."

Gray Wolf thought for a moment, then smiled. "Maybe, but I guess I'd like to think Leo's television spirits are taking a break. They're not needed anymore."

***

Driving home that evening, Daniel found his spirits raising considerably as he put distance between Badger township and him. Leo had received a proper send off and was, no doubt, now counseling with the other Lakota elders who had preceded him.

"Well, Mizz Paxton, I'm feeling a whole lot better right now. He lived a long time and I'll miss his orneriness. But what's important is he's at peace."

Linda smiled at her lover. "Welcome back to the living world. I'm glad to see your frame of mind is intact because I need to mention a couple of things."

"Okay. Shoot."

"Number one is, how old did Leo claim to be?"

Daniel thought for a moment. "Let's see, he was ninety-eight."

"Now, if he was ninety-eight, then he was born around 1895. Let me ask you, how could he remember Wounded Knee if it happened **five years before he was born**?

"Well, that's easy to—let me think—there's probably some reasonable ... Hell! That would make the old fart a hundred and eight! Imagine that. Leo Red Hawk vain about his age."

Daniel drove the familiar road, silently recalculating the years. Three times he tried, and each time rendered the same answer. Leo had stayed on earth a century and eight years. *Because of you, kola. He always said how tired he was of waiting for me to get married and raise a new Ihanbla Gmunka.*

"You said a couple of things needed mentioning. What's the other?"

Linda leaned her head against Daniel's shoulder and whispered into his ear. "You really need to have a talk with your son. David has a girlfriend and they've ... well, they've been intimate. He told me about watching her sleep. Suddenly, he was in her dream."